# One More Time, Jennie Darling

## Jerry Jaffe

Foreword by Paul McComas

iUniverse, Inc.
Bloomington

# One More Time, Jennie Darling

iUniverse books may be ordered through booksellers or by contacting:

iUniverse
1663 Liberty Drive
Bloomington, IN 47403
www.iuniverse.com
1-800-Authors (1-800-288-4677)

ISBN: 978-1-4759-2988-1 (sc)
ISBN: 978-1-4759-2990-4 (hc)
ISBN: 978-1-4759-2989-8 (e)

Library of Congress Control Number: 2012909683

Printed in the United States of America

iUniverse rev. date: 08/29/2012

# DEDICATION

To my wife, Dorlene, for her sense of humor, cheerfulness of spirit, calmness, and unflagging faith in all of my endeavors.

To my daughter Cyndi, my sister Alice, my nieces Gail and Carol, and my nephew Stan.

To Donna Allen, for her support and insight during the creation of this manuscript.

# ACKNOWLEDGMENT

I wish to thank Paul McComas, my line editor, guru, and friend, who held the lantern high in order for me to see where I was going throughout the publication of this novel.

*Keep saying "yes" when all around you are saying "no."*

*Jaffe, 2012*

# Foreword: "Dreams into Nightmares"
# by Paul McComas

Once I knew a girl who looked so much like Judy Garland
That people would stop and give her money.
-Elvis Costello, "Jack of All Parades"

The hardest part of writing a Foreword for Jerry Jaffe's brilliant debut novel has been coming up with the right title.

I considered "Textbook Storytelling," because in all four elements of narrative development—plot, characterization, setting, and theme—Jaffe shines. (I'll extrapolate on this shortly.) But "textbook" sounds too much like "by the book," which means "in accordance with established guidelines." And while Jaffe certainly is working within and paying homage to popular and well-loved literary and cinematic genres and traditions, his take on them is singular.

Then, I considered "Identity Crisis," for around one of these, the story does indeed revolve —"revolve" being apt, as the novel's protagonist spirals ever downward in his whirlpool of self-abnegation ... even as he believes he's rising ever higher.

"Be Careful What You Wish For" came to mind, but only after I'd read the fine back-cover blurb by my friend, Gary McLouth.

And surely, you can't derive the title of your Foreword from what some *other* author had to say!

And so: "Dreams into Nightmares." In *One More Time, Jennie Darling*, talented yet perpetually struggling lounge singer Steve Dennis dreams of fame and fortune, of recognition and runaway success. He dreams, in short, of stardom—one that will take him to Vegas, to Hollywood, and all around the world. For Steve, these dreams are fulfilled … but at what cost? It's a bit of a koan: If the successful expression of your gift requires the loss of your very self, then are "you" even there, in the end, to enjoy it?

The answer, Jaffe says, is a resounding "No"—and hence the nightmare. As Matthew 16:26 asks: "What profiteth it a man to gain the world but lose his soul?" Life is full of trade-offs, and a life in show biz more so than most; and Hollywood is, after all, "the Dream Factory," so fantasy and illusion come with the territory. Still, when artistry and artifice become as tightly entwined as the strands forming the ropes on Jennie's swing, then the ace "impersonator" may well find that the core of that word—his very *person*—has vanished … possibly for good.

Speaking of the swing: what a well-chosen central image! Jaffe was wise to insist that his cover incorporate this emblem of childhood innocence that, for Jennie and then Steve, comes to symbolize anything but. It's *Citizen Kane*'s "Rosebud," but with strings attached, literally and figuratively. Tied to its twin ropes, suspended in mid-air, the swing becomes a symbol at once of bondage and limbo, of captivity, lostness, and loss … all for the sake of stardom. As James M. Cain's classic *noir* novel reminds us, "The postman always rings twice." So it is with swings: when you push one forward, it *always* swings back.

Allow me to pivot and briefly discuss each of the four key

elements of narrative development as they pertain to *One More Time, Jennie Darling.*

I'll save "plot" for last, for reasons that my 14 years' worth of fiction-writing students could readily tell you, as they've all heard me "evangelize" on this point a time or two (or twelve). It boils down to this: important though storyline may be, it is *not* the place to begin. The most organic, credible, compelling plots aren't outlined; rather, they grow out of the interaction of the other three elements: characterization, setting, and theme. This triad yields a premise, and it is while exploring said premise—not before writing, but while and by and *through* writing—that a successful storyline emerges. Thus, generating a plot is—like so much in both art and life—more about the journey than the destination.

I don't know whether or not Jaffe knew how his novel would end when he started writing it. He may have had an inkling; he may have had more. Regardless, I can guarantee that he didn't know precisely how he was going to get there.

Characterization, to me, is key. If readers can't engage with the characters, it's hard for them to care, so why bother reading? If the people aren't compelling, then the story won't be, either. Happily, none of this is an issue for Jaffe; characterization is his calling card. He has "cast" this Hollywood novel with deftly wrought, credible, engaging people, from the "names above the title" to the "supporting players," all the way down to the "extras."

Let me introduce you to just a few:

There's our likable yet injudicious protagonist, Steve, who is relatable enough for us to empathize with him—yet foreign enough to keep the story moving into intriguing, discomfiting places. There's his wife, Stella, whose humor and heart win us over at once, and who becomes the book's voice of reason as Steve takes leave of his own; though she's not our point-of-view character, it's for Stella, ultimately, that we're rooting. There's Stella's *doppelganger* (use of the German very much intentional), Silvi, the love interest of both Steve's and the novel's Third Act—a frustrated, perceptive, sensual Berlin *hausfrau* who is, in turn, drawn to *and* repelled by Steve, for all the right reasons. Our hearts go out to Stella and Silvi alike—as well as to young Iris, level-headed daughter of a screen goddess, who must juggle college course work with parenting her own mother: the titular Miss Darling.

As for Jennie herself, the nominal resemblance to a real-life entertainment icon ("Jennie" to "Judy," "Darling" to "Garland") is no coincidence: by any other name, "J" is still larger than life, still calling the shots, still both impossible *and* impossibly talented, still the star not only of her own life but of everyone else's—and still stuck somewhere out in Oz, with no way home.

As you may have noted, most of the characters I've mentioned are women. Unlike most male writers of his generation (Norman Mailer and Philip Roth, to name two), Jaffe writes exceedingly well across the gender line; his female characters are at least as likable, complex, and real as their male counterparts, if not more so. In this sense, the author is a kind of literary Steve Dennis, ably and authentically slipping into the skin of the fairer sex … though in Jerry's case, there's a stable mind at the center and, thus, little risk involved!

Settings, too, are strongly evoked throughout this novel. From the dark, seedy "dive" bar of the first chapter to, in time, the ritziest of Vegas clubs and Manhattan theaters, and from New York to Hollywood to Paris to London and back again, Jaffe scripts a vivid, exciting 1950s spectacle of glitz and glamour, drama and dance, music … and mayhem. Steve has neither the time nor the patience for Dayton, Ohio—though more time there would surely do him good!—and so, neither does this novel.

Within the *mise-en-scène* of *Jennie Darling*, the colors are always a bit more intense and the lights just a little brighter than we'd like ... yet with the blackest of film-noir shadows creeping along the edges.

Theme? There are several. Two of them, I've already discussed: "Be careful what you wish for, because ... "—Definitely. "What profteth it a man," etc.—Without a doubt. But above and beyond these is another, and I'll defer to the Bard for its best expression: "This above all: to thine own self be true / And it must follow, as the night the day / Thou canst not then be false to any man." Lucky Laertes (in *Hamlet*, of course), to have a father as wise as Polonius; if Steve Dennis had been so fortunate in his own parentage, it might have saved him, his wife, and their child a great deal of pain, heartache, and loss ...

... But then we wouldn't have much of a story, would we? And we do; we have one *hell* of a story. I don't want to disclose too much, lest I rob you of the pleasure of discovery; suffice it to say that the plot moves inexorably into ever-darker places, though often with the ironic illusion of those places being diamond-bright.

While we're on the subject of illusion, consider the huge role that make-up plays in this narrative—and consider *its* relation to the concept of "illusion." For, as any savvy seven-year-old can tell you, something that's "made up" isn't real at all.

Jaffe's narrative is rife with the kind of plausible surprises that, to me, comprise the Holy Grail of fiction—and the hallmark of organic writing that "lets plot happen." The book is also cleverly and elegantly structured, with several chilling echoes and repetitions-for-effect, a few well-timed (and dramatically justified) point-of-view shifts to underline Steve's escalating identity crisis, and an italicized set-piece at the novel's dead center (Don't skip ahead; it won't work if read out of turn!) that takes your breath away.

This may be the story of a nightmare. But the *craft* of it, the writing itself? That's the stuff of dreams.

Having read, line-edited, and now written the Foreword for Jaffe's first novel, I chuckle to think back to our first meeting, a few years ago. Jerry was in the audience for "The Lying Game: Confessions of a Fiction Writer," an 80-minute performance that I presented—largely to retirees—at the public library in his town of residence, Skokie, Illinois. Apparently, he liked what he saw and heard that night, for he asked for my business card, then took me out for breakfast and a bending-of-my-ear. A couple of ironies come to mind (hence my chuckling): one, that a man whose first experience of me was "on stage"—where, if the reviews are to be believed, I can come across as intense—would enlist me to work with him on the story of an intensely driven showman. And two, that Jerry's presence at a learning-in-retirement program would pull him *out* of retirement and plunge him into a whole new career!

One final irony—no; less an irony, really, than an appropriate and most fitting happenstance: This talented, charming man, whom I'm honored to call my colleague and friend, professed to me early on that writing and publishing a novel was his "dream" … then jumped right into the oft-nightmarish process (writing, rewriting, inputting suggested edits, proofreading, etc.) needed to get there—with the quite-successful end result now residing in your hands.

"Dreams into nightmares"—? For Steve Dennis, maybe.

But for Jerry Jaffe? Nightmares into dreams.

**Paul McComas**
**Author of *Unforgettable*, *Planet of the Dates*, and *Unplugged***
**Evanston, Illinois**

ONE MORE TIME,

JENNIE DARLING

by

Jerry Jaffe

# CHAPTER ONE

About halfway up the block, Stella waved to him from beside their five-year-old badly rusted Buick. Drifting snow settled about his shoulders as he stepped out from a nearby doorway. Steve got in the passenger's seat, slammed the door and gave a quick backward glance to the brightly lit sign that headlined The Club Chloe:

STEVEN DENNIS MASTER OF SONG

"How was it tonight?" she asked quietly.

He looked at his wife, now sitting beside him, edging her way into the street, studying the traffic pattern. That pert nose would forever remain tilted, he said to himself. As her scarf came down, he could see her usually flowing shoulder- length blonde hair drawn up into a tight bun on top, surrounded by bands of rhinestones. She held her lips tightly together. He smelled the faint odor of an animal and realized it was the collar on her coat, wet from the snow. The advertisement had said the pelt was supposed to be genuine silver fox. He suspected that it was an unfortunate canine that had wandered into the furrier's by mistake.

She glanced at him out of the corner of her eye and repeated her question.

"Well, we had all of fifteen customers. Joe kept counting their heads, probably expecting them to multiply. I stayed at the bar in between sets watching Gus rearrange the glasses." He could visualize the pudgy, bald bartender in front of him, as sad-eyed as the rest of them, his eyebrows going up and down rapidly as he spoke of the club's ultimate closing.

"Janet going to be at the party?" she asked as a matter of fact.

"She's coming with Gus as soon as she finishes singing. The guys in the band are going together in a group." He looked at the few people on the street. Each time they exhaled, clouds of white shot out into the air. "Everyone from the club will be there, except Joe. He'll be too busy going over the receipts, trying to decide how he can make the place go for another few months."

"That isn't what he told me!" She looked at him and turned away to check the traffic.

He could feel a flush come to his face and was glad the inside of the car was dark. Couldn't anyone keep their mouth shut?

They pulled up in front of a white marble condominium where a slender black doorman in a dark brown and gold braided uniform greeted them. They told him they were guests of Jay Taggart. The doorman backed away swiftly to the intercom system and checked it out with Apartment 62A.

Steve turned to her. "If you think I like coming here for Jay's annual Thanksgiving bash, you've got it all wrong. I shouldn't have let you talk me into it." He was angry with Jay for not being the friend he always said he was. For all his big talk, Jay wasn't throwing any opportunities his way.

Stella was looking at him intently, her eyes narrowing. He guessed she was reading his thoughts. "Come on, don't be angry. Jay worked hard for his success. For twenty years he was at the bottom of the totem pole. He deserves everything he's got." She tightened the leather gloves about her hands by forcibly pulling them down.

"So I've got twelve more years to go," he gritted, shuffling about the wet sidewalk, waiting for the doorman to take their car.

She brought her face close to his. "But I don't know if I have." Then she drew herself up stiffly and moved the few wisps of hair that trailed about her face back into the bun.

The doorman handed them a claim ticket. As they walked through the oversized glass doors, their car was driven away.

"Thank God for the post office and the holiday mail rush," she whispered. "It's steady money, at least!"

"Yeah, but I was so goddamn tired from hauling mail sacks around, they practically had to haul me onto the stage. Of course those dozen people in the joint were really an incentive to get up there and perform. They didn't respond to the songs," he wiped an itch away from the bottom of his nose, "so I did some imitations. I ended up with Jennie Darling. That brought what was left of the house down!"

Her voice was determined: "You have no idea how grateful I am that my folks insisted I go to Business College for two years. I found out awfully fast that the stage was not for me. Even with ten years of dancing lessons holding me up. The only good thing that ever happened to me in show business was meeting you—"

"In the chorus of 'Two's A Crowd,'" he finished the sentence for her.

She grinned and her eyes brightened. The tightness usually around them disappeared.

The rosewood-paneled elevator doors opened, and they stepped inside. She still carried herself like a tall young girl. As they turned around, the highly polished brass mirrored them. He didn't look

so bad. He still had the baby face he had been lugging around
ever since he could remember. That had been his nickname once,
and he'd licked every son-of-a-bitch in the orphanage who called
him that until they stopped. Hell, he would probably die looking
like he was twelve years old.

He ran his palm over his head. The shock of light brown hair
first resisted his hand, then settled down.

"Is it so hard to tear yourself away from show business?"
she asked, looking up at the lights flashing through numbered
circles.

"My time has *got* to finally come up."

"Uh huh! How about the home and the kids we promised
ourselves?" She swallowed and shifted her weight, looking at him
almost wistfully. "I'm not as willing as I once was to do without.
I'm sorry about that. Really, I am."

"Quiet!" He planted a soft kiss on her lips and inhaled what
he knew was the last of that expensive perfume he'd bought her
on her last birthday. He'd have to buy her a new bottle as soon as
he got lucky over a game of spastic dominos during lunch hour.

"I guess I'm upset," she smiled weakly. "Today we got a notice
that the rent on our apartment is going up."

"What?" The loudness of his voice startled him. "They should
pay us for living there." He laughed because the whole damn thing
was so funny. "How can they charge so much for so little?"

"But there's good news for a change," she interrupted his
thinking. "Sam Sloan called me this evening. He said he would
try to get you a spot on Craig Henderson's show soon."

"Nice," he smirked. "He told *me* I needed brand new
arrangements just a few days ago. While we're at it, do you think
we could also find a writer who gives a money-back guarantee on
jokes?"

She broke into gentle laughter. The elevator was slowing down, and Floor 62 was coming up. The doors silently opened, and the couple stepped onto the heavy plush rug. Christ, Jay wasn't that much older than he, but had gotten into the business years earlier. Stella took his arm and they walked down the hall to the ten-foot-tall doors that led into apartment A.

The penthouse was already overcrowded at the door. Their host, well over six feet tall and towering over Stella, bent down to kiss her and wish her a happy holiday. Jay grabbed Steve around the shoulders and ushered them to the bar. That new goatee and moustache Jay was sporting didn't make him look any better, Steve thought—only more affected.

"Couldn't you get here earlier?" Jay moaned. "Wow, that combo's loud! I've got to get them to cut down the decibels." Then, to the young man tending bar, he said, "Give the good people what they want." The door opened. "Say, someone just came in who I've been trying to see for over a week. I'll be back in a minute. Excuse me." Jay kissed Stella and patted Steve on the shoulder lightly, then made his way for the door, where an elegant-looking middle-aged couple were waving.

Stella craned her neck. "A new crowd—there aren't many here that I recognize."

Someone behind Steve pinched his ear. "Did you come by mule train?" Janet came around to face him. "Gus and I have been here for hours. I didn't do my last set because Joe shut the place early." She looked around and pouted. "The action is getting faster. Definitely not better." She raised her half-empty glass. "'Tis the season—"

"For unemployment," he finished the toast.

Her voluminous breasts were almost falling out of the low-cut black dress she was wearing and they moved from side to

side as she breathed. She smiled. There was still something fresh
about her, in contrast to her otherwise tawdry look, accentuated
by a too-bright red dye job. "At least it's not a wake. Hot, isn't
it?" she questioned, running her hand down the luminous black
satin cape resting on her shoulders. "But I'll be damned if I'll
get rid of this wrap for even five minutes. It cost me a week's
pay."

A rush of people, led by a burly wrestler type, came to the bar
to refill their glasses, and jostled them. Steve was about to start
something but thought better of it.

"Steve Dennis—The Wonder Boy!" a voice rang out over the
noise.

Stella turned to see a tall, pleasant, sandy-haired man standing
behind her. "Nat!"

Steve grabbed Nat's outstretched hand and shook it firmly.
"Where in hell have you been?"

"Not hell; Mexico. Sometimes, though, I couldn't tell the
difference."

"Where's Gwen?"

"She divorced me in California and took the kids to Canada
to marry a stockbroker. But don't be unhappy about it. I'm not;
I'm free and easy and this time I can afford it. The market has
blessed me!" He gently patted his stomach, which was beginning
to destroy the symmetry of his tailored tuxedo jacket.

"Janet, this is Nat Graham. Janet is our singer at the Chloe,"
Steve explained.

"The late Chloe, that is," she grimaced.

"Is that joint still standing?"

"Air pollution is doing its best to hold it up. Damn," she
muttered as she was pushed into Nat by people hemming them
in on all sides. "Jay should install traffic lights in here."

A drum roll signaled an event about to take place. Small chairs were set together, and the lights began blinking on and off. "Jesus, we're going to have to sing for our supper." Steve pulled his mouth over to one side: "Well, at least they should be a more appreciative audience than the one I just left at the Chloe."

Jay strode into the center of the room. A wave of hand clapping started. Using volunteers from the audience, he did an impromptu off-color version of his question-and-answer show. His guests roared and stamped their feet as he played back and forth with sex-loaded one-liners.

A willowy white-haired blonde who'd been tailing Jay all evening was introduced next as a singer. She wasn't bad, but she was flat. She sang with everything she had, including her voice, but could not hold the crowd's attention. When she realized this, she stopped gyrating to the music and started to sing more loudly.

Several people in the audience began chanting, "Take it off, take it off." She held up the index finger of her right hand and kept on with her singing. Finally, in exasperation at her reception, she walked out of the performing area in a huff. The audience cheered loudly.

Jay leapt into the spotlight and called out, "Where the hell are you, Steve?"

The boisterous crowd began to chant, "We want Steve. We want Steve," and Nat shoved him forward. He caught reflections of rings and watches on the hands that moved him to the center of the room. When he got there, his tiredness receded and his senses snapped to attention.

"Why aren't you all at the Chloe?" he yelled. "We're so broke, we'll welcome anybody!" The remark drew a round of interested laughter.

"I've been there once," a voice called out.

"Once is enough," another answered.

"More than," Steve retorted, "but like it or not, you are going to be entertained by its *star!*" The small group behind him faked it, and he began to sing. He heard the beginnings of talk over his song and inwardly cringed. Damn it—he was losing them. But he would not sing more loudly to get their attention.

"And now for another fabulous entertainer. Here's Hip Reynolds, Singing Cowpoke Extraordinaire." He started to sing in the familiar twang of the current western folk hero, and the chatter stopped. Simultaneously he went into Hip's familiar lope as he continued with the tune. Great! He had them! When he finished the number, he smiled.

"I'll do Matt Dagger next—"

"*Everybody* does Matt Dagger," an icy voice called out.

"Everybody does him good, too," someone else added.

"Give them a load of Jennie Darling!" Janet's voice pierced the dark. He could barely see her standing off to one side. "Show them," she shouted. "Catch!" Her black cape sailed through the air and as it collapsed against him, he found her makeup bag in its pocket.

He turned away from his audience and quickly combed bangs across his forehead, pulling out a long lock of hair on each cheek. Bending to catch the light in the compact's mirror, he drew on lips and eyebrows. Then he wrapped the black cape around himself and turned around.

The room abruptly quieted. "Well?" He paused. "I'm here. What would you like me to sing?" He had them—again! The titles of Jennie's hit records came flying across the room at the same time, making it difficult for him to decide. He couldn't go wrong with any of them.

After he'd finished singing "Tip-Tap-Toe," in response to ear-splitting applause, he stepped forward and threw them an enthusiastic Jennie Darling kiss.

"'One More Time'," a voice called out as the noise died down. He vetoed the suggestion with a shake of his head. That song, written for Jennie years ago for her first starring picture, was as personal as her fingerprint. The crowd began chanting, "One More Time. One More Time." The combo segued into the familiar introduction. He wished they hadn't done that. Now, he'd end up looking like a horse's ass. The band played the introduction again. In resignation, he began the prayerful number. Everyone knew when to expect the cry in the lyrics, and they were not disappointed. He tenderly held onto each word and phrase.

Suddenly, he heard someone else singing on the other side of the room. Determined, he continued the duet. Damn! Some broad out there had her down better than he did. He heard a rush of whispers run through the crowd. He was losing them again. Someone was slowly walking toward him with a vaguely familiar shrug. She was touching shoulders and shaking hands as she came forward. Then it hit him like a wave slapping against his body. Nobody today had that kind of galvanizing charisma. Even in the dark, she was lighting up the room.

She slowly came into the lighted area. Her red-brown hair was cut short, falling carelessly about her head, the curl ends drawn onto her cheeks, giving her an elfin quality. Her large, child-like eyes were warm and friendly. She had performed the song times beyond counting, yet the words came out as sincerely as they had the first time she'd sung it. Steve could sense the audience anxiously waiting for his next move.

She came up to his side. Christ, she was almost as tall as he. She brought her hands up to her hair and extended her long fingers, each one crowned with a dark red nail. When it came to stage presence, anything she didn't know, she didn't have to.

Her eyes told him to follow her. Picking up the cue, he tried to anticipate her every move. A chuckle came from the crowd when he erred, but they did finish the song together. From behind, her hand pushed his upper body down in a bow, and when he straightened up, she kissed him.

The lights came on. The cheers were deafening.

"Thank you," she said humbly to the audience, then turned to him. "And, you, too—whoever you are."

A throng pulled her away, leaving Steve alone on the improvised stage. He pulled off the cape as Stella and Janet joined him, and he returned it together with the makeup bag. Taking a tissue from Stella, he wiped his face, still feeling the tingle of Jennie's magic. "She's really something," he murmured to himself.

After several minutes with the group that had taken her away, Jennie came toward him and smiled.

"To coin an oft-used phrase, 'Where have you been all my life?'" Suddenly she tightened as a number of people descended upon her. "In here!" She grabbed his arm and pulled him away from Stella and Janet into a nearby bedroom. After locking the door, she kicked off her shoes and worked up her skirt to straighten her stockings.

"Are you a transvestite?" When he said no, she continued, "Are you queer?" Again, he said no. "Well. *That's* something! Who taught you to do me that well?"

"No one, but I've seen all your pictures many times." He told her he had done it first as a lark, then began to use her in his act every once in a while.

"We even look alike," she peered at him, "except for the obvious. Do you do a straight-out mimic act?"

"I sing," he answered, flattered by her interest. "And I tell jokes. The other stuff is what I do when I get desperate."

"You should get desperate all the time. You've got it, Baby, and nobody knows more about talent than little Jennie. Where do you work?"

"At the Club Chloe. Don't blink while you're there or you'll miss my act."

"You're barking up the wrong talent. When I first heard you do me, I was pissed, but when you did it so well, I became fascinated. You should work up something wild to capitalize on that. It's too rare a gift to just let lay. In the Orient, it's elevated to a high art. Say, I'm going back to the Coast next week. Come out there with me! You can stay at my place and I'll help you work out an act."

She crossed her arms against her chest and waited.

"I'm married," he blurted.

"So?" she continued, nonplussed, "Drag her along. I've got a big-enough place that I almost own."

"Bring Stella?"

"Stella?" she echoed in disbelief, then paused. "Why not? Nobody named Stella can be that much trouble." She eyed him critically. "Look, Lady Bountiful is just not my sort of thing, but I *am* offering you a hand. If you're really going to do me, then do me first class. Nobody shortchanges Jennie Darling." She waited. "Well?"

"For years I've waited for a break, and here it is because of a dumb party stunt." He hadn't had anything to drink, yet was already beginning to feel light-headed.

"You can return to New York if you don't like the set-up. The trains and planes still go both ways." She stood before the mirror and brushed off her dress. "I'll give you my phone number." She jotted it down, then pressed the slip of paper into his hand. "Baby, you're going places!" Then she hit her forehead with her hand. "I'll be damned! I get the craziest feeling that I'm talking to myself."

As she unlocked the door, Stella burst in. Startled, Jennie jumped back and glared. Stella rested her gaze on Steve, waiting for him to say something.

"My wife," he explained.

She studied Stella appraisingly. "I take it all back." She stifled a grin.

He looked at her, perplexed.

"About the name Stella not meaning trouble, that is." She quickly drew herself up and walked directly past Stella into the living room, where she was immediately surrounded.

"What was that all about?" Stella asked as she leaned against the door jamb.

"Nothing much. She had too damn much to drink." He looked at the slip of paper in his hand, crushed it into a ball, and tossed it into the waste basket.

Then he and Stella left the room to join the rest of the guests.

# CHAPTER TWO

He hadn't noticed it before, but in each of the letters of the "Club Chloe" sign, at least one bulb was burned out. Steve resolutely pushed open the door and slammed into Gus. The paunchy man in his striped bartender's apron jumped back and expectantly held out his arms. His fat cheeks swayed back and forth until their weight stopped the motion. Then he grinned.

"What are you doing up here, Gus?"

"I'd be back at the bar if there were any customers. Hell, this place wouldn't draw a crowd if it were a union hall." He ran his hand over his freckled bald head, patting down imaginary hairs, then shook his head disgustedly.

Across the room, the group was beginning a set, and Janet, shielding her eyes from the spotlight, dedicated her number to the only two patrons in the club. The new song sounded a bit ragged, but what the hell: what better time was there to rehearse?

Leaning on the reservations lectern, Steve took a cigarette from the drawer and lit it. "How come you're still here, Gus?"

"I get tired of reading the want ads at home!"

"With those jokes, you should be the headliner here instead of me! How was Thanksgiving?"

"OK. The kids got on my nerves so I was kind of glad to get back. Where are you going when we close shop?"

"Not to the post office!" He brought his hands around the

sides of the stand. "I've got a few things working." He didn't mention that he had been dropping in at the offices of agents, ostensibly to say hello. Those assholes were always out for new talent, but old talent got all the breaks when you really came down to it.

"How's Stella?"

"Happy," he lied. "She told me to give you her best."

Since the club was nearly empty, Steve cut his act short. He used a few new jokes he'd just bought and let his imitations go with Matt Dagger. He knew Joe would complain about that, but it didn't matter. The tinny applause from the solitary couple haunted him all the way to the bar.

Someone came close and kissed him on the cheek. Janet's perfume still lingered after she'd moved away. "You're still here?" Steve asked. She looked tired in spite of her efforts to appear vivacious. Even in the dimness, he could see her light hazel eyes clouded over.

"Not for long. I don't have the guts to stay at this party and be picked off like a duck in a shooting gallery."

Steve took a swallow of her drink, swiveled off the stool and walked to the door as Joe entered. He stood his ground until the club's owner nearly walked into him.

"Oh, I didn't see you." Joe pulled his horn-rimmed glasses off his pockmarked nose. "Happy holidays, Steve."

"Why not? How long, Joe?"

"The truth?" He replaced his glasses.

"That's why I asked."

"One week for sure. Maybe two. Hang on for three." He rubbed his hands together as if it were cold inside the club. Years of being indoors had given his skin a waxy pallor in spite of his weekend attempts to acquire a suntan, either outdoors or under a sun lamp. His heavy shoulders drooped; he tried to summon a smile but it fell short of realization. "What a shitty business."

"Yeah, I'll start putting out feelers. Maybe Janet and I can whack an act together. I'll talk to her about it later. Ciao." Steve walked back to the bar where the musicians had joined Janet and Gus. As he approached them he heard ripples of whistling in the dark.

"Level, man," Bernie, the group leader, prodded. "We know what you were talking to Joe about."

"OK. One more week definitely."

Everyone drew a breath in unison.

He knew they were making plans they knew they could no longer delay, searching for paths to the next job. "Well, there are always weddings, bar-mitzvahs and funerals. We'll all scramble, and if we can do each other any good, we will."

"Steve!" Joe's voice sounded hollow in the near-empty room. "Telephone. Take it in my office."

Steve opened an almost-invisible door along the far wall and sat in Joe's chair, its leather panels pulling away from seams as a result of supporting great weight. As he picked up the phone, he heard Joe click off at the other end. "Steve Dennis," he said crisply.

"Where are you?" a female voice demanded.

Irritated, he replied, "Here! And just who the hell are you?"

"Jennie! Jennie Darling! And you should be here! I shouldn't have to spend my hard-earned cash to remind you."

Was this her idea of a joke? No, it couldn't be. Her voice had too much of an edge to it. What a sketch and a half! His free arm hit the desk with a dull thud. Clenching his teeth, he was too flustered to match wits.

She waited a moment. "What's holding you back? Who's holding you back? The Mouse?"

"The Mouse?"

"Stella!"

"Christ, I thought you were kidding."

"Jennie does not kid—"

"Hey, I just can't pick up and leave."

"The hell you can't. You can do anything if you really want to. Get off the pot and start moving west."

"Hey now, wait. This only happens when it's written into the script."

"In *my* scripts—in *my* scenes." There was an urgency in her tone, but it suddenly disappeared. Had it been there at all? "Well," her voice rose sharply, "do you come out here, or are you a professional second stringer?"

"Is this offer legit? Stay with you and work up an act?" It had to be a dream. Pretty soon the alarm clock would ring and shoot him into another day at the post office. "I don't believe it."

"Jennie does not kid," she repeated.

"All right." He paused and hoped she wouldn't hang up. This was a gift horse he didn't want to watch run away. "As of right now, I'm here for one more week. That's it," he said with as much finality as he could muster. "I'll fly out on the first orange."

"I'll get someone to help you with a booking so you can eat while we're drumming up a routine."

"What's in it for you?"

"Satisfaction!" she bellowed into the receiver.

He pulled the phone away from his ear for a moment, then brought it back.

"And a few other things I'm not quite sure about myself at this time. But we'll make this quirky town sit up and take notice. You're going to be my A-1 discovery."

"Deal me in! Give me your number and I'll call you back at the end of the week."

"Are you bringing The Mouse?"

He stopped to think. Would Stella leave New York for an opportunity as flimsy as this? He doubted it. Still, she might. After all, he had been chasing opportunity for years. Now, it finally seemed to be chasing him.

"I'll be looking for you."

Before he had a chance to reply, he heard the line go dead. She sure didn't waste any time, he thought, and replaced the receiver. Could it really happen as easily as this? Somebody opening a door for him without his pushing and shoving? One of the most extraordinary talents in the business was at his side to help him. The room around him no longer looked grim and drab.

Steve began to smile.

*   *   *

Stella leaned against the warm oven, tall on its giraffe-like iron legs, and absentmindedly twisted a dish towel. She avoided looking at him.

"Why get mixed up with her?" When he didn't answer, she started again. "Look I never seriously asked you to quit the business because I know how much it means to you. But linking up with *her*? I know what I would do, but I can't tell *you* what to do." She finally threw the towel onto the small kitchen table; it collapsed into a heap. "Hell," she blurted out in desperation, "do what you think is right."

He cradled her head in his arm and moved it onto his chest. She felt warm, small and very vulnerable. She certainly deserved more from life than their past decade of poverty. Resting his face in her hair, he looked at their shabby living room. It was so small.

He rarely used it because of the hemmed-in feeling he got when he sat in either of their two facing chairs.

"I've got to go to California. I've got to go!"

"I've got to stay." Her voice was so low, he almost was unsure he'd heard anything. "I'll be here when you come back. You'll be back." She pulled away from him. "You don't have to be in the business to know she's totally washed up."

"Temporarily," he corrected. "She'll make it back up the mountain. She's done it time and time again."

"No one will touch her! She's too unpredictable!"

"She's a genius," he said sharply. "In front of an audience, she's magic."

"The trick is getting her there, on time and sober." She wiped her hands on her apron. "The only reason she has time for you is because she has time on her hands. That's no secret. And, she's broke."

"It makes no difference. I'll learn from her. It'll be a new beginning for us, you'll see. What have I got to lose? There will always be a post office around somewhere, waiting. Hell," he paused, "you know you don't have to worry about me and Jennie—"

"I know—"

"What then?"

"It doesn't matter."

But he knew that it did, and she wasn't telling him why.

# CHAPTER THREE

Steve opened the drapes, and bright sunlight flooded the room. He pushed the button: the viewing screen disappeared into the ceiling, and the projector slid noiselessly down into the desk. Then he put the soundtrack of "Jamaican Lady" into the tape player. Swaying his head to the beat, he studied his reflection in the mirror. There was a clash of cymbals, then Jennie came on, pouring life into the rhythmic number. He let his head drop back loosely until he could feel her throaty vibrato; then he started to sing.

It was always an uphill struggle—phrasing short groups of words, then working several phrases at a time. But now, the two of them sang as one. When they finished on the same beat, the same note, and with the same inflection, he smiled.

He exchanged the tape for one with only the accompaniment and sang along with it a half-dozen times, then pushed down the buttons for "play" and "record."

The familiar pulse began. French horns picked it up in the background; a cacophony of bells jingled their way into the music, and then came what he had been waiting for. With the clash of cymbals, his voice became Jennie Darling's. It was a studied journey to that last yell, but he got there on time, purring, moaning, bringing the sound up from the center of his gut. During the bridge, he tried to go into her shuffle, but his feet were still too uncomfortable in high heels.

As he finished singing, he heard a screech in the driveway. A car door slammed shut. On her way into the house, Jennie furiously kicked a stone in her path: it hit and cracked the library window. She shoved the front door open with such force, it banged off the wall. In the middle of the foyer, she abruptly brought her hands to her head.

"Jeeeeeeesus Christ!" she screamed. "Louise! Where the hell are you?"

A scrawny, small, gray-haired woman of indeterminate age gave her a patronizing look as she came into the room, her thin lips tightly drawn and pursed.

"Get me a goddamned bullshot and give it plenty of character."

"OK, I know. A fifth of vodka and a half-ounce of bullion," Louise mumbled under her breath, then disappeared.

When she returned, Jennie grabbed the drink, spilling some as she let go of her coat. Stepping over the crumpled mound at her feet, she strode into the living room and fell onto the sofa. Her face was flushed. The veins in her neck stood out against pale skin. Why had she come home alone? And, in whose car? Something must have happened at the television studio.

Most afternoons, her current lover, Ron Pilda, chauffeured her home.

Maybe she could be humored out of her rage. It was worth a try. Steve came into the doorway. "Hey—I've got a surprise for you!"

"A dilly, I'm sure!" She covered her face with her free hand and held out the empty glass with the other. "First, a refill." When Louise came back with one, Jennie broke into an incongruous laugh. Lifting one foot from the floor, she pounded on the arm of the sofa with her free hand. "You walk so damn funny in those pumps."

Using his toe, Steve pried the slipper off the heel of his other foot. "Every time I take a step, that heel spike goes up my back. My calves are killing me! How can you walk on them?"

"Baby, I can't stand *without* them!"

"I don't think I'm man enough to do it. You deserve some kind of medal for going through life on these stilts."

"Get used to your working wardrobe. Hell, if you worked on a high-rise, you'd be walking in gunboats." She patted a place on the sofa next to her, working hard to control herself. "There are no worse things than that daytime quiz show. I feel like a whore every morning. If that MC doesn't stop upstaging me, I'll claw his eyes out if he doesn't get at me first with his knitting needles. Do you know how degrading it is to go out there and be 'cute' for sixty minutes a day for eight weeks?" She rubbed the sides of her body, exasperated. "God knows how long I can keep it up."

"Iris called—"

"My daughter?" Surprised, she tilted her head.

"She'll call again tonight. I told her you would be home then. She didn't ask who I was."

Jennie leaned forward, took a mint from an inlaid wooden box. "I wonder what she wants." A smile started to cross her face. "I'm real proud of my college baby." She started up from the sofa, but the effort was too much for her. "I've just *got* to hop a plane, and see her, or send her money to come here."

"Louise told me the income tax man called—" As soon as the words had left his mouth, he was sorry he'd said them.

"Again?" She sighed helplessly. "I've already told them to give me a little more time." She shook her head slowly and gazed about the room. "The bastards want to take this roof right off my head. To get work, I've got to look as if I don't need it, and how do I do that with Uncle Sam chewing away at my ass?" She shook her head as if to clear it. "I've just got to see Iris! Is that the surprise?"

As Louise passed the door to the living room, Jennie spotted her. "Louise!"

The maid came into the room with an air of resignation.

"Where was the green silk I was supposed to wear for today's taping? I had to wear the same rag I wore last Wednesday." She bounced off the couch so fast, she almost tripped. Then she drew herself up regally. "Couldn't you remember to send it to the studio? You are the last word in incompetence. Take two weeks' pay and get the hell out of here."

"Great. Pay me for the *first* week; *then* you can fire me." Louise's clear gray eyes stared through Jennie. "The reason you didn't get your green silk is because there was not enough money to get it out of the cleaners."

Grabbing both of Louise's shoulders, Jennie tried to shake her thoroughly, but the maid stood her ground and Jennie ended up almost leaning on her.

"You're stealing from me. Just like everyone else." She stopped abruptly. Supporting herself on the back of a nearby sofa, she began to laugh. "Hell, I can't even fire my maid because I haven't paid her. Do you know of a bigger joke?"

The doorbell rang, and Jennie raised her hand imperiously. "Tell Mister Pilda he can jolly well get his clothes out of my closets. Be sure to ask him where the hell he was when we finished taping. The director loaned me his car to get home because he knew I couldn't afford a cab. Christ, I wasn't made to star in … this farce!"

Accustomed to her tirades against her current lover, Steve waited for her temper to dissipate. What had happened to Ron? Ultimately, her anger would pass, and they would all play gin rummy, as usual, for nickels, until the early hours of the morning. Steve genuinely liked Ron. He was friendly, puppy-like, all physical and no trouble to have around—a perfect foil for Jennie.

She forced down the sobs, struggling upward as Louise returned with a gigantic bouquet of red roses in a vase and placed them on the table. Her eyes widened.

"The nerve! That bastard thinks he can make up with me. Huh, he was probably shacking up with some secretary he tripped over in the commissary." She turned to Steve. "But, it was nice— the flowers, I mean. God, they're lovely." She inhaled their scent. For a moment, her face became soft and pliant.

Then her voice changed register. "I'll bet that son-of-a-bitch charged them to my account. Oh, my God, the presents I gave him! The suits! The diamond watch! And he isn't even that good in bed. He's out!" she stormed. "I don't want him living here any longer. He didn't even have the guts to write an apology and include it with the flowers. Class shows, Stevie, and so does the lack of it! Louise!" she yelled. "Get these goddamn roses out of here before I throw them out the window!"

Louise appeared in the doorway. "This was on the doorstep. It must have fallen out of the wrappings."

Jennie snatched the pastel envelope as Louise took the flowers away. As she ripped it open, she called out, "Break the damn vase, too!"

Louise tucked some hairs at the back of her neck into the bun resting on top of her head, did a turn and burlesqued a curtsy. Her thin lips almost spread into a smile. She gave Steve a "What can I do?" shrug and winked, then left the room.

Jennie wiped the side of her mouth, lost in thought as she read the note. Had her companion of the past months actually found something to say? Suddenly, she ran from the room, only to return sorrowfully a moment later. "The flowers are already in the garbage … in the broken vase. Christ, it's absolutely terrible having a maid who follows your orders to the letter!"

Steve shrugged. "I thought you said …"

"The flowers weren't from Ron. They were from Mike Fallon, my old Metro producer. We did some fantastic, mind-blowing musicals together." Her high-polished nails darted up her arms. "Those were the years! The golden ones! I was protected, privileged, pampered—and I worked like a field hand. 'Jennie The Roman Candle,' they called me. He wants something." She looked at Steve warmly. "I said you would be lucky for me, Baby." She reached for his hands and held them tightly. "And I was right." She gently settled down again into the sofa and crossed her legs at the ankles. "He'll get in touch, and when he does, I mustn't appear too eager."

He looked down at her and ran his hand gently over her coppery hair. She was a real thoroughbred, and she knew the track like nobody else did. He reached to switch on the new tape.

Her head tilted in recognition. "God, I was absolutely flawless then." She spoke with detached admiration. "What a way with a lyric—"

"That's the surprise," he explained. "That's *me!*"

She squinted her eyes to see him better. After the final notes, there came the faraway screech of a car braking to a fast stop. She looked up at him quizzically.

"That was you, outside." He pointed out the window. "Racing up the driveway."

"Play it again!"

He did.

She closed her eyes and began to sing. He joined her, and together, the three voices sang as one.

\*    \*    \*

In the dining room, they listened to a cricket calling to its mate. Steve took another spoonful of tamale pie from the center of the table. Across from him, Jennie spoke quietly: "He should be calling within a few days if I know anything at all about Hollywood politics."

"Stella called."

"The Mouse?" Jennie raised her eyebrows slowly and started to laugh. "What have you been sending her through the mail? Cheese?"

In their conversations, Stella never inquired about Jennie, and Jennie studiously avoided referring to Steve's wife. Yet he surmised that Jennie knew he missed her, if for no other reason than having been celibate during the whole time he had been in California. Stella was weakening. When she realized he wasn't coming back as soon as she'd initially thought, she'd begun entertaining the idea of relocating.

At the close of each telephone conversation, he realized how much he missed her easy laugh. He wanted to reach out to her, to make love to her and to plan for their future.

"She's going to come out here when I get a job." After his performance today, he was anxious to start working the act to see if it had the pizazz Jennie thought it did. At first, he'd had mixed feelings about getting completely into her character and wondered what Gus, Bernie and Joe would say when they saw him wigged and in a gown. But, he would, after all, perform as himself during the second part of the act. The most important thing was for him to be seen, no matter how he did it.

"Yes," she answered. "The Scandal is a good place to get yourself launched. I know the owner ... very well. Everyone in the Valley goes there. God," she added, "I despise hamburger!"

"You're lucky you're eating meat," Louise replied as she took their plates from the table and quickly moved away.

"Lay off." Jennie circled one hand with the other. "This isn't the first time we've been down and out."

"You're right about that! If I had any brains, I'd have left you years ago."

"Lucky you haven't," Jennie snapped, turning her attention back to Steve. "If I can't get anything here soon, I may do a New York play." He could see she almost believed it.

"Or starve," Louise added, backing through the swinging door with the remains of dinner.

Past the full-length windows, lights were strewn like diamonds over the blue velvet curtain that was Los Angeles. Everyone in the business knew she was having trouble, but how much, they didn't want to know. On this lonely mountain top, she was stranded with her gargantuan pride. Steve was embarrassed to find he now felt more compassion for Jennie than ever before.

"How many times have you been broke?" he asked, eyes still on the view.

"You heard Louise. Many times." She ran her fingers absentmindedly through her hair, then walked around the table on legs that seemed too slender to support her. Jennie rested her arm on his shoulder.

He could hear her deep breathing.

"Baby, I owned it all once, and I don't even know where it went." She paused. "Yes, I do. I guess you have to be an all-time idiot to go through twenty million bucks before you're forty. Today, I can't put my hand on a single dime. I've nothing left." She looked around the room. "I've sold almost everything. The Renoirs, the Riveras and all but one fur to pay back-taxes."

She slipped her fist into her hand. "I was a money fountain, and everyone came around for a long, cool drink. My mother, my father, my sister, not to mention the keepers on the funny farms when I had to go there." She braced herself against the table. "Well, the hungry relatives are all gone now. There's only Iris and myself left.

"Maybe I'll go to England. I'll put out a few feelers." She pointed her finger at him. "It'll happen again. When the going gets good, all the ass-kissers in the world will be out again. You'll see!"

"Well, what did they say at the Scandal?"

"The job is yours. Did Louise alter those gowns for you? They'll bring you luck." Momentarily forgetting her own troubles, she patted his arm. "I'll get the greasepaint out and meet you in the rehearsal room in fifteen minutes." Then she strode out of the room like a young girl on a new adventure.

*   *   *

"You definitely need more padding," Jennie decided. Taking a pair of foam rubber breasts larger than the ones in the gown's bodice, she quickly made an exchange and stepped back. "Great!" Her eyes gleamed. "Turn sideways. Stand straight. Walk away from me."

On high heels, Steve stepped uncertainly across the floor.

"Don't clump! Put one foot directly in front of the other, in dainty, little steps. That's fine. Glide." She nodded approvingly as he executed a turn. As Steve walked around the room in a box-like pattern, she took a wig coiffed exactly like her own hair—short, with daggers of red at intervals around the sides. A blast of bangs fell carelessly over the front.

He sat down on the chair in front of her.

"Check your watch so we can see how long this takes."

He moved his face close to the brilliantly lighted mirror and watched her apply shadow to the hollows of his cheeks and the edge of his jawline. With white grease, she drew a line down his nose, then highlighted his forehead and chin. Squinting, she placed the wig over his head as he guided it into place with his hands. The change was startling. The anomaly he had been a moment ago was suddenly and clearly a woman.

"It's coming," she said. Studying the pictures tacked to the frame of the mirror, she carefully marked the curve of one eyebrow. "You do the other."

As he copied the eyebrow in carefully measured strokes, her look began to emerge. She applied layer upon layer of black to his lashes and brushed dark shadow onto the upper lids, then applied a stark white under the arch of the brow. He followed her movements, studying, concentrating, memorizing.

"I can't stand it," she groaned. "You're gorgeous."

She outlined his lips, then used dark lipstick for the top lip and a lighter one for the bottom. He blotted them, then held his lips taut as she applied a light coating of Vaseline.

"My God, you're really me."

In the mirror, staring at him, was Jennie Darling. He brought his hand up to his face …

"No." She pulled his arm down. "You'll ruin it." Spellbound by her own production, she continued to gaze at him as she backed across the room and shoved the rehearsal tape from "Jamaican Lady" into the player. "Do it." She leaned against the ballet bar, engrossed in her creation …

After he'd finished singing, Jennie remained motionless for a moment. A tear ran out of her eye. He lifted her hands gently and kissed her forehead. She hugged him tightly and returned the kiss. "You were magnificent," she murmured. "I couldn't have done better. Do 'One More Time'—"

"No thanks," he replied. "No one else has ever come close to you. It's yours, as much as Jolson's 'Swannee' or Garland's 'Over the Rainbow.' Doing it would be a cheap, second-rate stunt."

"You're not cheap, and you're definitely not second rate! You're me! As much as I am!" She sat down and crossed her legs, only to get up suddenly. "I need a drink." As she left the room, she called back, "I'll get you one, too."

He took a new tape and shoved it into the player. The familiar strains of "One More Time" began. In his mind, he could see her once again in her first starring role as Melinda, wide-eyed and braided, sitting in a farm swing, convincing a depression-weary country that wonderful things could happen to it as well as to the little farm girl who dreamt she was a princess.

He began singing the words, sending her voice into each corner of the room.

When she returned, her eyes lit up. "That song!" She sighed. "Beautiful little Melinda." Her eyes closed in recollection.

"Who," he questioned, "could ever forget her?"

*   *   *

In the dark of his bedroom, he was suddenly awakened. A series of wails outside his room died away. Then he heard footsteps and a heavy thud. He became aware of a small, consistent knocking on his door. Cautiously, he made his way across the floor.

Jennie, multicolored rivers of makeup streaming down her face, stared up at him. What the hell had happened now? She'd been happy a few hours ago in the rehearsal room. The sash from her robe had fallen to the floor; he knelt down to pick it up.

"Ron left," she mumbled. "He came and got his things. He actually left me." She swayed into Steve.

He held her firmly around the waist, led her to the kitchen, and seated her at the table. Going to the cabinet, he took out a saucepan. There was no need to bother Louise so late at night.

"I don't need that." She shoved away the warm milk he'd heated for her. He caught the glass just before it would have slid off the table. Her sobbing was quiet as she drummed her fingers on the tabletop. "Get me a scotch before I burst my skin."

He brought the drink into the kitchen, and she downed it. "There's a beer in the refrigerator." He brought her a can, which she quietly polished off. "There's nothing quite like a boilermaker to get it all together." Foam clung to her lips, giving her a whimsical look, but Steve knew better than to smile. Instead, he sat down quietly beside her.

"He actually moved out!" Her amazement at Ron's leaving baffled him. It wasn't the first time she had thrown him out, but he'd known it was only a matter of time before Ron would get tired of coming back. They both knew their relationship had nothing to do with love, but it did satisfy a mutual need. Still, striking out at him in anger hurt her more in the long run. Suddenly, he became aware that she was speaking. "Mike Fallon will call, won't he?"

He reassuringly nodded his head.

"I'm afraid he won't. Yet, I'm afraid he will. That scares me, too!" She looked around, almost suspicious of being overheard. "What if he offers me a shit deal? God, what am I going to do?" She brought her head down to her chest like an ashamed animal. "I've just got to get another chance." Her eyes flooded with tears, which then fell onto her hands.

"How much did you drink after we went to bed?"

She did not look up. With her thumb and forefinger, she approximated a one-finger shot. "That's all. No pills: nothing.

That louse came in as if nothing had happened. We fought, and he left." She grimaced. "That's it ... plain and simple!" She walked to the sink with the empty beer can, then turned around abruptly. "They all left me. Stevie, manage me. Please. Forget about your act, and just take me on."

He shifted his gaze to the floor, and she stepped away from him.

"Yeah. I know. You've just *got* to be a star. Well, I'm a Star!" she screamed. "And am I such hot stuff? Get me two blue pills from the bottle in that cabinet over there. Go on," she rasped. "I take that stuff like other people take vitamins. Christ," she slapped her forehead, "I've just got to pull myself together for tomorrow's taping. Thank God it's only for three more weeks." Like a child, she accepted the pills from him and the glass of water with which to wash it down.

"You'll feel better tomorrow," he said, helping her to her bedroom. There was no fight left in her. In the two months that he had been at the house, he had never seen her so disturbed. He swore under his breath at Ron, and at life in general, for treating her badly. She always said the harder she was bounced, the higher up she soared. Could she count on that happening tomorrow morning?

The alarm clock on her nightstand was set for five. He'd stay with her until then, just in case she needed something.

An oversized oil painting hung from the opposite wall: Jennie, in costume as Melinda, was peering out at the world, excited and alert, with vibrant health and hopes for the future. Her gigantic brown eyes dominated her face, and a delicately shaped mouth was poised to speak. The painting was named "The Sleeping Princess."

Nobody was ever that young and naïve, he thought, just before falling asleep in the overstuffed chair at her side.

# CHAPTER FOUR

Steve parked his newly acquired jalopy in front of Jennie's house with its sky-piercing carport looking like a theater marquee. A tourist bus had followed him, its occupants craning their necks and clutching their celebrity maps, looking as if they had just blown in from Kansas or Oklahoma. The bus hesitated as Steve pulled up the driveway, got out of the car, pushed the door open and walked through the side entrance.

What was so important that he had to be here so early? He would have come at the usual afternoon time to rehearse, but he'd rather spend the time in bed with Stella, who had arrived yesterday. Just thinking about her all-over softness gave him a warm glow.

"Jennie," he called out.

"In the rehearsal hall." Louise nodded over the load of sheets she was carrying. "We live again," she said happily. "No more hundred-and-one ways to make hamburger taste like steak." She parodied a curtsy and left the room smiling.

Jennie had been secretive during the past week. There were little hints. Before he moved to his apartment over a garage near Roxbury Drive two weeks ago, he'd overheard enough of her telephone conversations to know that something was in the wind.

Where she'd gotten the money to put on the spread for Mike

Fallon's dinner, he didn't know, but she had, and it was an elegant affair. Several backers came out with Mike for drinks a few nights later. They left the house hours later looking grim, but determined. Maybe she was too apprehensive to tell him about it, biding her time until she finally had some real news.

"Stevie, Baby," Jennie sang out as he entered. She was dressed in skin-tight black toreador pants with a man's shirt, many sizes too big, over her tiny frame. She extended her hands, and her red beetle nails flashed. Her face reflected excitement.

"I *told* you everything would work out. And it has! It has!" She came sailing up to him, putting her hands around his neck, and kissed him full on the lips. As she jerked away, that wonderful look of astonished delight came to her face.

"I *did* it. I *did* it! I'll never have to worry about money again. I'll be able to pick and choose and won't have to play games anymore." She let her head go back and come up quickly. "It's a dream coming true."

Stepping back, with one hand on her hip, she said, "I told them I wanted only top talent. And," she stopped for emphasis, "the full treatment! A limousine to take me to the sets. Kasavata to do my hair. He's an absolute genius." Her voice was warm. "Mervin Manning for my costumes." She crossed her arms and closed her eyes. "He knows how to minimize every flaw I've got. And Jack Rayburr directing. Joey Fantoni to do the choreography. Who in hell could pick a greater crew?" She bowed reverently. "All *I* gotta do is strut my stuff."

Suddenly, she turned serious. "It's me all the way. Just like in the old days. I get full approval of all footage. Who gets *that* today? And my shooting schedule doesn't start till noon." Delighted, she fell into the chair behind her.

"They've cleared with Metro to do 'One More Time,' and I've

got six new songs and six new routines to nail down. And, I'm going to make them all mine! It's going to be Melinda all over again!

"The picture's about a small-town girl who comes to the big city," she rambled on, speaking more to herself than to him. "She makes it big and marries a bandleader who leaves her for another babe. She hits the bottle, comes back and marries again. This time, her success intimidates the good guy she's married to. He gives her the ultimatum: him, or the business. She can't give up the business—he leaves her, and socko, that's the end!"

"It's your show all the way," Steve cheered, and reached for her hand. It was terrific to see her in such high spirits, planning for a future with all the excitement of a teenager.

"No money worries ever again. I'm getting a percentage of the gross, plus. But I'll have to get in fighting trim for the role. I've got to lose about ten pounds—"

"You'll disappear," he laughed.

"The camera will put it back on. We're going to do the dramatic portions first. They'll be the easiest to do, using the equipment at the studio for the most part, but," her voice rose, "they're going to build six new sets especially for me, just like in the old days. Intricate ones for the dance numbers: split levels, revolving stages, staircases, platforms—the works!"

"Is this what you wanted to tell me?"

"Can you think of better news to share?" She left the room and returned with a couple of filled wine glasses. "News like that can't stay on ice. It wasn't only that." Her voice softened. "Iris will be here in three hours." She looked at him eagerly. "Would you be a sweetheart to good old Jennie and pick her up?"

"Why can't you meet her?"

She took a short sip of wine. "I didn't tell you quite all of it."

She started to light a cigarette, but the match went out. She cursed, got it lit and shot the smoke out of her nostrils in two blue streams. "What I said was all true, but I had to accede to conditions."

"Oh?" He leaned forward.

"I can't screw up. No-how! Ever! But I'm older now and definitely smarter." He could hear an anxiety returning to her voice. "It's my last time around to grab the gold ring. That's why I can't pick Iris up. I've got to be at the studio within one hour for preproduction talks, and then I start my exercises." She lowered her voice to a confidential whisper: "I'll be getting enough money to live on. The check comes weekly. If I louse up, I get docked."

"I thought it was your picture."

"If I run even one hour over budget, the costs come out of my percentage. I've got to be on time—every time—for fittings, story conferences, rehearsals, everything."

He whistled. "They've really got you nailed to the cross!"

"But I stand to make three and a half million after taxes if it's the hit we expect it to be." She smiled. "Don't worry your sweet ass, because I'm going to let it all hang out. Nobody has seen me for a while under full sail. I've got Iris' flight number. You can make it to the airport on time if you start now. I'll make it up to you, honest. Please, baby, entertain her for me." She leaned over and hugged him.

As Steve headed out the door, Louise nudged him in the ribs and took a deep breath of fresh air. "The Gravy Train is running again," she almost sang. "I feel it in my arthritic bones. She's pulled herself up again, and she'll be brighter than ever. It's not right for anyone with her talent to beg for pennies. She's given too much happiness to the world. She's done too much for too many people and never got that much back. Remember that green-dress incident when she was going to fire me?"

He nodded.

"The reason there wasn't enough money to take her stuff out of the cleaners that week was because she visited Burt Marks and Sybil Proyer. They co-starred with her in *The Sleeping Princess.* Anyway, they're both broke and ailing. When she left them at the Actors' Home, she ordered a television set for Burt, because his had finally conked out, and she bought Sybil a new couch." She exhaled asthmatically. "They're not the only ones she shells out for, but when I tell her to stop, she shuts me up fast. No one knows all the good she's done—no one but me. And she'd kill me if she knew I'd told you."

He felt a sudden warmth for Louise—and more admiration for Jennie, as complex as she was talented. Sure, he would help her out—just look what she'd done for him! At the car, he paused and gazed back.

"Louise, how long have you been with her?"

"Through one child, two abortions, three husbands and a couple of nervous collapses," she replied, then went back into the house.

*       *       *

With Iris seated in the car, he slammed the door, placed her only suitcase in the luggage compartment, and walked around to the driver's side. It was a balmy Los Angeles day. For a moment, he watched the sleek silver planes float onto the runways. Then he got in.

The tall girl who sat next to him bore no resemblance to her mother, except for the soulful eyes that dominated her face. Though less effervescent than Jennie, Iris seemed to be more sure of herself. She folded her large hands over the purse on her lap and turned the full effect of her green eyes on him. "To Mother's?"

"Do you mind if we stop at my place first?"

"Where do I live?" she questioned him quickly. He gave her Jennie's address. "What's our maid's name?" she fired at him. "How many animals do we have with us?" When he answered "None," she broke into a sharp laugh. "You're kosher, I guess!"

"And you're pretty cautious," he grinned back at her. "I did speak to you on the phone. Remember?"

"Anybody could be 'Steve'!" she half-smiled. "I'm almost convinced you won't try to hold me for the ransom money she doesn't have. But, you'd never believe the nuts that have tried to get to her through me." She peered at the cars on the freeway cutting through the city toward Beverly Hills. Her elbow on the armrest, her chin in her hand, she asked, "Why didn't she come out to meet me?"

He glanced sideways and told her Jennie's good news.

She studied the houses flashing by. "Maybe she's got sense enough to hold onto some of it this time. I swear, there are holes in her body that let everything slip right through."

"She'll do just fine, but she's got to go into a disciplined regime."

"Like always."

"This picture is important!"

She scratched her chin. "They all were. Listen," her voice became firm, "I'm going to insist that I read the small print in the contracts. She only reads the large stuff."

"You have a lot of savvy for a kid—"

"I was *never* a kid." She searched in her handbag for a cigarette and pushed in the lighter on the dashboard. "I want her to do well because I love her very much. She can make it fine unless they start hounding her. If they do, she'll come apart." The cigarette smoke curled about her face. "Maybe I should come back while she's filming. Tell me: Is she happy?"

"Very—but she'll be very busy. Why don't you plan to spend some time with my wife and me, doing L.A? You know, Santa Monica, beach picnics—"

"Did they drain our pool because she hasn't paid the water bill?"

He laughed. "No, but you know how preproduction plans are."

"Too well." She shrugged her shoulders in disgust.

"How come you're not in the business?" He pulled the visor down to keep the sun out of his eyes. "You're pretty enough."

"Knowing what it's done to my mother, you still ask?" She looked at him incredulously. "Mother is a phenomenon. Applause keeps her alive. When everything else turns to ashes in her mouth, she goes on stage, flashes those brown Melinda eyes and gets waves of love washed all over her." She stubbed her cigarette into the ashtray. "So she goes through it all over again, after every divorce—after every bout with emotional exhaustion, every time anyone kicks her in the teeth. I know," she grimaced, "that half the women in the world think they would like to trade places with her. But their ignorance saves them.

"She's a piggy bank that you try to fill with love through a hole in the top of her head. The trouble is that somebody stole the cork out of the other end. Hey," she asked casually, "you sleeping with her?"

He shook his head and kept his eyes on the road.

"Then you're probably doing her some good." She fumbled with the catch on her handbag. "If only she could find a man who didn't want anything from her."

"How old did you say you were?"

"Twenty. On my next birthday I'll be forty-three."

"You're at Libertyville College, aren't you?"

She pursed her lips. "For two more years. I'm in advertising and computer programming—in case you're interested." Displeased with her remark, she faced him, an apology on her face. "I'm sorry, but I'm all wrought up about Mother. And I've only got a few days here."

"It's tough that you came in just as she has this deal working. But, Iris, this picture will put her back on top for good. She says it wraps her career up as nothing before has."

"Great! That will rev her up even more. I'm going to talk to her about putting the money in an inviolate trust."

"You can't right now. She's not making that much," he blurted out, and explained the financial arrangement.

"Hogtied," she snapped, then paused. "Tell me ... what have you got going with Mother?"

This girl was sharp. And direct. He brought her up to date on everything since the first meeting with Jennie in New York. He felt uneasy at being forced to explain himself.

She looked him over critically. "You do look somewhat like her. If she's willing to work with you, you've got to be super; the only thing she knows about is talent. When do I get to see her? This afternoon?"

"Soon." He turned off the expressway.

She looked at the houses in their varied pastel shades, and the corners of her lips curled up. They turned into Roxbury Drive with its stately mansions, each challenging its neighbors in style or appointments. The lawns were carefully manicured, but there was no sign of life.

"Land of Marzipan," she clucked. "You can almost believe that everything is going to turn out all right if you live here long enough."

\*   \*   \*

Steve took the steps alongside the garage two at a time and grabbed Stella by the waist when she opened the door. Damn, it sure was good having her here. Suddenly he wished Iris wasn't with him and they could be alone.

Stella glanced over his shoulder and saw Iris. "Other women—so soon?"

He explained about Jennie's daughter.

"She's pretty," Stella said as Iris walked up the steps. "Doesn't look at all like her mother!" That was her way of getting back at Jennie for calling him away this morning.

On the table in their sparsely furnished apartment, Stella placed a pot of coffee and some sandwiches. As she went for cups, Iris sat on the sofa and rubbed the back of her neck. "What time did Mother say she would be finished?"

"She didn't." He noticed the disappointment in Iris' face. "But if she's busy, we'll take you out to dinner."

She smiled and leaned over the table for a sandwich.

"I'm surprised myself," Steve said, "at how well my new act is shaping up. Your mother was the hardest one to pin down. The others fall in line because they're more limited in what they do—but not her."

"She's got enough talent for ten people." Iris glanced at her watch. "Does Mother have your number?

He nodded.

"Then she hasn't tried to call me yet." She bit her lower lip. "I hope this isn't the way it's going to be. Did I louse up your afternoon?"

"That's OK." Steve sat down.

From the kitchen, Stella called out: "Did you tell Jennie I was in town?"

"There was no time. I'd just gotten there when she asked me

to pick up Iris." He walked toward the phone. "I'll call Louise." He heard Stella telling Iris about the difficulty she might have in getting used to the casualness of California living because she loved the changing seasons and the keyed-up style of New York City life.

Steve returned to the living room. "No answer. I'll call back in an hour."

Iris pulled a cigarette from her purse. "My luck. One week out of school, and Mother's up to her eyeballs in work."

"Come to The Chimney with us tonight," Stella suggested.

He wiped his mouth, realizing that was the way the evening was going to end. Why in hell couldn't Jennie bug out of that conference early? She said she loved Iris so, yet she was ignoring her. Shit—he just couldn't figure it out.

"I can take you home to unpack and change before we go," he said.

"Sure. I'd like, however, a few minutes to talk with Louise."

# CHAPTER FIVE

"Did you see her at all last night?" Steve asked Iris in Jennie's living room the next day.

Her voice was low: "She woke me when she came in. We talked for about a half hour and got caught up on the basics. She was tired and I—"

"Yeah?"

"Knew she was tired, so we both went to bed." He could sense her frustration.

"Honey!" Jennie floated into the room. "I've been looking all over for you. I even checked the pool for bodies." She circled her daughter happily, kissed her, then abruptly became contrite. "I'm painfully sorry about last night. Louise!" she called out. "Coffee, and lace it." Looking at Iris for a moment, she added, "Don't bother about the lace—I'll take it straight."

She moved back and, planting her fists firmly on her hips, appraised her daughter. "Isn't she beautiful? And so smart, too!"

"Mother!" Iris became embarrassed and put down the crossword puzzle on which she had been working.

"Why shouldn't I be proud? I've got my baby here, and my best friend, and things are going great."

Louise announced that breakfast was ready, and Jennie grandly motioned for them to follow her.

"What the hell time is it?" She peeked into the kitchen and, satisfied, sat down at the dining room table to sip her coffee.

"I didn't know The Mouse was in town," she said to Steve.

Iris looked at her, puzzled.

"My wife," he explained. "It's your mother's idea of a bad joke."

"Now, now," Jennie began, "you once hinted that she was on the colorless side."

"What time do you have to go back to the studio?" Iris asked.

Jennie said the limo would pick her up shortly.

"Will you be back for dinner?"

"We'll dine together tonight, a deux," she beamed. Then the smile quickly turned into a frown. "I hope to hell it isn't a rerun of yesterday. We're having some storyline trouble. And with those damned commitments I've had to make—"

"Mother, promise me you'll behave yourself. The people out there in the dark still think you're Melinda."

"My saving grace." She interlaced her fingers and rested her face upon them.

"She's going to do a terrific job," Steve butted in, and they both turned toward him at once, acting as if they had forgotten he was there. "It's a great opportunity." He thought of everyone he knew back in New York still struggling for a foothold in the business, while here, everything was being handed to her on a silver platter. All she had to do was be on time and mind her manners. "I'd like a shot like that myself."

"You'll get yours." She winked. "That's another thing I know about."

Iris summed it up tersely: "No booze, no pills, plenty of rest, and available whenever you're needed—and even when you're not, huh?"

Jennie replied, "For your information, Miss Know-it-all, Wesley Adams is back in my life." She dropped two saccharine tablets into her coffee.

"For how long this time?"

"Never you mind." Jennie helped herself to a spoonful of scrambled eggs. "He was always good to me and for me. He saw me through some of my worst times with the studio. He is now an assistant director on the picture. So what do you think of that, Smarty?"

"I think the eggs are very good this morning." Iris helped herself to more, then glanced at Steve over the rim of her coffee cup.

"You two ought to have more time together," Steve said. "It's too bad all this activity is going on just now." He was glad that Stella and Iris had gotten along so well, right from the start; his wife would see that Iris wouldn't have too much time on her hands.

"I'll be back again at the end of the semester," Iris said as she picked at the remains of her toast.

"We'll be finished shooting by then," Jennie's voice sang out, "so let's go somewhere together and do something absolutely mad."

The phone rang; it was Wesley. The studio limousine would be along shortly.

"See?" Jennie put the receiver down triumphantly. "The Star Treatment!"

"I'm so happy for you, Mom." Iris quickly stepped up to hug her.

"I'd better get to the rehearsal hall," Steve said and stood.

"Can you stay for dinner—in case of another emergency?" Jennie asked.

"Stella will be waiting. I've got to get home."

"I'll be home early, Baby." She patted Iris on the arm. "And we'll spend the whole evening together. We'll spend a whole week of evenings together." A look of concern crossed her face. "I sure could use a drink." She got up halfway from her chair but then slumped back, shooting each of her companions a smile. "Never mind! You see: I'm changing my habits already."

As Steve left the room, Jennie suggested that Iris watch him rehearse. "It'll be fun, Iris. You've no idea how amazing he is— even without the makeup and wigs."

*       *       *

Steve fell onto the gym mat along one side of the rehearsal hall and rested, a towel loosely thrown over his face. He was conscious of his breathing and the rising and falling of his chest. No matter how hard you worked at it, rehearsals were never easy. He thought of ways to make the number better while bringing his heels up and down on the mat in rhythm.

The door opened.

"It's me," Iris called out. "Will I bother you if I watch?"

"Hell, no," he chuckled. "I'd like company—and a little criticism. I think I've got this job pretty well blocked out. Watch Myra Dormann in the film clip. When it's over, close your eyes and see if the mood still carries when I do it."

After he ran the film, he inserted the accompaniment tape into the player.

Iris folded her arms across her chest and closed her eyes. A smile played along her face as Steve began to sing. "You're terrific," she told him when he had finished.

"You haven't seen anything." He ran his hands through his

hair, which was wet with perspiration. "You should see me do your mother."

She cut him off: "Some other time."

"What's the matter, kid?"

She walked away from him and toward the wall upon which the ballet bar was attached. "She's getting caught up in it," her voice broke. "She's getting the feeling again that nothing can touch her. I can see it starting."

"You don't know what you're talking about."

She turned smartly. "I don't, huh? Assistant Director—hell! Wesley Adams is a studio watchdog! He's been put on the picture to see that mother behaves herself—and everybody knows it but her." She sighed hopelessly. "I haven't seen his orders, but I'm sure they read for him to do anything to keep Mother happy during the filming. Anything. *Anything!*"

"You're wrong," he said—but just how right was she?

She pulled at her ear, trying to make sense of what she knew to be true. "Why would they put him on her tail so soon?"

"They're not taking any chances on the picture going over budget." He surprised himself by realizing how quickly he could see the studio's point of view, and that bothered him, for his first allegiance was to Jennie. The studio had done nothing for him.

"Her health is too delicate for this business! That's what I'm scared of. I'm sure it's what she's scared of, too," She scratched her forehead. "But what's worse is what happens when she's not up to performing and has to. She can't jump up and down on command anymore; she doesn't have the resiliency." Her eyes drew him in as he listened.

"If they finish the picture on schedule," she continued, "and mother doesn't take any criticisms personally, she'll be rich, right on top again, and temper her demands. She only goes wild when she's insecure. It's her way of finding out how much they'll take from her, measuring her own importance.

"But she's very vulnerable," she confided. "And no one notices it because no one has the time or interest to care." She shook a cigarette out of her pack.

Steve noticed a slight shaking in her fingers. He let her light the cigarette for herself, giving her time to compose herself, impressed with her analysis.

"I care." He started to rewind the film clip.

She reached out for his arm. "Watch her for me, Steve. If she gets jumpy, call. I'll fly back immediately."

"Very few kids would feel that way." He placed his hand over hers.

"She *is* my mother."

"Kids have their own lives to lead—"

"She has no one else." Iris looked at him angrily. "Where are all those wonderful friends who just couldn't live without her?"

"She's too proud to call them."

"After the first twenty calls she made, that no one responded to, she became proud," Iris retorted.

"I didn't know," he acknowledged, somewhat flustered, then turned off the projector and inserted the film reel back into the can.

"To all of them she's just a cash cow, so they adore her. But she's my mother and I *love* her. There's the difference."

"This picture is the answer, though," Steve said. "She'll be up there again, and pretty soon everybody will be kissing her ass."

"That's the hell of it," she said grimly. "Either way, she loses!"

# CHAPTER SIX

J apanese lanterns strung alongside the Hawaiian buffet tables gleamed and swayed gently in the night breeze. At each end of the swimming pool, the catering service staff was passing out hors-d'oeuvres and keeping glasses full.

For her pre-filming party, Jennie was as they all had known her, light-hearted and ephemeral in a red and pink caftan. Steve mixed her a club soda with a twist of lemon, but even without liquor, she had no trouble seeming a little high. Each time she caught his attention, she winked. They'd grown closer since Iris' visit. The evenings she had promised her daughter added up to two, yet Iris had boarded the plane with no recriminations.

Jennie came up to him happily. "Let them eat, drink and be merry because Monday we start all kinds of tests. From then on it's work, work, work. What do you think of Wesley Adams?"

Steve glanced to where a tall man with glasses on a handsome, craggy face was addressing a small group. Even from a distance, he exuded an air of authority. His eyes seemed to be searching for something as they swept continually over the faces in the room. It was only when he walked that a slight limp became evident.

Jennie began again. "We fought and made up and then fought again, but we've got it together now. I had to do some fast talking to get Grant James and Caesar Valerio as my leading men. James was already signed to do something else, but Wesley put the pressure on and he's mine—in the picture, anyway," she laughed.

"Look at these guests," she went on, "they're so busy enjoying themselves, they haven't even missed me. Steve," she hesitated, "I'm grateful for what you did for me—and Iris." She brushed imaginary lint off his jacket. "Don't think that because I haven't said anything I don't appreciate it." She brought her hand up to her chest, and the dark red beetles lay momentarily on her breasts.

"Don't think about it." He brought his arm around her shoulder as she leaned into him. "It doesn't take much to pick up the slack around here."

"At the studio, Wesley does all of it," she said. "He steps in and takes over when I get tired of doing it all by myself." She changed the subject: "Where's The Mouse?"

"You said you'd stop that!"

"Just testing," she smiled up at him. "Are you ready for your debut?"

"What do *you* think?" In spite of his confidence in his ability, he felt a stab of anxiety at the thought of performing in front of a hardened film crew.

"I want them to remember this party. It'll help," she chuckled, "when we start going for each other's throats during filming,"

"A stitch in time buys a little help from your friends?"

"Exactly!"

"Tell Stella I'll be in the rehearsal hall, dressing."

He saw her watch him until he was at the door. Then, like a butterfly gathering momentum by fluttering its wings, she straightened herself, breathed deeply, took a pill from her miniscule handbag and washed it down with her drink.

Once the bones of the kahlua pig had been picked clean,

the coconut pudding eaten, and the dishes cleared away, the handymen began setting up a stage. In a corner, the Hawaiian band sang sadly of lost loves on beautiful islands.

Steve watched the stage crew out of the corner of his eye. Everything was being carried out according to plan. Carefully they wheeled in the hi-fi system and quickly strung a curtain across both ends of the makeshift stage.

He glanced at his watch. Months of rehearsal had gone into the act he had polished to a dazzling brightness. He was faultless on tape, in makeup and costume, when he was alone, or with Jennie. Onstage, might there be a slip-up he hadn't anticipated? He didn't want to be a caricature. The line that separated his work as an artist from that of a comic drag queen was too fine to tamper with.

Outside the window he could see and hear Jennie on the stage.

"I've been keeping off the sauce. See," she boasted, to a mixture of "yays" and "boos." "And, look at my newer figure—five pounds more to go." She turned sideways and received a round of applause. "And I'm going to entertain you, like it or not." They applauded heartily. "Give me five." She dashed across the stage and came down the side steps.

The band began playing once more, and she appeared in the doorway of the rehearsal hall.

"Follow me." She took Steve's hand and pulled him through the darkened house.

"I can walk on the damn things, but I sure as hell can't run," he protested.

When they arrived close to the stage, Jennie caught the eye of the band leader. He pressed a switch, and floodlights battered the guests' eyes. Then the lights went out. Steve quickly got on the stage.

From behind the drapes Jennie, through a microphone, told them she would do her routine from "Jamaican Lady." A burst of applause chopped into the black night as she switched on the tape. Lights strung into nearby trees illuminated the stage. The familiar beat began, with the French horns in the background. A brace of super-cold icicles thawed and crackled in Steve's body as cymbals crashed and he stepped forward, thrusting his hands into the light. His blood charged through his veins. Throwing his shoulders back, he dipped forward on one leg and, with his long, red fingernails, motioned the audience to settle down. The film veterans became very quiet.

He turned fast and the weighted bottom of the gown flashed across his legs, briefly outlining them before it fell back into place. Then, he lowered his head, brought his face up ever so slowly and began singing.

A surge of energy from the floor started to rise, forcing itself into his body. Gathering momentum, it shot upward. A blast of white-hot fire followed. He was sure a heart attack was on its way, but a few seconds later, a sense of peace cooled the heat within him, and calm pervaded his being. That was it! He knew he was having a sexual affair with the crowd, almost to the point of an ejaculation, and didn't want any of it to stop.

Suddenly the euphoria faded as quickly as it came. He now knew what connecting with an audience was *really* all about.

At the song's conclusion, he reached out with both hands and compressed a ball of nothingness until it was all gone, then opened his arms wide and lifted them high. The enthusiastic cheering continued as he took his bows and stepped back.

Keeping in Jennie's character, he returned to the microphone and said, "How about one more? How about 'Push The Clouds Away?'"

The applause that rained upon his ears made him feel omnipotent.

He began to sing softly. From beneath heavily lidded eyes he could just barely see Jennie on the other side. A gasp of surprise came from the audience as she made her way toward him across the stage. He met her in the center, singing, their voices melting together. The professionals had been thoroughly fooled! Still singing, the duo did a quick shuffle and, when they finished, bowed low from the waist.

Everyone stood up and shouted. Jennie took the microphone and motioned for them to be seated as she introduced herself— then pointed to Steve.

In Jennie's voice, he told them he would be back in fifteen minutes to sing as himself. In a burst of elation, he hurried back to the rehearsal hall.

Pulling the wig off his head, he handed it to Stella, who had seen it all through the window. She placed the wig on its stand, picked up two large pins, and thrust them into the styrofoam form, muttering, "Olé!" There was no mistaking her reaction to the audience's acceptance of his performance.

Steve sat down, took off the eyelashes and lathered cream over his face. When he stood up, she unzipped him. He kicked the shoes off his feet and walked to the wash basin, where he removed all traces of Jennie.

"Did you hear them?" he asked, not waiting for an answer. "That's the kind of applause I want. That kind of appreciation." He ran a comb through his hair, settling it. "Can you believe it? I had them fooled! Really fooled. Just think," he waved his hand, "a one-way ticket to the top of the mountain we've always dreamed about. Now, I'll go back and knock 'em dead with my own stuff."

"Right!" Her voice was on the brink of convincing.

"That's it. I've polished up the second half of the gig as myself. Here," he held out his hand. "Help me get these damn claws off."

One by one, she removed the artificial nails. She looked up at him and, in spite of her irritation, began to smile.

He finished dressing and stood in front of the mirror. "Christ," he murmured, "I've finally found a way."

They walked back toward the stage, hand in hand. Then he left her. Everyone looked at him in the bright light, trying to decide just where he resembled Jennie. When they asked him to speak in her voice, he refused, explaining that it would wreck the illusion. As himself, he now sang two newly arranged songs and enjoyed the applause he received after each one.

Immediately after his performance, Jennie came to his side with Wesley Adams in tow. "What do you think of this monster I've created?"

"I've never seen anything quite like it."

"He is special, isn't he? He's going to start at Scandal next week."

"With this act?"

"As of now! He can do Lily Jannings, Sherri Pickens and Myra Dormann," she added proudly.

"Who's your agent, kid?"

He replied that he had none.

"Jennie," Wesley suggested, "put Sam Markham onto—what's your name?"

"Dennis. Steve Dennis."

Stella walked over to them, and Steve introduced her to Wesley, who spoke with her for a few minutes and then left with Jennie on his arm. As they took the plates of food Louise had set aside for them, he and Stella noticed Jennie flitting from one guest to another.

"Doesn't she ever leave them alone?" Stella questioned under her breath. She had been watching Jennie with envy all night.

"Why don't you lay off? She's storing up a pile of goodwill for herself. She hasn't done anything to you and she got me the best offer I ever had. Right?"

Stella said nothing.

"Let's sit over there," he motioned, and led her to a secluded table on the other side of the pool. The stately black palms surrounded them like watchful sentinels. "You heard Wesley tell her to get in touch with an agent for me. I'm on my way, and you've got to make allowances for certain failings in people."

"It's enough that Iris does," she replied.

"That's not your business." He turned to her abruptly. "Let's not end the night this way."

A few people on their way out waved; the couple smiled back. But Stella's smile vanished when he returned his attention to her. What the hell was bothering her?

"Spit it out. You've had something on your mind the last few days."

"You're at her beck and call like a lap dog. You don't need her!"

"I do, and that's what you don't understand. She knows everyone and everything in this whole town and she's been kind enough—"

"And so have you," she added, folding her hands on the table in front of her. "You fail to see how dependent she is on you."

"Baloney."

"Baloney nothing. You've been good to her and for her, and vice versa. But now, she's going her way and you're going yours.

That's the way it should be. Steve, you've only got a freak act going for you—".

"That 'freak act' is going to pay off a lot of overdue bills," he seethed. "Christ, talk about cheering from the old home crowd!" He glanced over her shoulder at Jennie beckoning him. "Just a minute. Jennie wants to see us—"

"She wants to see you."

"Come on, Green Eyes. Let's go—together!"

*     *     *

In the library Jennie, leaning against the pale brick fireplace, bent over to push the starter button. A pilot light flashed over concealed jets in the sand, and a curtain of fire enveloped the imitation logs. She turned the gas flame down, then closed the brass curtains and turned to Steve. "Did Stella mind when I said I wanted to see you alone?"

He motioned that it didn't matter.

She pointed to the huge white piled sofa, and he sat down. Jennie was still standing. "I have a confession to make," she said apologetically.

He began to stand but she gestured him back into the seat. "I know the agent Wesley recommended, but I didn't want to tell you about him until the last minute." She took a sip of wine from a long-stemmed glass. When she caught his disapproving glance, she said, "A little is good for the vocal chords." "You're great, Steve. In time you could be absolutely phenomenal, but you've come to a fork in the road." She stopped and searched his face. What was she getting at? Then, it came: "Would you consider letting it all go to hell?"

Rather than say anything, he stared at the glass decanter on the low table in front of him.

"It would be better for you in the long run. And safer."

"You asked me before, and I said 'No'." Very softly, he asked, "Would you?"

She bit her lip. "I've gone too far to turn back, but you're just beginning." She began to play with the thin gold necklace around her neck. "You don't have that much to lose."

"How much is 'that much'?"

"Everything!" She gritted her teeth and took a step forward. "It's not going to go as smoothly as they promised. I need someone to help me."

"You can get anybody." He leaned forward and rested his arms on his knees.

"I want someone who sees things *my* way."

He laughed.

She cocked her head, trying to understand the reason for his outburst.

"Stella said—"

"The Mouse?" Her face became defiant. "What did she squeak out this time?" She ran her hand through her hair, her fingers slicing through the thick, coppery mass.

He stood up with his hands in his pockets, looking for a calm, low—keyed response. "As a pro, you can't ask that."

The corners of her lips twitched once, twice. She gazed at him for a moment. "OK," she smiled, drawing herself together. "I'll fight 'em off—by myself. I've done it before." She rose onto the balls of her feet and came down slowly. "I'm not sorry I asked, though. Still friends?"

"Always!" he said with relief.

She stepped up in front of him and held out her hand.

Instead of shaking it, he kissed it lightly—then kissed her forehead.

She smiled softly. "If Stella hadn't been first, I'd have set my cap for you."

"I wouldn't have been all that hard to get, but let's go out before she thinks—"

"The worst," Jennie interrupted, and led him back onto the terrace by the pool. There, Stella was waiting under a crescent moon, watching blue water lap against white tiles.

# CHAPTER SEVEN

At The Club Scandal, his billing read:

STEVEN DENNIS MASTER OF SONG

Out front were photos of Steve as himself, plus his characterizations of Jennie, Sherri Pickens, Lily Jannings and Myra Dormann, all done by Clyde of Hollywood, Jennie's favorite photographer.

As a result of an increase in business because of his act, the Club's management had given him a pair of huge garnet cuff links—his first tangible symbol of success. He fingered the jewelry before laying them on the dressing table.

Tacked onto the frame on top of the dressing table was the review of his act in the Valley Tattler:

Run, do not walk to The Club Scandal where an amazing thing is happening nightly. Steve Dennis, with a voice of unusual range and quality, does an impression of a female superstar each evening. I defy you to say that it is not the star herself. More than an impersonator, he is a consummate artist on the rise with a fantastic skill. I urge the ladies being portrayed to go to see how great they really are ..."

"Don't let the notices go to your head." Behind him, Stella rubbed the tension out of his neck. "Not even the ones Sam didn't plant."

He pointed to a Jennie Darling photo. "She's still the hardest one to do."

Stella took Jennie's emerald gown from a hanger and carefully laid it over a chair. Green feathers covered the bosom and hem, the effect suggesting something serpentine. He held out his hands. Into each one, she slapped a pair of surgical grippers holding artificial lashes. He applied them to each eyelid with a tiny bead of glue.

"What was the big problem that prompted her to phone you this morning?" she asked as a matter of fact. It was the first time she'd even acknowledged Jennie's call.

"She wanted my opinion on the title of her picture. There were three in the running. I chose *Star Fire*. That's the one she wanted, too." He leaned back, examining himself. "She told me it was sweet to be wanted back, but it's damn hard to live up to their expectations. They're going to advertise the picture with the slogan 'America's Darling'."

"As long as she isn't Steve's darling."

"She isn't!" He pulled off his undershirt. "The brassiere!"

She handed him the right one.

He slipped the straps over his shoulders, then brought his hands in back to hook it.

"Christ, I'm sure not going to be stuck with this act the rest of my life. No, siree." He roughly snuffed out his cigarette; the smoke curled about his hands. "I'll add more and more of my own stuff into the routine, and before they know it, only Steve will be on stage!" He adjusted the gooseneck lamp and seated himself, his face bathed in its harsh yellow glow. Stella seated herself on the arm of the sofa. He could see her observing him through the mirror.

"Well, now that *Star Fire* is going full blast, she should be out of our hair. I don't like her calling at all hours." She crossed her legs and leaned heavily on her arm. "What does she have advisors like Wesley Adams for?"

He laughed. "He's not her alter ego!"

"You're damn right. Nor are you."

"It costs nothing to give, and it doesn't hurt a bit. Finally, her future looks bright. Don't you do anything to change it. Stop sniping at her every time you get a chance." It was something he eventually would have to iron out, but he didn't want to start any kind of an argument right now. He glanced into the mirror. "I think she's great."

"When she behaves herself."

"Do you want everything?" He rested his hands on the top of the table. "She's right about most things—except herself. That's where I come in," he boasted. "I'm a compass that helps her keep on course."

"You've got it wrong. She sets her own course, then expects the world to adapt to her conception of where 'north' is."

There was no need to go on like this. "As long as you're going to have the house you want, the kids you want—"

"We want."

"Right."

"Speaking of kids, I saw the letter from Iris."

"She doesn't have anything to worry about."

"I wouldn't be so sure. Jennie's taking pills—

"Only to sleep better. Besides," he interrupted, "how did you know?"

"When we were called to her place two days ago, there was an open bottle of green ones on the kitchen counter. What a terrible emergency! A lousy bunch of costume sketches she just *had* to show you." She lifted her head disdainfully and looked back at him.

"She's got a figure problem—"

"More than just a figure problem," she corrected him—then softened her voice. "For her sake, I hope she doesn't blow this job. She is on some pretty strong stuff."

"She's nervous," he addressed her reflection through the mirror. "You'd be, too. So, if I can help her it's little enough, even if it bothers you some."

"Steve, I care about you so much," her words came out in a rush. "I know she made this big chance for you, but I'm leery of her, of the frenzy surrounding her—"

This was no time to continue sparring. Maybe she would get the hint if he changed the subject. "The wig."

Stella reached for it, handling it gently.

He slipped it down over his head, and the transformation was complete. He grimaced as he worked his feet into the high heels, but smiled his satisfaction as he then stood on them comfortably. Slipping into the costume Stella handed him, he stood still while she zipped him in.

He drew his shoulders back and up. "Don't tell Jennie Darling she can't do what she wants to—especially in her own home town."

Stella chuckled. "You sound as asinine as she does."

"Be out front," he whispered, "then come around quickly and help me out of this get-up."

"Drop the act, Honey," she said. "You're not on stage yet."

"Aren't I?" he said, and started toward the wings.

# CHAPTER EIGHT

When the band blared his fanfare, Steve drew his breath in quickly, leaned against the railing and strode onto the stage. Suddenly the noise died away, and the patrons looked to the bandstand to see Sherri Pickens confronting them. He picked up the microphone and let out Sherri's customary bellow:

"Who the hell did you expect—Maria Callas?" He heard a rifle-crack of laughter.

"Like the dress?" He did a full turn and flicked the gown's multicolored feathered train around him. "I didn't know which color to wear, so what the hell, I wore them all!"

The band picked up the cue, and he began a comic number that dovetailed into a more serious one. People at "ringside" were questioning whether there actually was a man under the masquerade.

As he finished his act, a voice from across the footlights yelled, "Take it off!"

Steve grinned and sacrosanctly touched the wig.

"How does he do it?" he heard one woman whisper from a front table.

"Damned if I know," was her escort's reply, "but his Sherri is better than the real thing. I know; I've seen her!"

Another spotlight suddenly shone on a table a distance away from the stage. The applause was continuing—but it was no longer for Steve. He brought his hand to his brow to push away the glare and looked out: standing up proudly, with her back arched, was Jennie. The clapping broke into a thunderous beat as she approached the bandstand, her expression sheepish, then hugged Steve and held his hand. She looked terrific, but he still wanted to strangle her.

Shouts among the crowd urged her to sing, but she declined. There was nothing Steve could do except give the signal for the leader to swell the music behind them. The lights blinked, and he led her to the wings. Amusement now overshadowed his initial anger at being upstaged, and he hugged her warmly.

"I wanted to see if you'd kept up with your homework. And," she pouted, "what do I see? That no-account bitch Sherri Pickens!"

"No professional jealousy, please," he groaned. "You were on yesterday."

"Yesterday? God, those nemmies are fogging me up again!" She drew back against that distressing thought. "Gotta talk to you before you go on again."

He began to protest but she grabbed his arm and led him around an outer corridor until they came to a booth in an alcove, shielded from view by imitation greenery. A bottle of wine was already on the table.

"I'm going back now to finish off Sherri. Then I've got an hour before I go on again as myself," Steve explained. "I'll change, and get right back. Then we'll have all the time in the world to talk."

She pulled him down and held out her glass.

Frowning, he filled it. "Save some for me," he said, then stood and stepped away, "and don't move!"

When he returned, Jennie was intently studying a small card.

She looked up at him as he slid into the chair next to her. "Well?" he asked.

"I have something for you." She shoved a card across the table top.

In the dim light he picked it up and studied the private entry pass, in his name, to the studio—to be honored at all times.

"I've still got the old clout," she crowed. "And if I've got it, you've got it!"

"You won't have it long if you don't get enough sleep. Where's Wesley?"

"I ditched him." Her voice betrayed her anger, and she shook. "Wesley's been riding me. They all are—but I'll make it. They don't call me 'The Iron Lady' for nothing! It's funny, but only four people *really* know I'm scared." Jennie paused, "Steve, you'll have to take me home tonight"

*Christ,* he thought, *she could do that film with her eyes closed if she would just relax.* What she needed now was a prod. He couldn't do her any good sympathizing. He wished he were more of a politician. Suddenly he became aware that her eyes were riveted on him.

"I ache all over from those damned exercises—I'm not as young as I used to be. And they're after me to lose weight even faster. But that's OK," she sighed, "I've got a pharmacy of my own in the cellar. I can counteract anything they throw at me!"

She didn't really have to rely on anything except her own God-given talent. If she couldn't convince herself of that, how could *he* hope to convince her? "Hang in there. *Star Fire* is going to put you up there forever!"

"I *am* up there forever," she replied coolly. "I'm just dead broke and flat on my ass down here. They're not giving me the number of retakes they promised, and it takes me a while to warm up." She brushed her bangs away from her forehead. "And the bankers are on every set. Every day! They hound Jack Rayburr to cut corners like crazy."

"What time do you have to be at the studio?"

"Eight! Another one of the conditions the bastards sneaked into the contract when my back was turned. They know I don't even open my eyes until ten." She finished the glass of wine and looked at him. "I'm damned ashamed of myself. I promised I wouldn't come here to cry on your shoulder, and I did. Christ," she yawned, "I need some fast sleep. I've got to be there first thing in the morning and twinkle." She laughed. "Sweet Jesus—a forty-year-old Tinker Bell: Can you imagine that?"

"Stop feeling sorry for yourself. I'd give everything for the chance you're getting."

"You sound like you're working for the studio!" She put her arms in the sleeves of the coat resting on her shoulders.

"You've got a terrific story."

She agreed that was true.

"And the songs fit you."

She almost smiled.

"Don't fight success!"

"I should sit back and enjoy it, huh?"

"Right." He'd hit a home run and was touching all bases.

She grabbed the edge of the table, and he could see her knuckles stand up like mountains. "They've just *got to* take it easier on me."

"The caviar comes later." He held her hand tightly. It was only a mild case of nerves. All she needed was a sympathetic ear—and he had two, always available.

"I just wish I didn't have to tell them how to do their jobs. I'm a fool to worry." She busied herself snapping and unsnapping the clasp of her handbag. "I know it, and you know it." Her mouth curled down at the corners as she looked at her watch. "Stevie, take me home. Do you mind if I sleep on the way?"

He settled his arm around her shoulder, and she snuggled into it.

"How will the Mou—uh, Stella get home?"

"Stella goes with us!" he said firmly.

"Of course, Your Majesty!" Jennie turned to him and winked.

# CHAPTER NINE

"It's Her Royal Highness." Stella held the phone out to him. "Sounds like she's under water."

He opened one eye and grabbed the receiver as his wife left the bedroom. "Steve," he rasped.

"They've run out on me, Baby," she slurred. "God, my head feels ten inches off my neck. Wait a minute; Louise is bringing juice and coffee."

He heard the sound of clinking glassware and looked at his watch: noon. "Are you on the set?" he asked through his own fog. He could only handle one thought at a time right now.

"Set?" she screamed, "I'm still in bed. They left me. Didn't even give me a chance. The limo left without me!"

He fell back onto the pillow and swallowed. "Isn't not being on time what got you into this pickle?"

"Lay off," she groaned. "I can take it from anyone except you."

"What happened?"

"The driver came to pick me up. I was out cold!" She seemed pleased that she was able to remember. "Louise came in two, maybe three times, to wake me up, but I'd been up all night, going over my lines. I guess I got mad. I told the driver to get his ass out of here or I would cut it off—and his job besides."

He shut his eyes tightly, caught between a laugh and a cry. "I can't believe it!"

"Try! Anyway, he made a call, and then he was gone." She paused for a moment. "Well, now the game starts: I sit back and wait for them to make the next move, which they should have done hours ago. They can only shoot around me so long—"

"Call in and say you were sick but you're OK now."

"I *was* sick! For God's sake, I can't even remember what I took. Let me put you on 'hold'." He heard a sharp click.

In the living room, Stella was steering the prow of an iron around the buttons of his shirt. Behind her on the mantel of the fake fireplace lay twelve large budget envelopes she had "forgotten" to put into the strongbox. She looked up at him, her face impassive. He was about to tease her about uncompleted projects when he heard a second click.

"They're sending the car back for me. I called and told them I'm well enough to work. What a joke!" She quickly changed the subject. "I'm going to put you on the conference phone so I can get ready. If I conk out, start screaming. I'm in the john now. Wait a sec'."

Her voice came on stronger when she returned to her bedroom: "I should never have taken those nemmies so late—I mean, so early in the morning. Lord, the circles around my eyes! Like an owl. *I* should only be so wise."

He heard a thump as Jennie cursed.

"I stumbled getting into my underwear. Louise," she yelled, "more coffee! Bless that girl."

"What did you wash those pills down with?"

"Look, are you going to help me, or not? I get all the hell I can use from the production people. All right," she snapped, "so I finished off a bottle of wine, too! Sue me; everybody else does!"

"Get moving—"

"I'm moving, I'm moving."

He stretched out his legs, aching for his morning shower. Jennie was coming out of it faster than he'd thought possible. What had she done—or taken—when she'd left the phone? He caught Stella's attention and, pointing downward, made a circular motion on the bedside table top.

She quickly came in with hot coffee and set it down.

"I've begun rehearsals for the production numbers. They're all so different—and each one's a back-breaker! Hey, I feel better already. I'm almost back. Baby, say, as long as we've got the time, listen to the lines for today's shooting. It's this scene in front of the elevator in the office building where she meets her agent. It's one of the high-comedy spots." She stopped. "Where *is* that damn chauffeur?" Then she told Louise to let her know as soon as he came through the front gate.

"It begins like this—"

\* \* \*

When he finally put down the receiver, Steve went directly to the bathroom and stepped into the shower. He made quick work of it.

"Why in hell can't that woman leave you out of her life?" Stella called out. "I'll breathe easier soon, when she's a continent away from us."

"Did you check with Sam this morning?" he answered, then stepped out and grabbed a towel.

No reply.

The towel wrapped around him, Steve came to the table, where poached eggs awaited him. "Sam?" he questioned again.

"Las Vegas is set! Six weeks headlining the Camel Driver Lounge. The Pyramid Hotel welcomes you warmly, as do all the blurbs in all the Las Vegas throwaways."

"Is that all you've got to say? You sound thrilled," he chided, and pulled apart a slice of toast.

"What's with 'Melinda' this morning that was *not* with her last night or the day before?" She sat down and took a swallow of coffee.

"It's beginning to be an endurance contest, even though she knows and does what's right for the film most of the time." He looked directly at her. "You couldn't care less, could you?"

"Not true. I feel sorry for her." Stella lowered her lids. "She's a pretty puny tiger."

"She has a new cameraman who's giving her some trouble."

"And a director, and a script girl, and a prop man. But she's got talent enough to pull it off, even if they shot it in the dark," she grudgingly admitted.

"Yeah. It's just got to be perfect."

"Perfect's not enough for her."

He thought for a while as he buttered a piece of toast. "I want to see her before we leave L.A. Come with me to the studio," he suggested, knowing she wouldn't. "She'll be glad to see you."

Stella shook her head. "As glad as she was to see the new cameraman, I expect."

"Well, then, I'm going alone. Have you finished getting everything together?"

She said that she had.

"Look, we've got a couple of days before we have to be at the Pyramid. Why don't you drive to Vegas with Sam?" He went on quickly, "Get everything in order and set up rehearsal schedules with the band. Just because it's the lounge doesn't mean it's not going to get the best I can give it. One day, it will be the Big Room." He extended his finger, tapped the side of her nose and kissed the fingertip. "Just wait and see. Whatever you can't handle,

Sam will." He looked at her straight on. "I've got to see how things are coming along with her."

"Be as interested in me," she teased, and reached for a piece of toast. She munched on it thoughtfully, "I know I shouldn't complain." Her eyes softened. "It's just that I'm anxious for a life where there's only the two of us. She's everywhere."

"Not there," he pointed toward the bedroom. All of a sudden, he couldn't wait for them to be together, their skin rubbing against each other, until relief blissfully shocked and separated them. He knew he didn't look twenty any longer, but at this moment, he felt like it.

He led the way into the still room. They could hear a heavy truck passing by, and they smiled together at the public noise invading their privacy. He sat on the bed, and her long hair fell over his face. Reaching up with each hand, he grasped the gleaming blonde strands.

"Do you really want me to go with Sam while you stay here with Jennie?"

"Jennie who?" he asked, and pulled her down.

# CHAPTER TEN

Steve drove his jalopy up to the main studio gate. The man who came out from a side hut looked like an out-of-work character actor. Steve presented his pass and waited. The gateman told him that shooting was on Stage 18, a quick turn to the right and as far down as he could drive.

In the distance stood facades of buildings with no sides or backs. Viewed head-on they were complete, but assorted neighboring buildings destroyed the illusion. Stage work was one thing—movies were a different world. He recognized some classic sets as he passed, and wished Stella were there to see it all with him. He put that thought away when he remembered her-less-than enthusiastic departure.

There was more activity going on further away from the main gates. Workers and costumed actors could be seen walking to their destinations. Steve tried not to be obvious as he searched their faces, looking for someone familiar, his excitement rising. It was his first visit to a studio, and he could sense the grand-scale opportunities that were won and lost with eye-blink quickness. He felt small and frustrated at the studio for intimidating him with its larger-than-life quality.

He pulled into an area designated "Visitors" opposite a battalion of parked limousines. There was no glow to the red bulb on the sound stagedoor, so he opened it and presented his pass to the guard.

He walked through several interior sets, stepping carefully over snakelike cables. Off to one side was a miniature lake with a paddle wheeler, carefully scaled down to match a port town just as meticulously detailed. He could make out the name "Mark Twain" on the front of the paddleboat, and he squinted to make the models take on the look of real life.

Kleig lights on rafters three stories up trained their beams on an area a short distance away. As Steve continued toward the heat and light, he could hear the sounds of an argument. The noise died away quickly when the director announced a take. Leaning against a prop wall in the dark, he watched the make-believe world become reality.

How did it feel being the center of every technician's attention? Probably like being in zero gravity. It had to be a hundred times more intense than performing in front of a live audience. He tried to imagine himself in that constricted arena of concentrated activity.

Jennie, shirt tails hanging out of her tight-fitting slacks, was pleading with her "husband" to see things her way. She cried softly, tears falling as he brought her face tenderly up to his. They kissed, and then she slowly turned toward the camera, shrugged her shoulders, and choked down a sob.

Without warning, she tossed her head back suddenly and yelled out, "Cut the son-of-a-bitchin' shot!" Rocking back on her heels, she glared at the director. "Didn't you hear me say that when I came close to the camera, you were to slap that key light on me full strength? Why didn't you make it on time?"

The director signaled the technicians to turn off the arc lamps. "Because it was coming along beautifully. When we dolly in for the tight shot, we can take care of it."

As far as Steve could see, Jennie was lit beautifully.

"That hot baby has to be on me on time. I couldn't feel the heat on my cheeks until I got into my speech, and by that time it was too late!" She spun around to face her leading man. "You know what I mean, don't you?"

He mumbled that he did and apologized with a glance to the director.

"Jennie," the director said, keeping his voice in a tight rein. "That was the seventeenth take. You're wasting big money."

She planted her feet firmly on the floor and yelled into the darkness: "This is *my* film! My future *is* this film! If it isn't a five-star winner, I'm dead meat. So, Roy, do you want to be the leading lady, and I'll direct?"

"OK, Jennie, the technicians are waiting."

"And I'm waiting too—for some inspired directing. You've been talking too much to your classes at UCLA, and you're letting the magic get away from you!" She quickly stopped. "Everything's riding on my back, Roy. Don't forget that or we'll all be out of work!"

He raised his voice: "Don't you forget we've all been covering for you for some while now."

"How dare you!" She drew her head back like a serpent poised to strike. "If I'm not lit just right, I'll come out of that scene looking like a fool. This is the dramatic part of the picture—just in case you didn't know! Turn on the lights," she called upward, then marched across the set. "I can't see my way to the trailer, and I've got to break—"

"A leg," the director chimed in.

"Up yours, too," she flung back at him—then stopped suddenly as she spotted Steve. Her anger faded; her posture relaxed. "Save me, Stevie," she murmured.

While the scene was being filmed she had looked young

and radiant, but coming toward him moments later, she was a distraught older woman. He realized then how good an actress she was.

"God, I'm glad you're here! A friend among enemies." Her body went limp as she fell into him. "See me to my trailer," she whispered. "I'm wearing my nerves on the outside these days and they're beginning to fray."

Past a maze of electrical cable was her trailer, the largest on the lot. When they got to the door, she turned to look at the crew milling around, then all but leaped into the vehicle.

"If it isn't one damn thing, it's just got to be another," she said when they were inside. "Wouldn't you know that the dance sets won't be finished? They couldn't get the right materials on time." She picked nervously at her nails. "That is the bit of 'good news' I got this morning before we started shooting. And we're just about finished with all the dramatic stuff!" She slumped into the sofa and rested her forehead on her slight fist.

"What about the routines?" Steve knew how much of herself she had invested in that area of production.

"They're all blocked out. They don't worry me." She raised her face. "I could wing it and no one would even know. The dances are physically harder than anything I've done before. But this new cameraman is strictly an apprentice."

Photographing her now, Steve knew, was a tough task relying heavily upon proper lighting and makeup. It was her dependence on others that made her feel insecure.

She drew one side of her face up in despair. "That lighting man is hopeless."

"How about the director?"

"Him? Ninety percent of the stuff I tell him to do, he does. But," she slammed her fist down hard on the sofa arm, "why do

I have to tell him? He knew more about camera technique when he didn't know anything at all about camera technique."

She walked to the refrigerator and took out a bottle of vodka, added a bit of vermouth, and began dividing the mixture into two glasses.

"Don't worry," she said, anticipating his remark. "Roy drinks on the set, too. We've both got each other by the short hairs." She took a sip and closed her eyes. "If only I could just calm down a bit. You don't know how good it is to see you." She circled the glass in the air, then brought it to her mouth.

He tried to imagine himself in the same situation, trapped by time and health, trying to deliver a carefree performance. The other problems that were bothering her, he didn't want to know about. If only she could be persuaded to trust the others a little more. Could she see it that way? "They took quite a few takes," he reminded her.

"All with the same mistakes. And who does the blame fall on if it doesn't bring in tons of money? Not that incompetent in back of the camera who should be shooting porn.

"Lord, I've just got to get something lined up financially until we start shooting those musical sequences." She met his questioning glance. "That's right! I am not being paid unless we are filming. Down time is on me!" Her voice broke into a croak: "What the hell is this world coming to?"

He studied the art deco pattern in the carpet. "Everyone's doing their best."

"It's not good enough," she growled, her face turning red. Then she lowered her voice. "Look, I know I'm unreasonable. But it's because I'm frightened." She smiled bravely. "That's today's best-kept secret."

She walked to the end of the trailer and returned with a nail file and a bottle of polish. Carefully, she sanded the end of one nail and applied a top coat of enamel.

"Forget what I just said." She screwed the top back onto the bottle and straightened up in her chair, "The wolf pack should be coming back for me any second. But my work *is* good." Her pride was unmistakable. "Hell, it's almost sensational. Can you stick around town to see what's been done so far?"

"I've got a few days before I open—"

"At the Pyramid, no less," she finished the sentence for him.

"Stella and Sam took all the stuff with them—"

"Stay at my place," she urged. "I'm living here at the studio in this trash heap. It's the only way I can get to the set on time. Please!"

He heard footsteps approaching. "Sure," he said without thinking, then stepped out of the trailer ahead of her and extended his arm.

Under perfect control, Jennie emerged, flashed a smile to the cameraman, kissed the director on the cheek and walked to her chalk marks on the floor. Her leading man disengaged himself from a small group and came to her side.

Roy asked if everyone was ready, and Jennie nodded in unison with her screen husband. He repeated her last instructions to the men on the catwalk. "Lights," Roy commanded, and the small area was bathed in incandescence.

Jennie threw Steve a kiss, which he returned.

"Camera. Speed," Roy called.

The clapboard was shoved in front of the players and snapped. "Action."

Jennie began pleading with her "husband," and her tears fell again. When she turned, the key light flashed on her with all its intensity amplifying the sadness on her face. She kept building the scene, letting the grief in her throat out a little at a time. Her last words were fired in a flood of anguish.

"Cut! Cut! It's all there! This is the *one.*" Roy bowed low to Jennie in admiration.

She clasped her hands in front of her, an ecstatic smile on her face.

*   *   *

The swim in Jennie's pool had been invigorating, and Steve enjoyed the leisurely morning. He told Louise not to expect him for dinner and left her searching for something to do in the huge mansion. Having followed the glittering sun on the expressway, he now turned from it and drove down the ramp leading toward the studio.

Jennie was anxious for him to see the work done so far. Her voice had been lively when she'd spoken to him about it last night. She'd also been happily surprised by a couple of weeks' work suddenly presented to her in a package tour of the Far East and was going to spend the rest of the night reading the small print in the contract.

The technicians were just leaving as Steve stepped onto the soundstage. A camera was being pulled back, and in the center of the set he caught Jennie regaling some of the crew with an anecdote. Her audience broke into guffaws as Steve approached. The richness of the theatrical color on her face made the natural hues around her fade into pastels. There was a quickness in her steps, an almost careless grace about her.

Mike Fallon, one of the producers, was with her, and he seemed very proud, his thick, craggy dark eyebrows raised in pleasure. Steve shook Mike's hand and felt the energy contained

within this powerhouse of a man who knew where he was and
never forget how he'd gotten there.

Mike took off his horn-rimmed glasses. "I hear you're making
people sit up and take notice. Must catch the act—"

"At the Pyramid in Vegas," Jennie added.

"Of course!" He put his glasses back on and stepped back. Did
Mike make everyone feel he was assessing them? Was that look
natural, or practiced?

"Let's get on with it," Jennie cried. "Race you to the projection
room!"

"Save your strength," Mike cautioned. "We'll take the car."
He turned to the small group surrounding them. "No one said
they'd be home early tonight—did they?"

*   *   *

Crossing her legs at the knees, Jennie stretched her foot out in front
of her, impatiently waiting for the images to flash onto the screen.
She pressed her palms together and then pushed them apart,
finally letting them fall to the chair's armrests. The cameraman
in front of her turned, holding two cigarettes. She took one. As
she leaned back in her seat, Steve lit it for her.

"I haven't seen it pinned together," she said, "but this editing
will tell us something." She glanced around at the staff and
laughed at her own nervousness.

A bell rang and Mike nudged Jennie lightly in the ribs. "Roll
'em, Paul."

The voice from the projection booth told him it would take
a few more seconds.

"They're gluing the negatives together with spit," she murmured
under her breath.

Finally, from the booth came Paul's voice: "Ready."

Mike pressed a finger on his armrest console, and the studio's emblem appeared on the screen before them with its musical theme. A shifting background of Jennie's past hits shot across the screen.

"Your Darling," a screen voice boomed; a dazzling young Jennie shot a radiant smile at the camera, then danced away.

"America's Darling," the sonorous voice intoned over another clip of film showing Jennie in a tight military gold-braided uniform, a little older, dancing across a stage erected in front of tanks on a battlefield.

"Jennie Darling," the voice triumphantly, lovingly proclaimed. In a golden gown with a black fox hem, Jennie draped herself against a series of outdoor museum sculptures in the soft light of early evening.

She held onto Steve's arm so tightly it hurt. A complete smile of satisfaction crossed her face as a montage of fast *Star Fire* cuts sliced into each other. The spectacle lasted about eight seconds while the announcer told the audience about the new picture.

Then as the screen went dark, she murmured, "Not bad for a rough cut."

Suddenly, against a background of deepest midnight blue, a ball of yellow flame hurtled into the air and exploded. The shimmering fragments slowly descended forming the words, "Jennie Darling." Against the same blackness, a second ball of green fire sped up to explode and spell out the words *Star Fire*.

"God," she whispered, "it's gorgeous."

Steve squeezed her hand; she shot him a happy look, then returned her attention to the crudely assembled film. Her fiery talent was more multi-dimensional than ever. As the story progressed, the atmosphere in the viewing theatre became more intense. Steve leaned forward and looked around. As one, the audience smiled, chuckled, or were concerned in turn.

The last days' shooting was in correct sequence. There she was, in all her emotional disarray. When she turned to the camera, her face contorted with grief, he felt himself involuntarily tighten up. She was magnificent!

"The background music needs quickening," she said, "it's not keeping pace."

Mike nodded and pressed a button.

She made several other comments, and when he agreed, Steve noticed Mike pressing the same button.

When the lights came on, the room's silence was shattered by a wave of excited babble.

"Well," she exhaled, "*now* I can relax!"

"Dust off a spot on your mantel for the Academy Award." Mike kissed her tenderly on the forehead. "It's going to be yours next year."

The rest of the staff flocked around her, busily talking. Those who had fought with her along the way were now eager to agree that the film had been pulled together into a rare tour de force. Damn it, Steve thought. She had been right about everything!

After they left the viewing room, Jennie drove him to the far side of the lot in a little yellow-and-orange-striped cart, canopied with fringe. The uncompleted dance sets were inside the three immense soundstages, she told him.

"I'm dying for you to see what's been done." She shoved open the heavy door. In front of a giant electrical switch panel, she chose the one numbered "Section 2." "Over there," she pointed, pushing a few other switches. In response to his look of surprise, she grinned. "I've been around these places as long as I can remember. I could even fix the plumbing if I had to."

She took his hand and led him to a surrealistic sky. Transparent fabric arches overlapped, causing textured shadows to fall on the floor all around them.

"We're going to have lots of carbon dioxide clouds hugging the boards, so I have to be damn sure of where I'm stepping. Especially there." She pointed to celestial stairs that sailed into the sky, then walked toward them. "You, too," she called.

He faked steps he didn't know, and found himself next to her.

"Up," she directed.

He followed her.

She snapped out the beat with her fingers.

When she stopped, they looked at each other for a moment. Then he held out his arms and she collapsed into them. My God, he thought, she's as fragile as a hummingbird.

When he released her, she gazed around the set. "That's only the appetizer. On the other side of this barn is the set they're building for the 'Steamer Trunk' number. Try dancing in and out of one of those when you've nothing else to do."

"In heels?"

"Naturally. I used to be able to do those numbers without twisting the seams in my stockings. Now, I'm going to have to work at it. They won't shoot these sequences for about twelve weeks." She drew back slightly. "Did I tell you I signed a Far East booking this morning?"

"Shouldn't you rest until the sets are ready?"

"I can't afford to. I'm on my time. No salary. Besides, I leave in ten days. The studio wanted to send a PR crew with me, but I said I'd meet them in Manila. I prefer traveling alone."

"And, *I* leave tonight. They're waiting for me. Everything's all set up for Vegas."

"Who are you opening with?"

"My Lucky Star," he teased.

She clapped her hands sharply. "Hell. And I have to miss it. How's Lily Jannings' accent coming along?"

He told her that it was pretty well mastered.

"Listen, even she couldn't always keep it on straight and sing. She sounded like a bassett hound in heat most of the time."

"The accent is tricky, but she's the easiest of all to do."

She blinked her eyes. "I'm so proud of you. Who would have ever thought I'd launch such a top talent?"

# CHAPTER ELEVEN

S teve knew Stella had sent him downtown to pick up his monogrammed shirts purely as a diversion. He'd been increasingly tense since his arrival a week ago and now wished that opening night had come and gone. Stella felt the pressure as much as he but kept it under tight control, almost unnerving him with her coolness. A tic in his right eyelid forced him to blink hard to work it out. As he pulled up to the hotel he saw the sign:

ILLUSIONIST/SINGER
STEVEN DENNIS
in the
CAMEL DRIVER LOUNGE

The letters of his name were smaller than those of Sammie Sauer, the headliner in the Big Room, but one day they would be just as big—if he pushed hard enough. He already had one foot on the first rung of the ladder.

He bent backward to glance up at the blinking lights skittering over the edge of the huge sign only to reverse direction a moment later. Then he gave his car to the attendant. Had Stella seen the outside sign yet? He hoped not. He wanted to be the first to point it out to her, so he ran up the service stairs to the suite and shoved open the door. "Stella! Come! Look!"

She came into the living room.

He raced to the windows and pulled the drapes apart, letting in the afternoon sunlight. Steve gestured outdoors. "Sweetheart, did you ever see anything so beautiful?"

She shut her eyes tightly and clasped her hands in front of her. Her face flushed a deep red. "It's gorgeous, Steve." She stepped back and ran from the room. "I've got to get the camera."

"You first," he said when she returned, and took the camera from her. She posed in front of the window and he snapped her with the hotel sign conspicuously in the background. After she in turn, had taken his picture, he fell onto the plush white carpet and reached out for her. "Opening night is going to be one helluva snap." He hoped he sounded convincing.

She joined him on the floor. With her head lying on his stomach, they discussed how they would spend the first million dollars. When she finished thinking of all the fur coats she might want and he got tired of trying to decide between the forty-two or sixty-five-foot yacht, he reached over and circled her breasts with his palms. Her breath came in rushes, and he began matching her excitement until, in a frenzied outburst, they pulled off their clothes and reached hungrily for each other. "I truly love you," he softly murmured. "More than you'll ever know."

An hour later, lying on the suite's massage table, Steve ran through his new material as the masseur worked the tension out of his back muscles. At the end of each joke he watched Stella's face to catch her reactions. She still grinned at most of them. That was a good sign!

Stella moved to the desk chair and rummaged through some papers on the stack, then swung around and said, "Sam sent some offers for you to look over. They came while you were out. If there's anything you don't understand, call him in L.A." Walking to the head of the massage table, she held out the papers for him to see.

Steve nodded, closed his eyes, and let his head fall back to the padded pillow. The future was too far away to worry about now. Only the present mattered.

She walked back to the desk. "You don't have anything to worry about. You've never been better!"

"I know that," he groaned as the masseur twisted his feet at the ankles. "But do they?"

"You were never meant to parade around in heels. Don't ever get used to them." She picked up some papers from the table. "You have a tuxedo fitting tomorrow."

He grunted an acknowledgement and looked up at her. "You're always there, always picking up the pieces, aren't you?" A glow of warmth spread throughout his body. A lot of good living awaited both of them directly ahead, and she deserved the credit for it as much as he.

She brought her head to one side and her pony tail loosely swayed.

Lately, he was sure she felt she was being taken for granted in the shuffle of activities surrounding him—but for now that couldn't be helped.

As the masseur patted him on the stomach twice, signifying the end of the rubdown, Steve pulled the towel around his waist and got off the table. Walking toward the apartment sauna, he dropped the towel on the floor and entered the dark wooden chamber to stretch out on the redwood bench. He heard the sounds of someone leaving. Just as he was beginning to feel accustomed to the steam heat, a rush of cool air startled him when the door opened. He shivered, then saw Stella, naked, coming toward him. She sat down and pressed her face to his, massaging his chest with hands as capable as the masseur's.

"Darling," she whispered, "don't ever forget you mean so much to me."

He lightly outlined her facial features with a fingertip and tenderly closed her eyelids. "I love you, Stella. Honest to God, I do." Holding her tightly, he felt the tremblings of her body. "I always have. I should say it more often and I'm sorry I don't. It's a fault, I know, but I promise to make you more aware of it."

As she began to cry softly, he lifted her off the floor, and her legs separated as she settled onto his slick body. She lifted herself slightly at the hips, and he guided himself into her, then held her by the waist and smiled as a sense of pleasure ran from his body through hers. "I need you more than ever, Baby. Don't you *ever* forget that."

Afterward, he felt relaxed and cool. Stella leaned forward, holding him within her. Minutes later she fell asleep on his chest, exhausted. He picked her up gently and carried her out of the sauna.

\* \* \*

"I'm going to knock them out tonight," he boasted to Stella in his dressing room. "The wig looks great! Where did you get it done?"

"Here in the hotel," Stella told him.

He glanced impatiently at his watch. A knock interrupted them; she went to the door and opened it. He heard the familiar backstage noises of moving scenery and people talking in half-hushed voices as he continue to apply his makeup.

"Telegrams," she said, slitting the envelopes open. "Here's one from Jay Taggart."

He felt the lines around his mouth relax a bit as she read the message. It was damn nice of Jay to remember how much good wishes meant on opening night. Maybe he really had Jay figured wrong.

"Here's one from the folks. And, Janet—"

Gus, too?" He cocked his head.

"Uh huh, and some from local people."

He listened to good wishes from old friends and new acquaintances. The word had certainly gotten around. A tube of dark base fell from his hand. "Dammnit, my fingers won't hold anything." He brought his right arm down to his side, holding it there, waiting for it to relax.

Then he switched on the bright lights around the mirror. His face looked like a grotesque mask with the shadows starkly applied and not smoothed. Spilling some lotion on his hands, he resumed his work.

"Nothing from Jennie?" It was odd that he had not heard from her, She should have been the first to send him a good-luck message.

"No, and—"

He raised his hand. "Don't forget Jennie is responsible for us being here. Don't get on her back. She needs every friend and every dollar she can get her hands on right now!"

Stella brought the remains of a sandwich to the dressing table; he nodded in acknowledgement. Pinching the skin in front of her neck in her fingers, she thought aloud: "Well, by the time she gets back, the sets will be completed, and she can finish the film—then sit back and collect all her money. She is excited about that; isn't she?"

"She is excited about the film, period."

Without his asking she began to knead away the tension at

the base of his neck. "I'm glad she's gone." There was relief in her voice. "I had to get that out of me before you turned into her. If I said it then, that would be the worst kind of bad form."

"It would." He grinned into the mirror at her. "It would."

\*   \*   \*

From the other side of the curtain he could hear the sounds of tinkling glass and overlaying conversation. His whole body was drawing into a tight knot. To interest, let alone capture, that mob out there was the master challenge. There was no place to run to now!

He stood waiting at the side of the stage as the band started a vamp. A soft layer of noise floated over the room. The announcer, in a burst of enthusiasm, caught the audience's attention and introduced Steve as the lights lowered and his musical introduction became louder. Then the houselights went out, and the curtains sped away from each other.

He came into the spotlight uncertainly, just as Jennie did, and caught the crowd by surprise. He could see Stella sitting front ringside, toasting him with a fruit punch. He stood still for a moment, then moved to the center of the stage. Amid the purple velvet awnings in the tent-like atmosphere, a round of interested applause began.

He opened his eyes wide and pushed his leg against the clinging blue-beaded gown as the staccato rhythm of "Jamaican Lady" started. Moving into his opening number, he filled the space around him with the special sound he had been coached to use. Without giving them any time to react, he went into the next song.

The audience was slowly giving him their confidence. The palpable feeling was coming to him in steady beats across the footlights. He began relaxing and absorbing the sensation of being on a slow drunk, light-headed and unsteady. Now that he had their attention he wasn't about to let it go, and his performance began turning into something effortless.

Quickly he went into "Nobody Loves a Loser." The wail was built right into that one. His voice gathered strength as he sang the lyrics, his timing perfect. From the faces of the patrons nearest the stage he could sense how successful he was. He was damn proud. He had every right to be. Dipping his knee, he rotated the upper part of his body while his hands rose to the ceiling.

Piercing this excited glow was a sudden awareness of the audience's attention shifting to a new focus. Tightness wrapped around his chest. He could feel himself being left behind. Something out there was breaking his communication with the crowd, and his voice started to reflect his upset.

Unexpectedly, a beam of white frost cut through the darkness and focused on Jennie, sitting on top of a table, singing along with him. She waved and looked radiant, acting as if this were the most wonderful thing in the world that could happen. Helplessly he continued along with her.

As the song finished, flash bulbs began exploding. Steve smiled until his face hurt. The crowd drove itself into a frenzy of clapping as hands lifted Jennie off the table and voices urged her up to the stage. She came toward him from the side steps, and she took his hand.

"Isn't he absolutely wonderful?" she called out from his side, then pointed to him. "That's me." He wondered if she knew he was ready to kill her.

He played along: "Isn't he the greatest?" Steve pointed at Jennie. "That's me," he repeated. "In fact, which one of us is the real one?"

The audience knew it was being treated to something special. From a distance, he heard the slap of glasses against table tops. The insistent beat was taken up by still others until he thrust his hands out, urging them to stop. Then, with his arm around Jennie's shoulder, he snapped his fingers.

The orchestra broke into the opening bars of "Mad at Madagascar," and the yelling in the room rose to another peak. The duo did an impromptu routine, then took a low bow, to the audience and to each other.

Several voices began shouting, "One More Time." He knew that each patron in the room suddenly remembered that Melinda was a special part of their childhood when the only thing in life that mattered was going to the movies on Saturday afternoons. She nudged him aside and faced the throng as a hush descended upon the room. "This one is mine, Steve. Maestro, please..."

Under the spell of her magical talent, she took them into her make-believe world. It was true—she was the only sleeping princess the world would ever know. She trembled on the song's last note, then slowly snuffed it out.

"That is my song until the day I die," she half cried. The spotlight went out, leaving her in darkness. Then the houselights came on to an ear-piercing ovation. It was impossible for him to show her any anger now!

They bowed low again, and as he raised his head he caught a glowering Sammie Sauer at the front door. There was no trace of the easygoing comic about him now. Sammie shot a glance of hate at the stage, spun around and left, with his coterie following close behind.

The backstage dressing room was crammed with people moving about as he and Jennie held court. The owner of the

Pyramid, Nate Komanek, was the first to offer congratulations, his eyes beaming with pleasure.

Stella put Steve's wardrobe away carefully. In contrast to Jennie's black-fringed gown, slit to the knee, Stella's simple blue frock decorated with a turquoise and white Indian design looked like a house dress. She felt out of place.

Jennie threw her hands up in resignation, and her voice danced up the scale: "What else could I do? There I was, getting ready to fly over that great blue puddle tomorrow, and Stevie Baby was opening without me." She swung around to plant a kiss on his cheek. "So I just chartered a big bird and flew in. And I'm so glad I did."

Stella stifled her anger each time it threatened to erupt by compulsively seeing that the ashtrays were kept empty. Steve knew she wondered how he could be so accepting of the fact that Jennie had stolen his opening night and that foot-stamping performance by the patrons wasn't all for him! She quietly let him know she was also furious at the hotel for asking him not to go on to the second half of his act, as himself. She was furious at him too, for agreeing to the request.

The nightcaps following the show went on for two hours. As the guests finally started to leave, Stella breathed a sigh of relief. Jennie, in a corner, was telling a trio about her upcoming tour. They seemed as elated about it as she.

"Doesn't she *ever* stop?" Stella questioned loudly, hoping Jennie would overhear. A sleek blonde suggested a silver bullet between the hours of dawn and dusk, then slithered to the group around Jennie and extracted from it the man with whom she had arrived.

"Stella, dear, pretty please." From the sofa on which she was sitting, Jennie held out her empty glass.

As Stella grudgingly replenished it, Steve noticed Jennie's hand wobbling.

"She's going to fly to Singapore on her own power pretty soon," Stella muttered to him, then recorked the bottle.

"Let's all go to the Safari Room for breakfast," Jennie called out.

Everyone except Stella thought that was a great idea. From the doorway, the departing visitors promised to meet them there.

"I could really go for a lox omelet," Steve said, looking at his watch. "Hey, it's practically morning. No wonder I'm starved."

"You go on," Stella urged him. "I'll meet you there in a minute."

He decided he'd better not ask why she wouldn't go along with them. There were things he knew she wasn't aware of his knowing. She hated those people out there, desperate for something to do and settling on him. But at least they were settling on him—that was something! He'd shake them off when the time came, but he needed them now.

In the Safari Room, he kissed Stella on the cheek when she came in and held out a chair for her, but she slipped into his chair, next to Jennie.

Jennie looked up, raised an eyebrow and smiled. She dawdled over the last of her omelet, washed it down slowly with coffee and asked for a refill. Then: "You had a little trouble with your second number, Steve, but you covered it beautifully. Have the orchestra give you a longer bridge. It makes the transition easier."

"Right. Jesus, I'm glad you reminded me!"

"Me, too," Stella said grimly.

"Maybe I should stay for tomorrow night's show." She looked at him expectantly. "I'll have to let the pilot know. Shall I cancel?"

"No," Stella said calmly. "The only thing that needs canceling around here is your current performance."

The temperature around the table plummeted.

Into the embarrassing silence Jennie tossed a good-natured laugh. "That line should be washed down with a martini."

"Try water," Stella said through lips that hardly moved.

Jennie, with her elbow on the table, leaned forward. "You should have stayed in show business, Stella. You are really one helluva comic!"

"I don't mean to be. I only want to be left alone."

"Well, then—leave!"

"Alone, but with my husband. You see," she began, pausing not for emphasis but for strength, "I've put up with the ménage-a-trois long enough."

Steve sat frozen in his seat, hoping Stella would stop.

The challenge caught Jennie off guard, but she rallied to face the affront. "Ménage-a-trois? What insolence! Anyone with half a brain would have been delighted with the turn of events I set into operation. Listen, you." She cooly pointed her finger at Stella. "If you had your way, Steve would still be at the post office, licking stamps. What kind of a wife are you, anyway?"

"The best! Jennie, you've got what you wanted. Steve has finally got what he wants. And it's my turn now. Stop sucking at him. Stick to your pills!"

Jennie shoved her chair aside; it hit the next table and fell into the aisle. She glared at Stella while she addressed Steve: "The best advice I can give you now, Steve, is to drop her. She is the worst kind of no-talent bitch! She'll only drag you down." She brought her thumb to her chest. "I know the kind well! If you don't dump her now, it will cost you years and a bundle to get out from under. Did I call you The Mouse?" She stared Stella down, eyes narrowing. "You are nothing but a plague-ridden rat."

Steve could feel the veins on the side of his head pulsating; his hands begin to shake.

"I'm ready to leave," Stella said to him.

"Cut it out. Both of you," he growled. Why wasn't Stella leaving well enough alone? Jennie would have been out of the hotel in a few minutes and things would have been just fine. Didn't she know better than to start something with Jennie, who could handle herself in a roomful of tigers? It was an unequal match, no night for a contest, and damn it, he didn't want to be a referee—nor have to make choices!

"He's become something in spite of you," Jennie continued in a loud voice, unmindful of the other patrons looking at them. "I showed him how to use his talent, not bury it in the sand. I made him something bigger than he was when I first met him. What have you done for him? I'm willing to stack my eight months against all your years!"

As Stella forced herself to stand up, the flat of Jennie's hand smacked hard against the side of her head. Stella's body twisted to one side, and Steve caught her to keep her from falling.

Stella stared through her adversary. "You've got a plane and twelve weeks of occupational therapy waiting for you, Jennie. Get going."

"I am truly sorry—," Jennie began.

Christ, she was even going to apologize.

"Let's go home, Steve!"

"—that I didn't do that sooner!" She snatched up her coat, shaking it in disgust, and left the table. Heading for the door with her lips drawn together, she called back: "You needn't bother to see me out, Steve!"

He couldn't let her storm out like that. She needed him as much as he needed her. Stella would understand. She would *have* to.

And he raced out the door.

# CHAPTER TWELVE

Steve scanned the group from under the heavily made-up Nefertiti eyes that accented Myra's Dormann's Near Eastern look. Meeting the press at close range was the tough one. Behind the footlights, distance and technical wizardry worked for him, but being interviewed in character required great effort.

"You really gotta see my act," he began in an incongruous Brooklynese sing-song. His hands came down his sides, and his smiled widened. "I was never modest, and the show isn't either."

Pencils glided over notepads, jotting down the insouciant remarks. There was not a single incongruity in the personality facing them. Myra Dorman was good copy—any time, any way!

"Well, it's not totally my show. Steve's, too!" He crossed his legs. "Make no mistake—we really do work at it. Success is *all* perspiration. Edison was wrong when he said it was only ninety percent." He laughed. "Can you imagine Edison being wrong about anything?"

Several reporters started to raise their hands, but he fended them off. "Time is growing short, so let me save you the trouble. My most frequent answers to the most frequently asked questions are: Number one, my newest picture is always colossal. Number two, I've no new romances. Number three, I'm still as strong as a horse. Number four, yes, you *can* see me in the lounge, but check the schedule; Steve only lets me out once every four nights." He let his shoulders slump, knowing the wig's straight hair would fall across Myra's face dramatically; then, he drew the audience into his confidence.

"But I have to share the bill with three others, equally talented! Good manners force me to say both 'equally' and 'talented'." Several of the reporters chuckled.

"Do you mind if I leave now?" he said in a changed tone. "I have another appointment coming up that I can't miss. Please stay. I'll send Steve out to talk to you in a moment." He grinned, then lightly jumped off the stool while the cameras snapped away.

"Your illusion is astounding, Mister Dennis," a tall, ruddy-faced reporter in a gray open-necked shirt said. "Won't you come out of character?"

"Whose character?" he answered sharply—but then his voice softened. "I really have to leave. Please wait." He left the room quickly through a side door.

He was well aware that these interviews were greatly responsible for the turnaway business the show was generating. Nevertheless, he didn't especially enjoy doing doubles on the days they occurred. He'd been offered a twelve-week stint in the lounge during the latter part of the year with a substantial jump in salary—but with the deals Sam was lining up, he wasn't sure he would have the time for it. It was great having things come to you, for a change. However, he was too new at the situation to take it for granted for more than a few minutes at a time.

In the dressing room, Stella had already laid out his new custom-made tan-colored desert outfit. He looked at her busily setting aside towels. There had been no word from Jennie since she'd stormed out of the hotel a week ago.

He still winced when he thought about that evening. Stella

had been boiling mad that he had seen Jennie to the airport, but he'd told her repeatedly he was worried that Jennie had too much to drink to make it to the plane alone. He couldn't remember his wife ever raging at him before as she had when he'd returned to their suite. For two days, she had been at his side with everything he needed—except conversation.

Finally, he'd succeeded in explaining that Jennie was overwrought and had lost control of herself. Stella told him to save his breath. Since that first crack into the silence, things had gotten better.

Sitting down, he pulled off his eyelashes while Stella lifted the wig off his head. At least she didn't resent him doing Jennie. In time, her anger would dissipate; they had too much going for them for it not to. Once he had the makeup off his face, he stood still for a moment looking in the mirror. These days, he was aware that his mouth turned up at the corners instead of down. There was no substitute for success! Stubbing out a cigarette, he got into his clothes and kissed Stella.

"Don't be too long," she said when he was at the door. He could still sense some strain in her voice. "There are two more contracts to go over before Sam comes in from L.A. tonight. Don't detour at the crap tables, either! There's still a lot of other business we have to go over. Steve?" Her voice became soft. "You constantly said things would work out. I didn't always believe it."

"It's my time. All acts have a life span. When this one is over, I'll go on as a featured singer, probably with a hit record or two behind me for starters. All I have to do is make my moves at the right time."

*   *   *

Sammie Sauer cut his act by ten minutes so people wouldn't walk out on him to see the startling new show in the lounge.

After the customary intermission following Lily Jannings' appearance, Steve returned as himself and sang a couple of jazzy upbeat tunes and some tender blues. Within the past week, paragraphs had appeared in the papers devoted to the second part of his act—but those reviews were not up to the ones about his impressions. He consoled himself with the fact that solid singing acts were the toughest ones to launch.

He came off the stage and walked through the audience, taking a drink off the tray of an obliging waitress. He drank it and stepped out into the lounge with the departing patrons, who were enthusiastically extending compliments. He felt somewhat irritated because no one in the main area of the lobby stopped him for his autograph. Next time, he would walk more slowly.

When he opened the door to their suite, Stella looked up from the couch where she had been sleeping. On the coffee table were the papers Sam had left and an opened cardboard box.

She glanced at him and lifted her eyebrows, displeased. "A package from Louise. Special Delivery, Insured, Registered." She opened the large velvet case to reveal a half dozen rings, assorted pins and two necklaces. "Jennie wrote that she would rather you use them in the act than leave them at home where they might be stolen. She said she would collect them when she came back. Here's her letter." As she handed him the single sheet of paper, her mouth hardened. "What did she do with her jewelry before? It's just an excuse to see you again."

Shoving his lower lip out, he let the brief note slip from his hand after he'd read the last line. Better not let Stella see the faintest hint of a smile cross his face. It was Jennie's way of letting him know that she wasn't angry any more. Picking up the pieces one at a time, he examined them and put them back carefully.

"You don't need them in the act." she informed him.

"I know." It was time to change the subject. He motioned to the table. "Did you go over the legal stuff? Any hooks in it?"

"I did. No hooks. I only went as far ahead as a year and a half. We need a little time after that to catch our breath. Also, Sam said he would stop in tomorrow afternoon. He's really earning his commission. There's certainly enough to go around, at this point."

"Did he say anything about the New York Americana yet?" That spot would solidly launch him on the East Coast.

"He's still working on it." She lit a cigarette and drew on it heavily. "Things are good now," she admitted.

He looked down on her. What was she getting at?

"Steve, remember the night Jennie left—"

"I want to forget it," he cut her off quickly.

"No." Her hand with the lit cigarette in it went up. "What I mean is, that I said we were all going to get what we want."

"So?"

"Well," she said simply, "what I want to get is pregnant. Things can't get any better than they are now."

Why in hell did she want to bring that up? This was their time to enjoy living—not get stuck with a kid who'd cramp their style every time they turned around. It was the worst time to bring a child into their world. "Wait a second. What about the traveling we have to do? You can't lug a kid around like a suitcase."

"You can lug a baby around any way you want," she countered. "Don't be surprised if one of these days—"

"You're not, are you?"

"No such luck! But let's both of us mull it over, for now." She closed her eyes as though the subject was ended. "Speaking of news, there is a *London Post* contingent here to catch the act, and they would like to photograph you tomorrow as both yourself and Lily Jannings."

He expelled the air from his lungs in a wheeze. "I just did her, and I don't want to go through two makeups in a day." He'd just done that trick with Myra. "They'll have to wait. If they don't like the idea, tell them to shove it."

"I'll be sure to," she humored him. "Lily's opening at the Palladium, and they want to put a photo of you alongside one of her as a comparison shot."

"Not tomorrow. I've got a golf appointment with Sammie Sauer. I don't know what time I'll get back. Explain—"

"That it isn't ingratitude for the exposure they're giving you, but just that you're very tired."

He smiled at her. Stella really had a knack for grinding down his rough edges. "It's amazing to me how much I depend on you." He sat on the couch next to her. Placing his arm around her shoulder, he played with her ear.

"Flattery will get you everywhere." She tilted her head up as he leaned down to kiss her forehead. "They weren't interested in the glossies I said they could have."

"What they *really* want is to catch me in a slip-up. Putting on a bad show. Wouldn't that make a great column? They should know better," he grinned. "Once in costume, I'm the real thing."

"Just don't come to bed in your work clothes," she laughed.

"Never fear!" He held her tightly and kissed her again. The suite was beginning to close in on him. He wanted to be out in the cold, early-morning air. He longed for the shock of that fresh, healthy feeling. "Come on. Let's get the hell out of here and watch the sunrise over the desert. Just you and me and that new, expensive white convertible!"

Momentarily, he thought of their courtship days, and he remembered the mornings they'd met the sun at Jones Beach while planning their future.

At the closet, she threw a coat loosely over her shoulders. They walked through the casino, where Steve waved to the stone-faced croupiers. His step was buoyant and he felt more satisfied than at any other time in his married life.

Out in the steely gray of early morning, daylight was making its first appearance.

# CHAPTER THIRTEEN

It had been four days since Sam hit him with the news of the studio strike. A day later, *Variety* came out with the complete story. How long, Steve wondered, would filming be held up? Bad breaks swarmed around Jennie like hornets.

"Did you get everything packed for Chicago?" he asked Stella as she left the living room.

"Relax! We're traveling to the Windy City with twenty-three pieces of luggage. We are also in hock for upwards of fifteen thousand dollars. Do you really think it was wise ordering new costumes just because unemployed Paul Dudley came here from the studio with a portfolio full of sketches?"

He knew she hated being in debt, no matter what the amount. His own attitude had never rubbed off on her. Steve held out his arms.

She settled into them. "Your wardrobe is more dazzling than mine. Can I take them in, here and there, for myself, later? It's a unique opportunity. After all, what else is a husband for?" She circled his shoulder with one arm, then trailed a fingertip down the bridge of his nose. "Steve, how about visiting the family in Dayton right after we finish working Chicago?"

"What?" Taken by surprise, he looked directly at her. "What's to do in Ohio?"

Stella flinched.

He wanted to shoot directly into New York and spend free time at their old haunts. That used to be her style, too! She *had* changed! Well, still, nothing had been said about the baby recently, and that was a relief.

Then again, maybe some fresh air *would* settle them down before the New York opening. Besides, they hadn't seen her parents for well over a year. It was time to check up on things. Even on a farm, people grew older.

"On second thought, Stella, you're right. You always had an inside corner on brains."

The tightness in her body slackened.

He hugged her, then took a step back. "Where are the jewelry cases?"

"With me."

The ring of the phone interrupted their conversation, and she answered it. "Manila!" she exclaimed. "It's Jennie," she muttered. "Is that as far as her guts could get her?"

Stella handed him the phone and sat down at the opposite end of the small table. Crossing her arms, she rocked her upper leg back and forth, concentrating her attention on the call.

Jennie's woeful voice rang out across an ocean and two continents: "Stevie?" The connection was sharp and clear. She started to speak several times, but only succeeded in mumbling to herself.

He knew what was coming and wondered how to be both sympathetic and firm. The news of the studio strike had finally gotten to her. "What's the matter, Jennie?"

"If you don't help me, I'm gonna kill myself," she wailed. Then came the clink of glass.

"She's drinking," he whispered in an aside to Stella, then returned his attention to the call. "Hey, this call will cost you a fortune. Get on with it!"

"I'm going to cancel the tour. Now!" she yelled. "They're pushing me. No headliner should be treated this way."

He stood up, carrying the phone with him as he paced the floor. "Have you heard from anyone?" He was instantly sorry he'd brought the matter up.

"Nobody at the studio gives a damn about me!"

"You're drinking."

"I'm only groggy," she protested.

Suddenly, he knew what the matter was. "How many pills have you taken today?" He waited while she counted, lost count, began again. "For Christ's sake," he shouted, "how many have you taken?"

"Enough to make everything nice. Stevie, kiss Iris goodbye..." Her voice trailed off.

Stella folded her arms and gazed at him.

He returned the stare, not seeing her. "Jennie!" His voice bounced off the walls. "Pick up the goddamn phone and keep talking." He saw Stella's eyebrows draw together as she tried to construct the conversation at the other end. "Listen, damn it, I don't care what you've got in you. Just stick your fingers down your throat, and throw up the whole mess. Now!"

He thought she said, "OK." Then, he heard her heaving. Her heaves became longer and deeper. Steve waited. When she blurted out that she was "covered" with the foul-smelling stuff, he told her to "wash up and take a Benzedrine."

"Two's better," she replied.

He closed his eyes to push away the time until she returned to the phone.

"You have no idea how bad it's been, Stevie," she began. "I've had the runs ever since I crossed the International Date Line. My best friend has been any nearby toilet. The doctors

gave me something to hold me together, but it hasn't been
working and I'm weak, Baby, really weak. Do you know they
can't even rig the swing right? I *have* to come down from
the top, Little Melinda, singing 'One More Time,' or there's
no Jennie Darling show! I got stuck up there like a big-assed
bird," she laughed unsteadily, "so I dragged myself to the side
stairwell, then to center stage and just blubbered there like a
fool. Those Oriental sons-a-bitches took my signature act from
me! Wait a minute."

He heard her lay the receiver down again and hoped she
would not forget about it.

"I just had to use my relaxing spray," she explained when she
came back. "Stevie, don't ever let this happen to you! They're
only getting away with this because I'm too weak to fight back,
so I'm coming home. I have no choice; the sets are practically
ready anyway—"

"Don't do anything on this tour you'll be sorry for," he
interrupted, hoping his anxiety would not give him away. "Listen,
Jennie, for *Star Fire*, for yourself, keep your name out of bad
press." Intent on countering her with cool logic, he grabbed the
cigarette Stella offered him and took a long drag. Then: "Come
back to the States after you've worked Hawaii—"

"My last stop." She coughed and caught her breath. "Even
with the PR crew underfoot, I'm actually alone, and I hate it. If
anyone really cared, they'd be here with me." There was a silence
that lasted too long.

"What about Paul Rigdon?" He had seen the picture of Jennie
and the young actor waving happily to the press before boarding
her plane at the L.A. airport.

"That no-talent bastard ran out on me yesterday!" He could
tell she couldn't believe that. "I promised him a screen test, but

how could I fix one up for him in the Orient? He doesn't even know Japanese, and his eyes don't slant!"

Steve slumped downward, his free arm falling on his knee. At least she could still joke about rejection.

"Christ, he even said he loved me." The ache in her was still evident. "He's on his way home with the money I threw at him. I should have made him swim back! I'd just love to let go of everything."

"Jennie," he tried, again, "remember Iris."

"She'd be better off without me. Richer, anyway! I was never a real mother to her."

"You have a picture waiting," he argued. "You'll have everything all over again—"

"Promise?" Her voice picked up some brightness.

"In spades." He was finally getting there. "Come back with a finished tour, and we'll get you feeling great again."

"Will you be at the airport to meet me?"

"It's as good as done!"

"Oh, to be a top draw again, with first-class treatment all the way around! *That* thought might bring me out of it. I'll be OK. Don't worry." She suddenly seemed more confident. "How are you doing?"

"Great." He grinned, even though he knew she couldn't see him.

"Whom do they applaud the most?"

"Need you ask?"

"Good!" She'd become deliberate, now that the crisis in her mind had been brushed away. "I'll hit Singapore and Tokyo. After that, Hawaii, and then home. Now, I have to pull myself together. The show starts in a few hours."

"Don't do anything rash, and don't take anything strong!"

"Don't sweat it, Stevie," she assured him. "Jennie is just fine. I'm glad you're doing so well. Keep it up. By the way, I adore you for listening."

"Be a sweetheart and finish out the tour in style."

"In style," she echoed softly, then hung up.

He handed the receiver to Stella, and she replaced it on its cradle. He tried to be angry, but couldn't. His sense of compassion overrode any feeling of exasperation he felt concerning Jennie's actions.

Stella walked into the kitchen, then returned with two cups of coffee on a tray with cream and sugar.

Abruptly he got up and walked toward the window, only to spin around. "I don't need coffee; what I need is a drink," he barked, and at once became angry at himself for behaving like a son-of-a-bitch.

*   *   *

After the late show, Steve decided to have something to eat before returning to the suite. He was elated that Sam had signed him next into the Bonaparte Room in Chicago. It drew a warm and discriminating clientele and was a good place to break in new material before New York.

He could hear the ringing of the slot machines long before he opened the door leading to the lobby. He walked leisurely over the luxurious red rug. Was there time for a quickie with Lady Luck? A croupier pushed a drink into his hand.

"Thanks, Kyle. Anybody who doesn't like scotch straight doesn't like scotch," he said, enjoying the extra bit of attention. During his stay he made it a practice to know as many of the staff as possible on a first-name basis. They were a good group—

worked hard for their money and entertained no unreasonable illusions.

"I caught your first show," Kyle said, lifting his shoulders confidentially. "The scuttlebutt around these parts is that you're Big Room material." Abruptly Kyle turned his attention to a couple that had sauntered to his table.

Steve moved into the huge, red and black football-length room, which was sectioned into areas devoted to blackjack, roulette, and craps. Off to one side stood row upon row of slot machines with red and yellow lights on their tops. There was not a single machine that did not have someone in front of it courting Lady Luck, and in the noonday bright arena, no clock was in evidence. Occasionally, a shout of triumph would come from patrons as they hit a winner.

"Stevie!" a deep baritone voice called out from behind him. "Baby!"

Only Jennie had ever called him that! Surprised, he turned to see the lean, power-packed physique of Wesley Adams. Wesley's other hand ran over the buttocks of a vacantly staring blonde who had a black beauty mark ground into her left cheek. Her otherwise prim white dress' neckline ended just above her navel, exposing the inside curves of her lush breasts.

"I got in today," Wesley explained. "I was just on my way to see you."

*Why*, he wondered. The only thing they'd ever had in common was Jennie.

"Steve, meet Betty Graham. A graduate of the Fuck You Academy of Acting. We're here to do postgraduate research!"

The blonde smiled, and Wesley grinned back. Then, she returned her attention to the slot machine and screamed: Silver coins avalanched all over the floor, a siren blared and the light bulb on top of the machine swung around rapidly, indicating a major jackpot.

"I thought I was only going to help her get rid of my money," Wesley said in a bored tone, peering at the display area of the machine, "and she comes up with three cherries! Hell, I didn't think there was a virgin left in Las Vegas!" He patted her fondly on the behind. "Daddy is going to leave with Stevie for awhile. Come to the Safari Room when you run out of money, Sweetheart."

She threw Wesley a perfunctory glance.

"I caught 'Lily Jannings' tonight," Wesley said once he and Steve were seated in a small booth off to one side with a view toward the restaurant's entrance. "She was never better." Wesley studied him for a moment. "You are really quite a phenomenal talent."

"I didn't get the usual back-breaking applause," he confessed, and wished Wesley would reveal the reason for his visit.

"Peasants! What the hell do they know about art, anyway?"

The waitress brought them both coffee and cheesecake. Steve watched Wesley dig into his dessert. "How come you're not at the studio patching up the strike, Wes? It's mid-week!"

"What have you heard from Jennie?"

Lying, he replied that he had not heard anything.

Wesley wolfed down a piece of cake and washed it down with coffee. "That's good! Then she hasn't heard about it. By the time she does, the strike might be over. I know you would be the first one she would contact if she found out." Wesley's face took on a dour expression. "But, it doesn't look like it's going to be a short strike, and anyway, her sets are still uncompleted. Can you see her," his gray eyes blazed, "back here stomping around, not being able to work and wound up to a fever pitch? You just don't know Glitter City politics, Steve. Who do you suppose arranged the tour? We couldn't have her just churning around, all dressed up with no place to go. Besides, they *love* her in the Orient."

"How much of the picture is actually completed?" For a moment Steve wondered if the picture could be released as is— then realized how stupid that thought was. He felt Wesley reading his unspoken thoughts.

"What is a Jennie Darling film without our little dolly singing and dancing her heart out?" Wesley shut his eyes in mock reverence. "Those twinkling toes have danced a trillion miles across the soundstages since she first got into the business." Leaning forward, he let his hand support the weight of his head. "It was a fluke that we didn't have the sets ready in time. Now that we have the special materials, we can't get the workers to put them together." One side of his mouth turned up. "The irony of it all is that she had nothing to do with the current hold-up." His voice conveyed some sympathy. "But, she's been responsible for every other crappy thing that held up production!"

"Is that all you have to tell me?" Steve started to rise. "You are all a bunch of son-of-a-bitchin' leeches feeding on her, and you won't give up while there's an ounce of blood left."

"Now wait, Goodie Two-Shoes, before you start running off in all directions." Placing a restraining hand on Steve's shoulder, Wesley forced him down into his chair. "What you don't know is that I'm bucking for her every chance I get—"

"Is that right?"

"Yeah, that's right! For your information, I've been barely less than a husband to Jennie and much more than a lover. And," he raised his voice for emphasis, "the smartest thing we ever did was not to marry. That's why I will still do everything I can for her."

"What makes you think I would hear from her?"

"Because there is something going on between you two," he

smiled wryly. "That's why the big brass picked up the tab for this trip."

"Sorry, but I can't contribute anything," Steve said sharply. The big brass knew where to contact Jennie. If they were too damned chicken to tell her about the strike, he wasn't about to. Maybe the studio would open up in a couple of weeks, contrary to Wesley's opinion. He hoped so, or they would all be at each other like a blood-crazed school of sharks.

Wesley looked over his shoulder at someone at the doorway. "Betty's back!" He gave a short laugh. "She's run out of money! Well—since *you* can't help me, on to other matters." Wesley rose from the seat, signed the check and added a cash tip. He shoved his chair back and stood up.

The blonde walked toward them, her breasts swinging from side to side almost in slow motion. "I don't have anything left."

"Yes, you do! Honey, what do you say we go upstairs and do something more interesting than losing money?"

At the elevator junction off the main lobby, Wesley and Betty disappeared. Steve watched the metal doors clang shut and looked at the dial marking off the floors until it stopped at the thirtieth. He didn't feel much like gambling now. Irritation for Wesley and the studio continued to rankle him.

"Barrie," he called to a nearby cocktail waitress. "Get me a double scotch, will you? I just got some news that needs drowning."

# CHAPTER FOURTEEN

"And a child shall lead them." Stella waltzed into their huge Michigan Avenue hotel apartment.

Steve turned away from the window and reluctantly smiled, then stepped back and let the air out of his cheeks in a slow whistle. A baby? Already? What a goddam bust!

He pulled her toward the couch, reached down and softly stroked her hair. She looked so damn happy that he felt guilty not matching her feelings. But she should have waited a little longer. In a way he was excited about it, too, but he knew their world would never be uncomplicated again. "When did you find out?"

"Today. I've just come from the doctor's office. That's why I didn't stay up for your late shows in Vegas. I got my morning sickness at night." A glow came from deep within her eyes as she looked up at him. "You are happy, aren't you?"

"Let me get you a drink," he said without thinking.

She brought both of her hands back and lifted her hair off her shoulders. It fell back down again in a blonde cascade. "Orange juice, please. I'll leave the hard stuff to you from now on. Steve— Mom and Dad will be thrilled when I call them tonight. Let's stay with them before we push on." Suddenly she grabbed her stomach and, just as rapidly, released it.

"Labor pains already?" He was trying to sound light-hearted but was secretly alarmed.

"No such luck. Only nausea! It's quite common in the early weeks." She leaned back into the sofa and took several deep breaths.

"Be sure you rest more," he said firmly, hoping she would have an easy time carrying the child to term. He'd heard stories from Gus and his wife of how bad it could be.

"Don't worry." She patted his knee. "Have you been downstairs yet?"

"No, they're waiting. Are you sure you're all right?"

She nodded and looked around the room until she got to the ebony grand piano. "I don't see your arrangements. Where are they?"

"I sent them down." He looked out toward the lake where sailboats were tilting in the wind. "To be able to have time to go sailing—if I could sail," he chuckled. "It's one of the things you have to remind me to do when we're up there and we have all the time in the world." He stopped for a moment, then began to speak again. "We'll *make* the time. We have to, now that we're parents."

"Hurry down," she said, "so you can hurry back up."

He held her protectively, then walked to the bar and poured himself a glass of scotch over two rocks.

"So early in the day?" she called out, and started to frown.

"It's pre-opening tension." He winked back at her. Taking a small swallow, he let the fire plummet to his stomach and slapped the glass down hard on the counter. "By the way, verify Sam's reservation for the suite next door, will you, please? He'll be in tomorrow on the eleven a.m. plane."

\*   \*   \*

Sam reached for his coffee, took a slow sip. "So, Stella, what do you think of these offers?"

She jammed her cigarette into the ashtray. "I don't want Steve to work so hard at not being himself."

"There's more than work laid out on this table. There's also opportunity! I didn't come here just to see how you're doing at the Bonaparte Room, Steve. Chicago is not my favorite city." He mopped his sweaty brow with a napkin and pulled a cigar out of his inside coat pocket. Methodically, he sliced off the end and lit it, rolling it around in his mouth, savoring the smoke and feel. He drew the features of his face together. "These concessions aren't easy things to make, Steve. I don't deny that. In a way, I can't blame you, but you have to develop the fine art of compromise. It isn't like they're asking you to sign your life away. Play the act for all it's worth, and *then* you can do something different. You're an artist. What does it matter in which medium you create?"

"How will that act ever get him known as himself?" Stella asked, arms crossed.

"Where did Steven Dennis get all by himself? Yet as a mimic—"

"Illusionist," he corrected, pointing his finger directly into Sam's face. "I'm an actor. Just as much as any other actor playing a part. And I'm goddamn good at it!"

The startled agent moved back. "So, who's forgetting it? Act! And keep on with your act because it's the damndest one anyone has ever seen." Sam brought the cigar to his mouth and wrapped one hand over the other. "Don't let go of something that's been so good to you, Steve. Build it, use it, and you'll be your own legend in time!"

Steve raised his hands up in fists. "The illusions were only a gimmick to get me started! They were *never* meant to be an end in themselves." Then he got up and started to look out the windows to the lake.

"Relax, Steve. When the audience is tired, they'll give the act the old heave-ho. They're fickle." Sam grabbed his arm and pulled him into a chair. "Look, Steve," he said kindly, "the right time for you will come. Believe me. It's happened to Sinatra and others. Those aren't bad acts to follow—even if you are doing it backward."

"He's rehearsing constantly, perfecting and checking out different routines, Sam," Stella explained. "With the baby coming, he'll have to slow down."

"He will?" Sam's voice cracked. "I thought that was your department, Stella." He stood up on legs that only the kindliest soul would have considered straight. His shoulders sloped down into a roundness at the midsection, that then tapered to his knees. He looked like a pair of parentheses. Sam took Steve's expression for an acquiescence. "You'll sign?"

Steve's smile turned down. Damn it, Sam was all for pushing the real him out of the act, too!

"Steve," Sam blurted, "use your head. They come to see Jannings, Pickens, and Dormann, and—God help us—Jennie Darling." He brought his hands up into the air. "A new male singer, they can see any time! It's legends they want." Sam shaped the air in front of him into a ball and threw it to him. "So—give 'em legends!"

The cushions of the chair whooshed as Sam settled into them. "I've got to know. Immediately! What the hell! Tomorrow, the clubs might be hot for puppets. Grab the green while they're holding it out!"

"They've really been after you about cutting down my songs?" He knew he was drawing his face into a grimace.

Sam took another sip of coffee and sat back. "Male singers, they can get anywhere. But you know they barely let the first part of your act off the stage. And you're making more money than you ever dreamed you could."

"We are *all* making money, Sam," he interjected.

"And spending it like we have Fort Knox in the basement," Stella said, clearing away the uneaten sandwiches.

Sam walked to the huge floor-to-ceiling windows and looked out at the lake. The dusk shot dark shadows into the cotton-puff clouds that were forming in the distance. He stared at them, a short, small man considering his options.

"You can mail me the contracts by special delivery." Sam swept the inside of his mouth with his tongue. "You'll sign them, won't you?"

"Tivoli in Copenhagen, Sans Souci in Paris and The Appian Way in Rome. Impressive, isn't it?" Steve commented, fingering the contracts. He looked at the abstract patterns the black print made on the white pages. Suppose he cut down on the illusions but made up for it by reworking his part of the show, using special material? Other entertainers had worked in new acts by gradually easing out current ones, with no one the wiser. If he did it right, people would recognize him as a special singer with an easygoing delivery before they even knew it.

He looked at Stella. "We can't turn off the money fountain. I'll learn to handle my part in a different way."

Stella shrugged her shoulders.

Dammit—it was easy for her not to compromise. She didn't have a civil war going on inside her most of the time. How in hell did she think they could manage on less with a baby coming? She wouldn't be able to work! Even if she did, what she could make in an office wouldn't begin to make a dent in their financial obligations. Why couldn't she see that he had no choice?

"It's fantastic money," he said, almost in a monotone, "and we *have* waited a helluva long time for it. I waited so many years for anyone to want me. My tongue got dry from hanging out of my mouth for so long."

"Those contracts represent years off your life," Stella reminded him. "You can hold out! There's no need to book yourself so far into the future."

He stood up and gestured with his arms at the surroundings. "Look around. Neither of us is complaining about the furniture any more."

Sam shifted uneasily in his seat.

"Give me the pen, Sam!" With an exaggerated flourish he signed the contracts. They were ending the conference on too heavy a note and he didn't like it. It seemed like a bad omen. "You won't fuck me over with drafty dressing rooms like you did Jennie, will you?"

"Jennie!" Sam snorted. "They don't have drafts where she's going to be booked!" Sam looked down at the floor, then shifted his gaze up to Steve. "She had lawsuits pending before she even started the tour. It's going to take some campaign to get her off the hook this time after running out on her backers. You know she did, don't you?"

"Iris was here last week and told me all about it," he said grimly. "Libertyville University is only a couple of hours away."

Sam slouched forward. "Jennie's crazy,"

"She's crazy frightened," Steve rallied to her defense.

"Who isn't? Look," Sam rapped on the glass table top with his pen, "the people she ran out on won't take it lying down. The only thing going for her is that they still need her for *Star Fire's* unfinished numbers, which cost more than a mint." Sam relaxed, and the redness in his face receded.

Steve folded the contracts and handed them to Sam in a neat pile. A pile that represented his future.

"I kind of thought Jennie might have contacted you," Sam said casually.

"She didn't!" Glancing at his watch, Steve checked to see how many hours he had left before show time. He knew Sam, long used to the mannerisms of performers, was aware that it was time to go.

"Who are you doing tonight, Steve?"

"Sherri Pickens."

"Is that so? I hear you do a better Sherri Pickens than she does."

"Sure. She was born that way, but I had to get there by dissecting and studying all of her shtick. Sam, why not stay and see the show?"

"Stay, Sam." Stella came over to him. "We'll share a table at the dinner show. You can catch a later plane to the coast. Night flying is cheaper!"

"And darker! And scarier!"

Stella smiled. "Planes with agents in them don't crash. It's against God's law. I'll ring you in time for dinner." She led him to the door.

Before he left, Sam turned back and assured them, "You've made the right decision."

"A percentage of that decision is yours," Steve reminded him, then headed for the bedroom.

* * *

Steve was rehearsing an especially tricky number with Myra Dormann; at several points in the recording, he had to lift the tone arm to reset it, singing the phrases repeatedly until he had them right. Then he sang into a live mike, stopped, snapped off the machine, and replayed the recording. Great—he had her down cold!

The telephone rang. He was about to ask Stella to answer it when he realized she was out shopping for maternity clothes. As he picked up the receiver, he heard the familiar voice:

"Stevie, Baby, it's me! And guess where I am?"

"Switzerland," he replied, unsure whether to be happy or upset. He recalled Iris tearfully telling them that Jennie had left the Orient for Zurich with a married French politician she'd met at the Tokyo Grand Hotel. "Wherever you are, that's no place for you to be! And, how come you called direct? Suppose we weren't in?" His voice had developed an edge in spite of his efforts to keep it calm.

"It's my dime," she laughed, and the next words rushed together. "Look, Angel, be happy for me. Everything is wonderful and I'm really in love this time. I'm also going to make money. Pots and pots of it. I've signed for ten weeks at the Palladium. You know, London is my lucky town. At least they're civilized in England. Don't ever perform in Japan," she cautioned. "All that rice will give you beriberi." She burst into a series of delighted giggles. "Be delirious for me, Stevie—"

"How can I be when you ran out on your contract?"

"What's a contract?" she questioned nonchalantly. "It's only a piece of paper! I've been through too many lawsuits to be frightened by one more. Don't worry, I can take care of it.

"He's a beautiful person, Stevie. Honest to God! Anyway, I'm going to hire a public relations firm to do a whitewash job on the tour affair. The important thing is that I'm well and happy, and in love. Don't tell anyone I'm here. They'll find out soon enough and I'll be able to handle it once everything has cooled down. Wasn't the Palladium booking a lucky break?" She obviously wanted to get on to the positive aspects of her situation. "I've already shipped my props and costumes. At least they know how to rig a swing in London."

"What are you on?"

"Nothing—oh, a few vitamins. I gained some weight. I always do when I'm happy. But I'll be OK and ready for the picture. By that time, I'll have shed this flab. Anyway, my guy likes me on the plump side."

"The studio likes you slim!"

"And I like myself just as I am! I'm finally coming out of the tunnel, Stevie. I'm not even insomniac," she sighed. "Take my word for it: a good screw is better than a Nembutal to put you out at night—any time. He's gorgeous, Stevie—all over! Please, don't turn into a naysayer like those studio clods. Be happy for me."

"Is his wife still high and dry in Tokyo?"

"Come on. She's in Bombay with a guy who imports and exports—don't ask me what. And, don't pick on me. If you keep that up, you'll get a transoceanic earful!"

"Jennie, come on back and get things straightened out."

"For what? A studio strike? I'd end up by hammering the damn sets together all by myself, nail by nail."

"Calm down."

"I'm not up—not after talking to you," she griped, "And, by the way, I'm only drinking wine at dinner." Her voice turned tender. "Baby, the only reason I called was because I thought you'd be happy for me. For Christ's sake, be happy for me!"

"I am. I am, Jennie, but come back. Bring the politico if you like, but come back."

"I will," she said soothingly, "but first, I have a contract here. They've always loved me in London. I'm not going to let them down. Not *Jennie Darling*. And, he's coming with me. By the way, he's paying for this call, so we can talk for hours!"

"Well, thank God you found someone with his own bank account!" he laughed. "OK, stay there then, but ease up! At least you sound better than the last time I heard from you."

"That's why I called. I forbid you to worry about me any more. Promise?"

"Yeah—and you'll slow down. Promise?"

"Sure. I'll call you from London after I open. Where will you be?" After he told her, she whistled. "With you in Chicago and me in London as little Melinda, we'll knock them on their asses." Abruptly her mood shifted: "I'm going to call Iris right now. Check up on her in the next week or so, will you? I'd appreciate it." She hung up before he could say goodbye.

The call bothered him. He hung up the phone, trying to separate her happiness from her anxiety, frustrated at not being able to get through to her. Damn it—she hadn't heard a word he'd said. He'd thought he could make some sort of an impression on her, but he was wrong. She was acting like a schoolgirl going through her first crush.

"Shit."

He left the hotel through the Oak Street exit. The walk to the Chicago Athletic Club, where he had an appointment to play tennis with a professional instructor, was just long enough to allow the lake breezes to clear his head.

# CHAPTER FIFTEEN

New York was a lot dirtier than Steve remembered, and it hadn't been that long since they had been away. As he walked slowly around Manhattan's theater district, he realized the Club Chloe was just a short distance away. He decided to see what it looked like now, and quickened his steps along the familiar streets.

Turning the corner near a rundown coffee shop, he saw the front sign. Many of the bulbs were out of their sockets, and the paintless metal was rusting to a dirty orange. Jagged blades of glass had infiltrated the outside display boxes; he pulled at one box, which fell away from his fingers and shattered with a clash. Stepping away from the shards, he wondered where Joe was. Was Janet working? Where was Gus pouring drinks? He felt a sense of emptiness as he thought about them.

The open door caught his attention. The lock had been broken, probably recently, and the door was slightly ajar. He stepped inside the deserted building. It was dusty and dark inside, but he could make out the outlines of surroundings he once knew well.

A scurrying noise raised the hairs on the back of Steve's neck; he froze until he'd located the sound: a large rat darting across the floor. Shoving his hands in his coat pockets, he stared ahead to the raised platform, where he could see himself breathing life into pathetic material. He would tell Stella to get in touch with the old crowd, but viewing the past here hurt just too damn much! He walked out and hailed a cab.

When he got out of the cab, he overtipped the driver because he remembered his own grueling, penny—pinching years. The man mutely took the money and sped away. Directly in front of Steve loomed the Americana Hotel. Off to one side—under his portrait, in the center of a display setting—was an announcement surrounded by scrolls of gold and black on crushed velvet.

COMING—ILLUSIONIST STEVEN DENNIS

"First class," he murmured. It was first class, too, of the hotel to provide him with a four-room dressing suite adjacent to the stage. Star treatment was something he had not experienced before, and he didn't take that pleasurable feeling for granted.

"Look," Stella called out from the living room as he entered their apartment. She held up a sheaf of telegrams. "A celebrity is in town!" Setting them down, she interlocked her fingers behind her head and leaned back in her chair, fixing him in her gaze.

He walked to the table and read the first three messages. "Can I have a scotch?" He would read the rest when he was in a better mood. As she went to the bar, he called out, "Make it a double! I've just been to the Chloe."

He sat down and sipped the offered drink. He'd never thought much about it before, but he had traveled far in just under two years.

"You should have gone to the post office, too, and done the complete tour," she teased, trying to lighten his mood. "Come on, is success all that hard to take?"

"Hell, no!" he yelled, and found that he was relieved by his outburst. He got up and began pulling the shirt out of his pants.

"You've been too restless lately, and for no good reason." She went to his side and slipped her arms around him, lightly touching her lips to his cheek.

He drew his fingers down the side of her face. "Just as soon as I open, I'll be all right." He wanted another drink but squelched that thought as she took his empty glass.

"Let's do some shopping," she suggested. "That will get your mind off things. We won't have much time after you get into gear. In another day you face the press."

"Oh, happy day."

"Well, it won't be as though you're just starting out. Quite a few of the reporters have already seen you in Vegas." She circled the rim of his glass with a fingertip. "You'll win them over without even trying."

"Are you trying to flatter me?"

"Just being truthful! By the way, I promised the folks we would call them tonight. We should have stayed in Ohio longer." She paused. "I'm glad I didn't tell them anything about the baby until they could see for themselves." She posed in front of him, turning to the side so he could see her slightly distended figure.

He got up to pull her down onto the sofa next to him. She looked more beautiful than ever, and he couldn't remember having been crazier about her than right now. Christ, she had stuck with him through all those black and bleak moments.

"Let's take in a play each night before I open. After rehearsals, we'll walk during the afternoons, and finish the day with a late dinner. Let's be so busy that we'll fall flat on our faces into the bed at night."

"Why, that's the best offer I've had today!"

*   *   *

When opening night finally arrived, Steve sat with his elbows on the dressing table and stared into the mirror, watching Stella in back of him getting everything in order. From a ledge of wig boxes, she selected one with "JD" monogrammed in shiny brass letters on a black plastic background. He pulled a cigarette from the pack, blew the wind out of his cheeks, and shoved himself away from the table. Days ago he'd given up trying to hide his underlying tensions.

"The regular green shoes or the topaz?" she asked.

He told her either would do, then changed his mind and told her to select the topaz ones for luck.

Over two pins that stuck out of the front of the wig stand, she hung the topaz earrings. "You shouldn't have come down so early," she said, and pointed to the newspapers. "It's stage fright in your own home town that's doing it. You read yourself how you knocked those reporters off their feet." She forced his chin up so he'd have to look at her. "Cheer up!"

"Do you think my own numbers are too jazzy? Hell, it's too late to do anything about that right now." He realized he hadn't given her any time to respond.

"Relax, Sweetheart. Everything is going to be all right."

The telephone rang, and she took it. She listened intently for a moment without any response. He watched her face. Who would be so goddamned stupid as to call him now?

"Jennie," she said finally. "I can hardly make her out." She shut her eyes, trying to hear, then gave up and held the receiver out to Steve.

He took it eagerly. A transoceanic call to offer congratulations for a smash opening was Jennie at her best. "Jennie?"

An almost inaudible voice answered: "Save me, Stevie, Baby! You promised you'd save me!" Her crying blotted out further conversation. In frustration, he glanced up to the ceiling—meeting Stella's gaze briefly on the way down. "I'm a goner," Jennie coughed. "You have to fly out now and save me." She coughed again. "I'm a goner—"

She was so out of it that she didn't remember it was his opening night. What the hell had happened since they'd talked a few days ago? Tonight, he couldn't take it! He had more than enough to be concerned about.

"Jennie, get yourself to a doctor," he said, alarmed. "You're in no shape to do anything else."

"Steve!" She took on an authoritative air. "Leave it all and save Jennie, or there ain't gonna be anyone left worth saving. You can be here before you know it. I can't talk any longer," she gasped, "I have a show to do. *For God's sake, come!*"

"I can't. I'm opening tonight."

"Thrills and spills," she laughed.

He checked the wall clock: just enough time to get ready. "Pull yourself together, Jennie. I can't fly out now."

"You must!" Her tone was now one of panic, "I need help *now.* Don't worry about your contract; I'll tell you how to get out of it. Oh, Baby, if you do this for me, I won't ask you for anything else ever again."

"I can't come now. It's my opening night!"

"You have to!" she screamed back. "I'll wait for you, and we can go on together. We'll be double dynamite! You owe me that, at least—"

"Jennie, I can't."

"I'll wait for you at the airport. You can be here in hours. I need you badly, Stevie." The words were indistinct, fuzzy.

"What have you taken this time?" he demanded.

"What's that got to do with anything?" she blurted out. "I'm trying to remember. Let's see, I took a pepper-upper, I guess about an hour ago. It should have worked by now." She tried to muffle a cough.

"What did you wash it down with?"

"Water, I think," she said slowly. "It must have been water—it had to have been water!" The words sounded flat. "Stevie, that phony politician is no more. His wife came back, and do you know what?" She didn't wait for his answer. "I gave him back to her. That crazy bastard wanted all of us to live under one roof.

"Like ring around the rosy—all fall into bed—together! Too much," she moaned. "Absolutely too, too much. Steve, come!" The line went silent.

His stomach began a slow churn. She sounded as bad as she had when he got the call from Manila. Only for her, he thought, would he give up precious time tonight. He avoided looking at Stella. "Jennie?"

She murmured something he couldn't make out.

"Stick your finger down your throat."

"I've no time, Stevie," she moaned. "I've got to pull myself together. I'm on in moments. Say," she croaked, "did I tell you they love me here? Won't let me off the stage." She sounded pleased with herself— then changed her tone. "Did I tell you I sent that bastard packing? He was no good—absolutely no good! Did I tell you why?"

Damn it! Every time she reached out for a handful of happiness, life kicked it out of her fist. He realized he was close to canceling his opening night and flying out to be with her. That was a crazy thought—even for him.

"You ungrateful sonofabitch! You owe me everything! Everything!" An icy tone came into her voice. "Never mind, I can do it all by myself. I've done it before. I'm the only person I can depend on, anyway."

"I'll fly over on my first night off!" He slammed a palm on the table top; it stung. He had to make her understand. "I will!"

"Sure you will."

"Don't go on. Get a doctor." There was no one in London he knew who would keep an eye on her. His best hope was to get her to help herself, because both of them were running out of time.

"How can I call a doctor when *you're* on the phone? Jesus, what time is it?" She stopped. "So, I'll be fifteen minutes late! They've waited longer. They love me at the Palladium. But you don't." Her voice became imperious and steadier. "I've got to go. I don't disappoint *my* friends. That's strictly your department!" The connection broke as her receiver came down with a bang.

"What is it with Melinda now?" Stella asked

"I don't know. I don't think she does, either. I don't think anyone does. But, God damn it, she needs someone interested enough in her to bring her around to realizing that she needs a rest." He buried his face in his hands for a moment. "Make a plane reservation for me for Wednesday morning, for London. I'll be back the next day in time for the show."

"I hope you know what you're doing," was Stella's almost-audible reply.

There was nothing else he could do, he decided as he made himself up.

*     *     *

*The weather was damp outside, so Jennie pulled her mink from the closet and slung it over her shoulders. Where had she left her purse? She blinked her eyes, trying to locate it, as the room took little jumps in front of her.*

*"Friends! They all stink," she muttered, weaving her way across the room to the phone.*

*"It's Jennie Darling. Get me a cab outside the front door." She didn't wait for an answer but spun around and nearly fell. Automatically, her hand reached out to clutch a floor lamp, and she stiffened against it for support. God, her head hurt. Wrapping her coat around her tightly, she grabbed her purse off a table and swept grandly out of the room, and then the hotel.*

*In the cab, she focused her eyes on the meter and reached into her bag. The pound note was lots more than the charge would be, she knew, and tapped her feet impatiently on the floor. Damn Steve for wasting her time on that telephone call! She drew her wrist up to her eyes to see the time and hit her nose with her hand. She swore aloud.*

*When the cab pulled up to the stage entrance, she shoved the money at the driver and told him to keep the change. Tilting her head upward, she clutched her coat at her neck to ward off the evening chill and charged toward the stage entrance. She heard a mixture of backstage chatter and music when she opened the door. Pushing the door manager aside, she plunged forward.*

*"You are quite late," the stage manager informed her. His florid head bobbed nervously. His blue eyes raced from side to side above his white walrus moustache, giving his face a humorous look.*

*A shoe dropped off her foot. She began to fall and thanked him when he caught her. Then she hobbled the short distance to her door. "I'll be on as soon as I change."*

*"People are leaving," he told her.*

*"Fools!" She felt her strength returning. "Keep everybody away. Keep the orchestra playing. I'll be out in seconds." He tried to say something, but she cut him off:*

*"Do—as—I—say!"*

*He backed away from her in disbelief.*

*"And send somebody onto that goddamn stage to tell them that Jennie is coming. Jesus Christ, my throat!" She grabbed at it and stormed into her room. With the door still open, she screamed out, "Get that dresser in here, fast!" She thought for a moment of going on as she was, but decided that was asking the audience for too much.*

*Muffled chants could be heard through the heavy stage curtain. The singsong phrases blended into one another. Suddenly, she was furious at herself because she had let them down. She had let herself down, too. Then she became frightened. "They can't leave me. I won't let them."*

*The fear began devouring her. She held her arms against her body, trying to steady herself, and began to perspire. Rummaging through her bag, she found the bottle with the red pills. She fumbled with the cap until she got one into her hand and swallowed it without water. She shivered at its bitter taste but knew she'd be flying in seconds if that damned thing worked as it should.*

*She slid out of her coat and dress in one motion, then kicked them away. She flung her remaining shoe off her foot and grabbed the back of the vanity chair. Reaching for her chloroform spray, she squinted at the label to see if it was the more powerful one and shot several sprays deep into her throat. She slathered cold cream over her face and, just as quickly, rubbed it off.*

*"What a bastard—not to come!" Then she returned to the moment and quickly applied the heavy theatrical makeup.*

*There was no waiting for the dresser any longer. She pulled the nearest gown off the rack and, balancing herself precariously, inserted one foot into the costume, then another, then rustled it up her body. She reached back to zip it up, but her attempts to grasp the tab were futile; the gown fell away from her. She caught it and pressed it against her breasts with one arm.*

*Stretching her features, she began to apply mascara to the artificial* lashes she had somehow managed to put on. When they looked dark enough, she pulled the skin over her temples sideways and extended a black line over her lids. She blinked several times and crowned her achievements with the darkest shade of lipstick she could find on the dresser. Hell, she looked great!

She then located a pair of shoes that matched the color of her gown and unsteadily put them on.

The manager opened the door.

"It's a fiasco, Miss Darling," he howled. "They're leaving."

"Nobody walks out on Jennie! I'm getting on that swing, and Little Melinda is coming down to that stage singing 'One More Time'."

"You are in no condition to perform," he protested. "You're drunk!"

"How dare you?" she screamed, and pushed him aside. "Where the hell is my swing?" Shielding her eyes, she spotted it high above center stage, camouflaged by the heavy velvet drapes. The familiar melody of her tunes buoyed her up, and she grinned. "Zip me!" She brought her hands back to lift her hair at the nape of her neck. She heard the sound of the zipper locking her into her costume, then turned to him. "Don't you ever tell Jennie Darling what to do! Not as long as my show pays your salary!"

"You shouldn't—"

"Shut your sniveling little mouth," she yelled, and groped her way to the steps that would take her high onto the catwalk where the swing was anchored. The well-known surroundings gave her renewed vigor. Placing one foot in front of the other, she panted her way to the top. At the landing, she took a deep breath and gazed down at the stage crew directly under her. What the hell were they looking at? Hadn't they ever seen a star arrive late for a performance before?

The orchestra started the symphonic arrangement of "One More Time" as she seated herself on the swing and crossed one knee over the other. She lifted one hand to touch her cheek, careful not to smear *her makeup. What was it they were saying down there? Her makeup was* what?

*As she got comfortable, she waved her hand toward the electrician. At the board, he shoved one lever forward and pulled one back. The curtains parted slowly, and the stage below her became drenched in shades of pink. She pressed the lever on the swing's right side, and it began its downward trip.*

*"Open those goddam curtains faster," she ordered through a broad, sparkling smile.*

*As she started to sing "One More Time," coming down to center stage, she saw the last vestige of the audience getting ready to leave. Stunned, she stopped the swing halfway in its descent and peered out into the vast theatre, now completely lit. With her feet dangling in the air, she felt like a little child. Stragglers turned momentarily to look at her on their way toward the exit doors; she had to make them come back.*

*"Don't go," she pleaded, "it's me, Jennie, I love you and I'm going to sing for you. I'm going to dance for you. No," she begged, face awash with sweat. "Stay! Don't go!"*

*Her arms shot out to coax them back to her; thrown off balance, she fell forward. Her past life began swirling about her in slow motion; she saw herself singing and dancing. God, was she ever so young and so beautiful? But the words of the songs ran together and didn't make any sense. That was silly! She began to laugh. Then the floor came up and hit her.*

*It was the hardest knock she'd received in her entire life.*

\* \* \*

The bedroom was midnight dark, but Steve knew that outside it was bright and sunny. It was almost one in the afternoon by the travel clock on the glossy white highboy chest facing the bed. What a night! Who had punched him in the gut? His body ached as if someone had hit him with a two by four, and a wrecking ball was doing its business in his head. "Ugh," he growled to no one, and flung the blanket back. He had to get up. Where the heck was Stella?

The phone rang several times, screaming into his ears. "Stella," he called out; no response. He then pushed the receiver into his ear. "Steve here."

"It's me, Sam," the words rushed at him, "you in bed? Get your ass out fast, and turn on the TV. Bad news! Real, real bad! Catch you later!" The call was severed by a sharp click.

The bedroom door opened and Stella walked toward him. Midway, she stopped. "Jennie's dead!" She paused for a moment to let the news sink in. "Her story—it's on every channel!"

He shut his eyes tightly and grabbed his chest as he fell from a great height into a bottomless hole. An animal groan escaped his lips.

Stella waited, uncertain how to proceed, then spoke. "I'll open the drapes. You didn't sleep well at all last night, what with all that tossing and turning. Did she get to you, even in your dreams?"

He tried to reply, but the words weren't there.

"I'm very sorry—for her, *and* for you—but she never had a chance ever since she became Melinda."

On the breakfast tray she carried stood a tall vase holding a single long-stemmed daffodil. Steve studied it, noting how fragile it was, then looked up at his wife, larger around her midsection and finding it more difficult to move around quickly.

He turned his attention back to the TV; he switched from channel to channel but found no further news. "Damn it." He turned off the set.

"Don't blame yourself!"

"I was the last one she called!"

"Only because you were the last one in favor. She used people—a lot. You don't remember that part of her, but I do."

"Don't kick her when she can't defend herself," he snapped.

"You're upset and I can understand it, but don't deify her even though you loved her." Stella bit her lower lip and returned his look of surprise. "You did. I know you did, and in the back of your mind, you know you did, too. Maybe not the way you love me, but a genuine love, nevertheless. Don't talk me out of that thought. I'm a woman and I know what I'm talking about."

"She was so scared," he started to explain. "Why the hell do you think she was acting so nutty? She had everything under control but her fears, because there was so much at stake. Maybe it takes a dedicated performer to understand that."

"It's always a pity when you have only one thing to pin your hopes on." She faced him head on. "But performers aren't the only ones with problems."

He looked around the room. "Have you forgotten she was the one responsible for all of this?"

"No, I haven't." She waited a moment, then said, "You had a hand in it, in case you've forgotten, as did I, and *that,* I haven't forgotten. What the hell, this conversation is going nowhere. Get dressed. Your things are laid out on the bedroom chaise. You have an interview at five."

"Call them and see if I can beg off."

"What kind of nonsense is that? The reporters will only get back at you later for doing that to them."

"I can't do it," he argued. "Not until I'm up to it. You should be able to understand that better than anyone."

She started to leave the room.

"Jennie should have known I was on her side," he called after her, and felt a little better for having said it.

"Don't try to convince me," Stella replied tartly, "and don't bother convincing her. If she didn't know it then, it's a cinch she doesn't care about it now. I'll be waiting for you as soon as you get dressed."

The living room, ablaze with sunshine, seemed to mock his dark feelings. He poured himself a short glass of scotch as Stella looked at him. There was no sense trying for any more conversation at this point, so he turned away and slowly sipped his drink.

*     *     *

"It's news time," Stella said, snapping on the television set, not bothering for his reaction.

Sitting in front of the set with his forearms resting on his thighs, Steve watched the coverage. He was conscious of every breath he took and gritted his teeth hard. Stella held a lighted cigarette out to him; he took it with no acknowledgment.

The announcer sadly informed the public of the death of Jennie Darling, the "show business meteor whose shimmering presence had captured the world's attention for decades. After being dogged with bad luck, a major new picture signaling her comeback, *Star Fire,* was soon to be released. Illness had forced her to cancel a tour in the Far East, but she was looking forward to other professional commitments when she plunged to an accidental death from her swing at the Palladium Theatre in London. Her daughter at this moment is flying to New York with her body."

Immediate revivals of her movies were being scheduled nationwide, and a tribute to her as a permanent luminary in the entertainment world would be presented later that week on the same channel.

The announcer signed off with: "The world will never forget Little Melinda, 'The Sleeping Princess'. May 'The Sleeping Princess' sleep happily ever after."

Then a commercial for kitchen cleanser flooded the screen with bright colors and raucous sounds. Steve pressed the off switch. Now, the death dance would begin. He pulled on a cardigan sweater, then tapped his fingers against the table top.

On the phone, Iris had said it would be as simple a ceremony as possible.

He had to give the kid credit for the way she was taking over.

"Iris can stay with us," Stella said. "We have the room. She'll have to have some place where she can receive visitors," she thought aloud. "I'll see that there's plenty of food around—but we'll hold the liquor low."

He sank down onto the sofa—only to get up again in exasperation. He needed to settle down, fast! "Where are the happiness pills?"

"We're fresh out," she replied patiently, "I'll order them tomorrow."

"Can't we get some today?"

"I'll see. Look, you're being—"

"I know, a big prick, and I'm sorry for it, but just bear with me for a little while."

She bit her lower lip and began making a list on a note pad.

He broke the silence: "When she died, a part of me went with her. I never realized we had something going."

"I did." She stopped writing. "Say what you will, Steve, but she was an unhappy person. She went so far so fast. I wonder if she had any happy days in her entire life. After all, the show has got to end some time, and the audience has got to leave. All their collective love doesn't match the love of one individual for another. The dimension of depth is what's missing." Her eyes narrowed. "It baffles me how anyone ever confuses one for the other."

He came to the conclusion that he had been working up to all day. Very quietly, yet with finality, he said, "I'm not going to do Jennie, ever again. I've started to cut down on the illusions anyway. So far, no one's noticed."

Stella held her pencil in mid-air. "I think that's wise." She softly added, "Very wise."

"Do you suppose there's money enough for a decent funeral? If not," he said, "we really should take care of it—and see that Iris has enough to live on until the estate gets settled." He gritted his teeth until they hurt. The pain felt pleasurable. "Christ, that fantastic house of hers will be sold for peanuts to pay bills and back taxes. It's like picking a carcass clean."

Stella came to him, knelt, and pressed her face into his chest. He felt her slide against him and move away a little with each exhalation of breath.

"You won't run into difficulty, will you?" she questioned. "I mean, if you don't do Jennie?"

He knew what she was getting at. There were contracts, and that could mean lawsuits.

"It would be obscene if they held you to it."

"Anyway, I've been thinking of doing Claire Keller and some razzle-dazzle flapper stuff. She lives in town. Maybe she'll help me out with it." He rubbed his hands together, feeling their generating warmth. "Jennie out—Claire in!" He shook his head in disbelief. "Life really is a crock of crap."

"If we don't start cheering ourselves up, how can we possibly do anything for Iris when she arrives?" She took his hand in hers and softly kissed his cheek.

# CHAPTER SIXTEEN

The world mourned the death of Jennie.

An overcast sky marked her arrival at the Village Green Chapel and continued to lie heavily over the city. Stella held Steve's hand throughout the small private service in the late afternoon.

In the open coffin, Jennie's hair beautifully surrounded her face, and her lips were fixed in a smile of utter contentment. She wore a plain white cocktail dress. The tiny feet that had danced across every silver screen in the world now resided in unadorned white satin shoes. Two beaded butterflies rested on the soft yellow pillow cushioning her head, and her hands held a spray of yellow orchids.

An attendant quietly lowered the casket lid, an indication that the visitation period had ended. Iris leaned into Steve, then steadied herself. A black lace scarf was loosely crossed around her neck, its ends hanging down the back of her dress. Her skin was ashen; her usually vibrant brown hair was drab and without luster. She tried to smile once or twice but couldn't manage it.

Arrangements had been made for a late-afternoon dinner at the Four Seasons, and Steve was informed that the limousine was waiting. Small groups were forming outside, and he felt a vague uneasiness about this. As he guided Iris toward Stella, he hoped they would not have any trouble leaving the chapel.

"Let's go from there," he suggested, motioning to one of the arches with a lighted exit sign hanging under it. "It's nearer the parking lot." He turned to Stella. "Honey, would you see that the limousine is brought around to that side?"

She nodded and left them.

Through the stained-glass windows he could see shadows, and he wondered if people would remain there all night.

"They want to be the first to see her tomorrow morning at the public viewing," he explained to Iris.

She shrugged and, lips pursed, gave him a tolerant glance.

"You've got to remember," he said, "she belonged to everyone."

"That was her trouble," Iris added. "No one person was enough. Steve, I want to get it over with as quickly as possible. Displaying her is like—"

"Iris, this is something that *has* to be done. We owe it to Jennie. And to them! Those people out there have lost someone they loved."

"They are not alone," she muttered.

"You *have* to accommodate them," he insisted.

"Have you got the speech for Wesley Adams?" She looked at him through eyes red from crying.

He tapped his chest pocket.

"Good," she said. "I hope you skipped as much of the schmaltz as you could." A tear rolled down her cheek.

He pulled out a handkerchief and handed it to her.

She touched it to her face lightly. "Do you mind taking over from now on?"

He took her arm. She was doing just great! Handling a funeral almost alone was no small job, especially for a kid still in college.

They moved through a passageway, meeting the minister at the exit door. Reverend Moore's wide blue eyes, set in an unlined, full, almost florid face, were a comfort to him. The minister told them he would be there at six in the morning and firmly took Iris' hand. Then he held the door open for them as they stepped out.

"There they are!" a voice screamed.

"She doesn't look a bit like her mother, does she?"

Trapped, Iris backed into Steve and moaned.

From out of nowhere about fifty people suddenly appeared. Several held the *New York Daily News* in their upraised hands. Its four-inch headline shouted:

JENNIE DEAD!

On the front page were photos of Jennie entertaining GIs on the battlefronts and one familiar shot of her accepting an award from the President.

The crowd surged forward.

"She's not dead, tell me she's not dead," an elderly gray-haired woman said, and touched Iris' arm.

Iris drew away from her as if she had been burned. Flustered, she raised her fingers to cover her mouth as her eyes filled with tears.

Steve had feared that something like this might happen, yet knew of no way to prevent it. He found Stella and motioned toward the limo with his head, then handed Iris to her. "Please," he turned around to face the spectators, "pay your respects tomorrow. There will be time then."

Iris unexpectedly gasped.

Steve spun around to see what had happened.

A very short man, almost a dwarf, was holding onto the back of Iris' coat. "We want to see Jennie now," he pleaded. His face was deeply lined and pained, his eyes bloodshot. "Tell us it's not

true. We don't want her to go." He seemed unaware that he was
holding onto Iris' coat, tugging away at it.

Iris screamed, giving vent to her agony, and brought her hands
up to the sides of her face. Sobbing, she pleaded with the man
to let go.

"To the car, fast!" Steve shouted at Stella, and swiftly yanked
Iris' coat out of the man's grasp. As they pushed through the
crowd toward the black sedan, he tripped, but managed to shove
Iris forward just before he hit the ground. A sharp heel ground
into the small of his back. In a burst of agony, he rolled over and
thrust out his arms, clearing a space around him until he could
stand again. Then, arms outstretched, he cut a path for Iris and
Stella to get to the car door.

A tiny child walked in front of Stella and looked wide-eyed at
Iris, who was still crying. Stella moved the child to one side and
helped Iris into the cab.

"It's publicity for her new picture," an irate male voice rang
out with authority. "She was always a space grabber."

"How dare you!" Stella stormed, eyes blazing. Then she
lowered her voice: "I wish it *were* just a press agent's gag."

Inside the limousine, Iris shut her eyes and bit her lower lip.
"Is this the way it's going to be?"

"No, I'm going to see that they have a full police cordon
here tomorrow morning, starting at five." He slumped forward
and supported his elbows on his knees, beginning to take deep
breaths. The inside of the sedan seemed very confining.

*       *       *

During dinner, Iris picked indifferently at her food. She looked
better with her hair freshly brushed and a light application of

makeup on her face. The Four Seasons crowd was better-mannered, yet oblique glances were constantly aimed at their table.

"You should write a thank-you note to *Variety*," he suggested. "I've never seen such a tribute. They practically devoted the whole issue to her."

"Steve is right," Stella said.

"I realize it can't be a private affair," Iris said, "but I want it to be dignified." She contorted her lips and brought her hand down the side of her other arm. "She had so little dignity left at the end."

"Do you want to go back to our suite?" Stella asked. "The television coverage is enormous. Perhaps you'd like to watch some of it?"

Iris looked at Stella, her expression a mixture of weariness and distaste.

"Every time I turned on the tube today," Steve said, "there she was, from the time she was conceived on up. I didn't know they could do it so fast!" He concentrated on a torn piece of cuticle around his nail, slowly picking it away.

"I saw pictures of her I didn't even know existed," Iris added. "To them out there," she waved her hand, "it's big news—but I don't want to see any of it. I just want to go to bed."

\*    \*    \*

As she came out of the bedroom, Stella shook down a bottle of pills and put it back in her purse.

Steve looked at her from over the rim of his drink.

"Iris is almost asleep," she said. "Tomorrow is going to be rough—for all of us. One day of public viewing should be enough."

"Right!" He carefully folded a piece of paper into an airplane and sailed it across the room. "Let's get the papers." He picked up the telephone.

Once the newspapers arrived, he spread them all on the carpet. Jennie's picture was splashed over front-page layouts with in-depth stories that concentrated on her run of hard luck. He hated the circus air of excitement settling around the proceedings, yet was mesmerized by it, too.

He got up and, with his hands jammed into his pockets, stalked the room. Somehow, it didn't seem real. Things were happening too fast, and he seemed to be sleepwalking through them.

"Tomorrow night, I have to go up on that damn stage and be funny." He was silent for a moment as he thought of the Myra Dormann routine. "Funny?" he repeated. "That's a joke in itself. I'm going to take a shower and boil the hell out of myself and see if I can loosen up."

"That's a good idea," Stella agreed as she looked up at him, then continued reading an article about Jennie.

A half hour later, he came into the living room in pajamas. From her chair, Stella groaned wearily and removed her glasses. She placed the last of the newspapers next to her feet, on top of a neat pile.

"I'll be able to sleep tonight," he told her. "I've taken something to see to that."

*   *   *

Along the outside wall of the Village Green Chapel at seven in the morning, hundreds of people stood in line. The macabre effect was heightened by placards bearing the names of "Jennie Darling

Fan Club of Newark," "Jennie's Star Boosters," and others Steve couldn't make out. One sign, taller than the rest read:

DON'T LEAVE US JENNIE—WE LOVE YOU!

He helped Stella from the cab to the locked door, upon which he tapped. The door opened to reveal the benign face of the funeral director with his graying sideburns and moustache. Stella and Iris went into the building first. Before Steve could enter, someone grabbed his arm and held it. He turned.

The wide-eyed round face of a gray-haired woman, stricken with grief, asked, "Are you somebody special?"

"Of course. And," he paused, "so are you! Everybody is," he added kindly. "Are you somebody special?" He turned to a man standing by quietly. The onlooker replied that he was.

"Are you?" he asked a woman with a print scarf tied under her chin. "Are you?" He singled out several people around him. Even as he did so, he had the feeling of watching himself from the crowd. Why was he saying all this? Where had it come from? The words seemed to belong to someone else.

Finally, he addressed the originator of the question once again, and took her hand. "If you are alive and breathing and have hope for the future, you are somebody special. Don't ever forget that! Jennie never did!"

The woman backed away from him, smiling.

"Where is she? What parlor?" a man rasped from a distance.

"I'll be back to let you know in just a few minutes," he called out, and quickly slammed the door on the crowd—then looked at the somber man facing them.

"Don't worry," the funeral director said. "We will take care of everything. Let me show you in."

As they walked into the huge viewing hall, Steve could see waist-high stanchions supporting corded velvet ropes to establish flow patterns up to and away from the casket. Two series of tall candles were lit, at the head and foot of the bier. A recording of Jennie singing spirituals from years earlier was piped into the room. The yellow orchids she'd held in her hands the day before had been replaced by pink tea roses, and a pink cushion had been placed under her head.

"She was etched into the national framework as deeply as the Capitol Building in Washington," the director said in reverential tones. "No one will ever forget her soulful eyes and that angelic face." Looking at the body in the casket, the director smoothed out a wrinkle in the pillow just above her head.

The man's performance was too much for Steve. "I want to be alone with her for a few minutes before it all starts." He looked straight ahead at the huge stained-glass window of The Last Supper. "Alone," he repeated softly.

Stella, jolted by his remark, hesitated, then escorted Iris out of the chapel.

The director silently shut the doors in back of him as he left.

Steve knelt next to the casket, head lowered, wondering how it might have been if he'd told her he would cancel his opening and fly to London when she phoned. God, she was so fired up with pure talent! From his breast pocket he took out a silver coin with "Good Luck" engraved over a horseshoe. It was the one she'd given him on his opening night at the Club Scandal. He held it until it felt warm, then slowly stood up and carefully placed the coin inside her folded hands. Then he walked quickly to the doors, where Stella and Iris were waiting on the other side.

\*    \*    \*

The days of public viewing extended to three. The casket was sealed, and Jennie was sent on to be buried in Forest Lawn. Rumors began to circulate about her cause of death. One of the most vocal groups maintained that she had not died at all but had been paralyzed and badly disfigured by her fall, and would spend the rest of her days in a private sanitarium. Hearsay had it that plastic surgeons had been called in to perform cosmetic surgery, but nothing at all could be done about her paralysis. Still others simply said she would be back entertaining again, some day.

Jennie Darling kept her peculiar hold on the world—even in death.

# CHAPTER SEVENTEEN

In the steam room of the New York Athletic Club, Steve briskly rubbed one palm over the other arm. A thread of loose skin peeled off; he tossed it to the floor and pressed a cold, moist towel against his head. The morning rehearsal of the Claire Keller routine hadn't worked out too well, and he couldn't seem to localize the trouble.

An attendant opened the glass door; as the cold air rushed in, steam clouds moved toward the ceiling. "Phone, Mister Dennis," the attendant called.

Covering himself with a towel, Steve left the room and picked up the receiver. "Hello?"

"Stella told me where I could reach you. She didn't seem well when I called. She said she'd just gotten up from a nap."

"Wesley! Wesley Adams!"

"You win the silver dollar, Steve," he chuckled. "I'm in town and staying at the Plaza. We're practically neighbors. How about getting together?"

"How about an early dinner tonight at our place before I go on?"

"How about my room before you turn in for the night?"

"OK. But Stella won't be able to make it. She goes to bed pretty early these days. Keeping tabs on everything wears her out a lot faster than it used to. Something on your mind?"

Wesley laughed softly. *"Quien sabe?* We'll have a drink, for old times' sake. By the way, I stopped at Libertyville College before coming here." He paused. "Iris told me to give you and Stella her love. She said she couldn't have made it through the funeral without you."

"Wes, I'm getting a draft here, and I've got a massage coming up in a few minutes. Are you sure about dinner?"

"No can do. But I'll see you tonight," he said, and hung up.

The last time Wesley had come to see him was to get news about Jennie. What kind of information was he looking for now?

\* \* \*

Somehow, Steve wasn't as relaxed on stage as he should have been. That, he decided, was the reason for the light applause. Sherri Pickens could have been more effervescent, more boisterous, but all of his illusions were mourning Jennie, as was most of the audience, so he cut his singing act short. On his way out, several audience members shook his hand and complimented his performance.

At the Plaza, he knocked softly on the door to Suite 2301. Wesley opened the door partway and stared at him for a moment before opening it wide and inviting him in. Deep in discussion were Mike Fallon, Jennie's old Metro producer, and Sam. In back of them, staring at the ground, was Joel Grannit, the studio head. In a smartly tailored black suit, six feet tall with a shock of red hair crowning his massive head, he stared at the floor. Steve rocked back on his heels, feeling trapped, as they rose to greet him. Wesley shut the door. If he'd had any idea this was a friendly get-together, seeing them all together dispelled that thought.

"Sit down, Steve." Mike motioned to an overstuffed green velvet armchair.

It was not an invitation, but an order, and Steve didn't like the tone of it. He slowly sat in the chair.

"I want to speak to you with all humility and truth," Mike began, pressing his palms together as he walked around the room. It was funny—him being able to afford anything except getting the limp out of his walk. Mike's breath was shallow, his eyes brilliant, and his expression worried. "I have a film falling short of its promise that is not only going to kill me, but bankrupt me before I die, as well as the studio. Yet this film has the brilliant potential of a diamond, Steve. *Star Fire* is over four million dollars in the red." He paused to let that fact sink in. "Everything has gone out, including Jennie. We could fake a few close-ups," he went on rapidly, "that wouldn't be as hard as it might seem. But we also have dialogue to rerecord that didn't come across clearly the first time around." He clapped his hands together like a mandarin. "But we don't have the musical numbers in the can." His desperation rose like air bubbles though water. "That's the clincher! Everybody is hounding me, wanting to know when *Star Fire* will be released!"

Wesley rescued the producer: "He's telling them it has to be cut with great care. Every frame—lovingly." Tall, graying, suntanned Wesley. He had the answers to everything.

"So I tell them," Mike picked up the conversation, "I'm working day and night on it because it's Jennie's finest effort. A repeat of Melinda; that's when the world first stood up to applaud—and never sat down." Suddenly, Mike turned around and faced Steve squarely, beads of perspiration shining on his forehead.

"What he's telling you," Sam started to say, "is that I'm coming to you, on my hands and knees, begging you to finish the film.

As Jennie." His voice became a whisper. "It will be done under the strictest secrecy the studio ever managed. Closed sets—they are nearly completed, and you are the only one, the *only one*," he repeated, "who can rescue the whole project." He wiped the corners of his mouth with his fingertips, then rubbed them across the front of his expensive suit.

"No one will know," Mike continued. "In makeup, you look like her twin. You could fool her mother."

"But I'm not good enough to fool the camera," he said. Somehow, he'd figured it out just after he'd entered the room. They were goddamn fools to even ask him.

"Trickery," Mike countered, "is what movie making is all about. Let us worry about that."

"I promised I wouldn't do her again!"

"That is a promise you must break! If you don't, the film will go under and take us with it. You've got to save us. You've got to save Jennie. It's her crowning achievement and without you, it will never see the light of day. If you do, it will bring closure to her career. You've got to break your promise."

*The only thing I've got to do,* he thought, *is break out of this craziness.* An idea glimmered in the far corner of his mind. "I don't dance."

"If you can walk, you can dance." Mike's carefully manicured nails gleamed as his hands cut the air. "You'll learn fast! We'll scale up the scenery in some shots so it will give you the appearance of her exact height. You've got to put Jennie's professional life in order! It was the one thing she couldn't do for herself. More than anyone else, she would want *you* to do it!"

Steve swallowed hard, and Wesley slipped a drink into his hand. Nodding thanks, he swallowed, grimacing as the liquor burned his throat.

"For certain, the talk is all over town that she's gonna get the Oscar for this film," Mike confided, "and that film is gonna grab every other fuckin' statue on that stage. It's that great—so far! You know! You saw the rushes!"

Steve took another swallow and leaned forward, his hands on his knees.

Suddenly Joel Grannit raised his head and began to speak. "Son, Jennie is still a big, big, star, but not yet a supernova like Garbo, Dietrich and Crawford." His sonorous voice filled the room. "You have the power to elevate her to that level. You have the power to make her a permanent, dazzling luminary in the entertainment pantheon. For her sake—for God's sake—son, give her what is due her! She couldn't do it for herself, but you can do it for her. Don't let her down!"

In their wrongness, were they also right? What good would an uncompleted film do Jennie? That would put her back at square zero again, even in death. But the film would make a pile once it was released. Iris would never have to worry about anything for the rest of her life. It began to make some kind of crazy sense. He just might be able to pull it off. The thought now seemed almost reasonable.

"No one must ever know," Mike added. "You'll live in a trailer on the lot during the entire filming."

"A studio prisoner, huh?" He rubbed the side of his nose. "I need time to think."

"We can give you everything else but." Mike looked down at him. "Remember, Steve, you owe her."

Steve took the force of that statement head on. "Don't judge me, Mike," he said curtly.

"Fine, but you are the only person in the world who can do this for her."

Steve supposed that being the only person in the world who could rescue the project should have made him feel important. It didn't. He imagined Stella's reaction to the idea, then pushed that thought aside. "How long will it take?"

"As you know, we have six numbers scheduled. We'll film them in fifteen-second segments and splice them together. It will be harder to do that way, but we can control quality and movements better. Figure filming about a minute each day, including Saturdays and Sundays, and ten to twelve weeks of shooting time."

"Maximum or minimum?" he questioned.

There was no answer.

"But I don't and can't dance," he repeated. "I can sing, even do close shots, but there's a limit. Even you have to understand that."

"Leave everything to us."

Joel walked over and placed his hands on Steve's shoulders. They seemed to weigh a ton apiece; the feeling made him squirm.

Joel spoke again: "There's roughly one quarter of the filming still to be done. You'll get twenty-five percent of what Jennie was getting. That's fair!" He waited for a response, then added. "Iris will get the other seventy-five percent. After that, you'll be rich enough to pick and choose what you want to do, and where. I've got Vegas connections. You've played the Lounge," Joel became confiding, "how about the Big Room? The Lotus? Sinatra, Lee, Sammie—they all play there. Hell, they practically live there."

"Me, the singer—or the Act?"

"Your call!"

Steve looked past Mike at the lighted city that stretched out beneath them.

"She was dying like hell to finish that picture," Wesley said. "The only reason she was chomping at the bit was because she couldn't. There is so goddamn much riding on that film! She can go out of this world riding a rainbow if you want her to, Steve!"

"If you don't," Mike interrupted, "we will send you the master reels to burn at a Black Mass. That's all they're good for now." Mike put out his hand to stop a response from Wesley. "Heads you win and tails you win. Those odds include both Jennie's and Iris' future. Not to mention yours!" Mike sat down and pulled the glasses off his face quickly.

Steve thought of the fortune in those film cans. Things were coming to him way too fast. Joel wasn't joking about getting him into the Pyramid—yet he would not have to be grateful in accepting his help; it would be his due, for he would be saving them millions. *Tens of millions.* Besides, the studio knew how to do things. They could work the cameras around him and fake the dancing, he knew. Everybody would come out of the race a winner.

"Make arrangements to get me out of here so I don't suffer professionally."

They nodded in unison, as if they were all wired to the same puppeteer.

Steve leaned back, resting his head against the cushions of the chair, and thought aloud. "I can do it all, except for the dancing. Even simplified, her numbers aren't easy."

"All you have to do is want to do them." Mike grabbed the sides of his chair, driving his idea home. "We're getting Joey Fontani to shove you around the floor for every number. He's the best choreographer money can buy, and he'll have you doing things you never dreamed you could do."

"You can do it," Wesley prodded from behind.

Torn between a frown and a smile, Steve glanced at Sam as his mind raced backward and forward in leaps. He remembered working with Jennie at her home; he recalled her Las Vegas visit. Now, the promised Lotus Room at the Pyramid seized—and held—his attention. Christ, what an opportunity—a show wholly built around himself. He never could have made it alone. Never. He buried his face in his hands and thought about his final conversation with Jennie, when she'd pleaded with him to join her. If he gave her the next few months of his life, the slate would be wiped clean. It would be the final payoff! In fact, the whole gig would give everyone a new start.

He raised his head and stared at the faces about him. He didn't entirely trust them—but he didn't need to, because they needed him. As he suddenly thrust his arm out, their eyes quickly followed its motion. He remembered how he used to swirl a biscuit in the air in front of Teddy, his mongrel dog, and how the animal's head followed the treat. The same goddamn thing was happening here.

"I'll do it." He sat up ramrod straight in the chair. "Get everything cleared away for me. We can be in California in three weeks."

"In one," Joel insisted.

Sam took the cigar out of his mouth slowly, tilted his head and peered down at Steve. "What about Stella?"

He could feel his expression hardening. "What about her? Her career is being a mother. Mine is stocking the pantry. You said so yourself, Sam." Christ, he was in the exact center of things—airborne in a balloon heading straight up, to … to where?

"To Jennie," Steve toasted, lifting his glass. She would have been proud of him. And so very grateful!

They all joined in and downed their drinks simultaneously.

# CHAPTER EIGHTEEN

The playback recording on Stage Twenty was suddenly silenced. Steve cocked his head at Ben Felton, who motioned him back to his starting position to wait while lights were adjusted.

It was here on the Marshmallow Sky sound stage that he'd first heard his recording as Jennie coming over the loudspeakers. He had never sounded better. But now, ten days later, the recording sounded like a military drill.

"From the beginning," Ben directed.

Steve walked to the white staircase in costume, his feet encased in ankle-strap heels.

"Ready?" Ben yelled.

Steve shot the director a hand signal.

"Lights! Camera!"

"We're rolling."

"Speed! Slate!" The jaws of the clapboard snapped together. "Action!"

Steve assumed the classic Jennie stance: left arm reaching for the ceiling, right leg extending to the side.

He mouthed the opening phrases and immediately went into the routine in time with the beat.

Two chorus boys stepped up alongside Steve to support him as he eased into a back bend. Holding their arms tightly, Steve placed his left foot on the next step and came up slowly.

"Cut," Ben commanded, and they all froze. Steve pulled himself out of his pose, "Steve, lift your right leg higher, and faster! Get the lead out of your ass. We've been over this before."

"Do I do anything right?" he blurted, looking down at him.

"Fuck you. You knew I wasn't a dancer when you hired me!"

"You're doing a helluva lot better than you think, but it's perfection I'm after."

Steve smiled through gritted teeth.

"Take it from where Cliff and Mike come in. Ready? Remember, lift that right leg high. Point!"

The music blared and the camera began dollying in. With his grin fixed, Steve grabbed the arms of the chorus boys and, using them for support, kicked so hard his leg cramped. No stopping now. He could see Ben looking at him, coldly. The director's hand twirled in a circle. Steve did his turn smartly, falling into Cliff's arms on beat, and flashed the camera an incandescent smile.

"Cut," Ben shouted. "Steve, try a right circle instead of a left just after you come up. You have enough time."

"That isn't the way we rehearsed it," he protested. "I'm not an improviser. I rehearsed this number, this way, day and night for ten days. I'm bone-ass tired and my ankles are killing me."

"I know you're tired," Ben replied. "But it's all over except for the shouting. Tell you what: let's wait until tomorrow and see how good the rushes look. Till then, one more run-through in fifteen minutes, then call it a day."

"Yeah, it's a day—my day! And, it's over!"

No one moved.

The set became unbearably quiet. Suddenly, the lights went off. The quick transition from dazzling white to near-darkness temporarily blinded Steve, but the chorus boys led him down the remaining steps. He would do anything to get back to the trailer.

He'd been working since six in the morning, and now, twelve hours later, he was at the same place where he'd started.

With a towel wrapped around his neck, he approached Stella, seated on an upholstered sofa in the trailer. The masseur had just left. Steve sat down next to her, moaning in pleasure, and flexed his ankles.

"What you need is something to relax," Ben suggested from the trailer door. "How about a little wine?"

"I'll get some," Stella offered, and waddled to the trailer.

Steve shook his head. "Ben, what is going on here is beyond belief. These routines are monkeys on my back. Even when I'm standing still, I find myself moving. I don't sleep much at night, so I go to the set to rehearse. When you get here in the morning, I've already gone through the number a half-dozen times."

"It shows," Ben said warmly. "It shows!" He fished into his pocket and came up with a small green bottle. "Take two of these at night. Don't take any alcohol afterward or you'll drift away." A knowing smile crossed Ben's face as he pressed the bottle into Steve's hand. "They don't take long to act."

As Stella approached them, Ben cautioned him again. "Remember, no alcohol."

* * *

The next afternoon, the technicians ran take after take in the projection room. Seated in an oversized viewing chair, Steve checked himself for small slip-ups. There were none; he moved his body with full assurance, always keeping his hands and feet extended. The positive expressions on the faces of the crew affirmed that he'd nailed the number. Several times, even he became lost in the illusion.

"That's a lot of stuff going on up there," Stella said, pointing to the screen. "To me, anything that moves more than three miles an hour seems to be going faster than sound."

He patted her stomach approvingly. He was looking forward to their extended vacation after the filming as much as she. By then, the baby would have arrived.

"That stuff you gave me did the trick," he confided to Ben, who was sitting next to him. Now, it was no trouble summoning the energy he needed for the numbers, knowing he could always count on sleeping through the night. There was a lot of magic in those jumping beans.

The lights came on; Mike stood with his back to the screen, facing the others. "People! What you are seeing here tonight is an absolute miracle. So wonderful, we can't lose it. From now on, we shoot in sequence, in costume and full makeup." His eyes lit up. "Jennie is not dead. She is here, finishing this picture!" Mike turned to Steve. "Sorry, but there is no 'Steve Dennis' any more. Only Jennie Darling—and everybody must concentrate, believe it, and translate that thought to the screen."

Steve gazed at Mike, listening attentively.

"You have all done a magnificent job in keeping faith with this project. No need to tell you to continue; I could not have wished for a more expert crew—and your bonuses will reflect the company's appreciation."

*   *   *

In the trailer, a knock on the door interrupted Steve's watching the late, late news. Mike came in without being asked and sat down at the small dinette. He poured himself a ginger ale and brought the glass up in a salute. "I just came in to wish you continual good luck with the rest of the numbers. The last one was a winner!"

Steve nodded.

Mike suddenly glanced at his diamond Rolex. "Sorry, I didn't catch the time. Shouldn't Jennie be turning in?"

"Aren't you overdoing things?" Steve inquired. "Jennie is dead. If you don't believe it, take a ride to Forest Lawn."

"You are very wrong," Mike corrected. "She's right here. Anyway, I'll be around if you need anything, want anything."

Steve snickered. "With you around, I don't need a mother. You're at me more than Stella—and she never took a back seat to anyone. Now, get the hell out of here."

"Nervous about all that's coming?"

"Usually," Steve admitted.

"Then take one of those blockbusters Ben gave you from the green bottle."

"Are you ever going to leave me alone?"

"As soon as the film is in the can. Good night." Mike softly shut the door behind him.

"When the film is in the can, *I'll* be in the can—throwing up!"

*   *   *

Stella, exhausted, climbed into bed. Steve knew she was concerned about him now that the pressure was mounting.

"Something to drink?" he asked.

She motioned affirmatively.

He ran the water, filled a glass, and handed it to her. She took several small sips and then reached up to kiss him, placing his hand over her stomach to feel their kicking child.

*   *   *

In the fitting room, Mervin Manning helped Steve into a body stocking and then the silver beaded costume that weighed thirty pounds on the hanger. Mervin took several steps back, one hand on his hip. "What the hell have you been eating since the last fitting—hog jowls? For Christ's sake, a beaded dress doesn't have any seams!"

A knock on the door interrupted them, and Ben let himself into the fitting room.

"Angel Face here is getting a fat ass," Mervin said unhappily. "Practically had to use a crowbar to get him into this rag—and it's one of the looser ones."

Ben scowled. "We'll get you some appetite suppressants and I'll have the studio prepare a diet. No more late-night snacks." Then, he left.

Steve sat down in a dental chair, and the makeup man swung a huge magnifying glass in front of his face. The nose on Joe Heller's face took on the dimensions of a gargantuan strawberry. Steve closed his eyes as Joe went to work.

The towel was finally removed from Steve's head. Jennie's wig came off its stand and was firmly anchored into Steve's own hair. "OK, Beautiful—no undue face motion," Joe warned, "until you're in front of the camera and it's rolling."

Steve took a last-minute glance at the mirror in front of him. The transformation was flawless.

Joe looked at his watch. "They should be picking you up now. I'll go along with touch-up stuff to make repairs." He grabbed the handle of his snakeskin attaché case and smiled.

"Thanks, Joe."

"Don't mention it, Jennie."

Steve stiffened as he went to the door. "Joe, you should know better than to swallow that line of crap."

*    *    *

Steve emerged from the limousine to see huge bouquets of flowers placed outside the doors of the soundstage. It was a nice gesture, but it didn't do anything for him. Jennie, though, sure would have enjoyed the attention.

"From the crew and company," Mike proudly told him, "but let's get to the set fast, before the magic fades."

*    *    *

"Ready?" Ben called, and Steve replied that he was.

"Places, everybody."

Steve yawned as he stepped over some electrical cables haphazardly lying on the floor.

"Let's not have any slip-ups," Ben reminded them. "Time is money; we don't want to do any more takes than we have to. The bankers in New York are starting to surround our little stagecoach, and I don't need another battle with them."

"Are you OK?" Mike's voice behind Steve was tinged with concern.

"A little sleepy," Steve replied. "I'll be all right as soon as I get on that damned carousel. The stuff I took last night really kicked me into another world."

"There's a line of coke in the second stall of the john if you need a jolt," Mike softly whispered.

"Don't sweat it. Everything's going to be just fine."

Steve wanted to turn around and tell Ben to shove off, but then he thought the better of it.

Pots of dry ice hidden by white cloud forms were spaced along a carefully marked path. Ben signaled, and water began systematically dripping into each container. A mist formed and hugged the floor, giving the area an ethereal look.

"Lights," Ben called. They came on all at once, hitting Steve hard with their heat.

"Ready?" the voice came up to him, and he waved he was. Jesus Christ, Mervin was right. The gown *was* holding him prisoner.

"Camera. Speed. Slate." The clapboard was placed in front of him, and the set became deathly quiet. Then, the two black jaws cracked together.

"Action!"

The music started, and a vivacious Jennie descended the stairs: singing, dancing and making love to the camera. *I can't screw up this take. I just can't,* Steve told himself.

# CHAPTER NINETEEN

"They knew what they were doing when they shot 'Marshmallow Sky' first," Steve groaned. "That one was the easiest to do." He let his shoulders slump, then closed his eyes, trying to forget the pain in the small of his back. "They're doing everything they can to erase the line between Jennie and me, but I'll be damned if I'll let them do it."

He tapped his fingers on the blue and orange Mexican tablecloth. "I didn't know it would be all that hard! So, tell me how bad I was today?"

"I can't." Stella's voice carried undisguised admiration. "Because you weren't. You're doing yourself proud."

"Great!" He felt a rumble in his stomach, which he tried to ignore, but it got the better of him. "Am I hungry!"

"No wonder. You forgot to take your diet pill." She went to the kitchen cabinet and returned with one. "Wash it down with juice."

He held out his hand. "Make it a Bloody Mary."

She looked at him disapprovingly but poured a half inch of vodka into a glass, followed by tomato juice.

"You really do hold me low on the booze, don't you?"

"'Glitter Baby' is a very intricate number."

"You're telling me! I have to be all over that goddamn stage at the same time. I don't have an unjarred bone in my whole body.

That reminds me, I've got to do my sit-ups." He got down on the floor with a feeling of resignation. "Do you think a bared midriff is my style?"

"With a long blonde wig, anything goes. Did it hurt yesterday when they ripped the hair off your stomach?"

"A little, but it's over before you know it. I didn't know what actors had to go through to look that great on the screen. It's a gigantic freak show." He gestured toward the walls. "This trailer is the only place on earth where I can be me. Outside, I join the rest of the crazies."

*   *   *

After midnight, in the projection room, they were viewing the paste up of the "Bombay Blonde" number.

Flashing around the screen with the speed of a whirlwind, hands beckoning the camera in nervous animation, was Jennie in a draped midriff gold costume. The long blonde wig spun about her face in one graceful motion. She slid to the floor, rolled over onto her back and swung upward. The playback ended with her leaning against a six-foot-high gold Balinese statue that stared, unseeing, out of black obsidian eyes. The set blacked out behind her. Then she, too, vanished. When the lights went on, even the grips and electricians stood up to applaud and offer congratulations.

"Thanks. Thanks a lot, everybody, but we have yet to hear the clink of cash making music at the box office," was all Steve could say.

"Have no fears." Mike pulled off his glasses and wiped them quickly. Replacing them, he gave everyone a toothy smile.

The fatigue hovering about Steve was becoming more difficult to shake. Off camera, when he showed signs of being tired, a

capsule was handed to him. Then, a burst of energy hit him and
his body tingled. Sleep was no problem either, with the stuff he
hid among his underwear in the bureau drawer.

Occasionally, his heart began to beat erratically. But as
suddenly as that started, it stopped. Stella wasn't aware of this
development, and that was just fine. The important point was to
get the damned thing off his back and into the can—the faster,
the better!

The routines already filmed faded into an indistinct blur; he
could only consider what was to be done during the next hours.

\* \* \*

In the trailer at half past two, sleep eluded him. He couldn't recall
if he had already taken something. Holding the medicine bottle
up to the light in the bathroom, he counted the remaining pills,
trying to remember how many should be left. When he couldn't,
he took one for good measure and sat at the kitchen table, waiting
for it to work.

It was so dark and cold. Hours, it seemed, had already passed
as he waited. He began to shake.

He popped another pill into his mouth and picked at the lobe
of his ear. It occurred to him that Jennie did that, too, when she
was disconcerted. Jennie! She should feel damn grateful for what
he was doing. And, Iris, too!

He hadn't had his fingerful of scotch that evening. He
should have reminded Stella about that before she went to bed.
That was why he was so restless! He flicked the light switch
and, as illumination flooded the table top, saw a glass filled
with water. He reached for it—and heard a rifle shot go off in
his head.

*  *  *

The alarm ring banged in Steve's ears. He tried to stop it, but something held him fast to the bed. He opened his eyes but could see only straight ahead.

Stella nudged him. "Time to shine, Honey."

He tried to speak, but words didn't come.

He heard her yawn. "You slept so soundly, I didn't want to disturb you, but now, I have to." Then, she shoved him.

He tried to stop her and raised himself slightly, only to slump down.

"Steve?" He sensed her beginning panic. In her nightgown, with her unwieldy stomach, she crawled over him. "Steve!" She began to hit his face.

In defense, he murmured something and tried to move away.

"My robe, my slippers, where the hell are they?" She must have found them because he heard her open the trailer door.

Then he heard her fall.

"Didn't you see the refrigeration cable?" a voice yelled out in consternation.

"What's wrong?" another voice called. It sounded like Ben's. "Jeff, what happened?"

"The lady tripped over a cable."

"Are you OK?"

"Yes," she said. "But Steve—"

"Stay put," Jeff ordered. "This area is still dark. Don't move!"

"I'm OK. My palms sting, that's all. "But—"

"Let us help you up."

"My husband isn't moving," she shrieked, "you've got to help *him!*"

"Get Feldar," Ben yelled. "On the goddamn double. Steve will be all right, Stella. I promise."

She moaned softly.

"Let's get you into this chair. Stay here," he commanded. Then Steve heard his approaching footsteps and the opening of the screen door.

"Sawbones is here," Jeff called out.

Steve heard everything, but he still could not speak. He raised his head slightly and looked straight ahead.

The door swung open, and a stranger—the doctor?—approached the bed.

Ben followed the doctor, and Stella was right behind him.

She held a cup of coffee to her chattering lips. Ben dabbed the perspiration off her brow and wiped away liquid that dribbled down her chin.

Steve saw a tall, lanky, white-haired man coming toward him. He shot a ray of light into Steve's eyes. It hurt like hell.

"He'll be all right; he's just overworked. Please leave the trailer. I want to examine him further. I'll call you in when I've finished."

The doctor injected several hypodermic shots into Steve's chest and one into each arm. Steve felt a warm flush, followed by a cool one, and then the warm flush returned. He began to breathe deeply, and slowly moved his head, arms and legs in succession. Doctor Feldar went to the trailer door, opened it and said, "Come back in about an hour. He's going to be just fine."

"Are you sure?" Stella seemed unable to believe such good news.

"Absolutely! Just don't go in now!" His slender hands smoothed down the sides of his gray-streaked hair with one motion. He lit a cigarette for himself, and one for her. "Simple exhaustion, rigid dieting—we've seen this before. It looks a lot worse than it is."

Forty-five minutes later, Steve opened the door, walked up to her and grinned sheepishly.

"How can you be up and on your feet so fast? I don't know whether to laugh or to cry." She began to do both.

Steve chuckled. "Just tuckered out," he explained, and rapidly straightened up. "But I feel absolutely great now, ready and able to get to work. Honey, do you want to go to Makeup with me?"

"No—you go on alone." She grimaced. "You're acting as if nothing happened."

"It didn't!"

"Time's flying," Ben said. "Let's go."

"Wait!" Steve disappeared into the trailer and returned with Jennie's wig in his hand. "I feel naked without it." He turned to her. "Make yourself something hot to eat. And get some rest. I'll see you on the set at nine."

\*　　\*　　\*

The makeup chair seemed to have spikes embedded in it, and Steve wriggled as Joe Heller went through the familiar routine. Several times, he asked Steve to stop moving his head. "I'm keeping it as still as I ever have," Steve retorted. "God," he sighed, "to be finally free of this number." His head felt like it was about to go sailing right off his neck.

"Eyes open," Joe ordered.

A frown flew across Steve's features. In the mirror, Jennie looked like a clown. Joe should know better than to make him up that way! "You've got the eyebrows too high," he spat out.

"You're looking at them from too low. They're perfect, just like every other day."

"Too high," Steve insisted, "and the lips, too angular."

"I get paid for knowing what I'm doing."

Steve glared into the mirror, displeased. "Then you should be paid in shit because that's the kind of job you're doing. Fix those damn eyebrows and lips, or you'll be sorry." He shook his head. "Christ, no one can tell you people anything."

Joe swirled his tongue around inside his cheek; his eyes narrowed. "It stays that way, Sweetheart!"

"Up yours," Steve growled and, reaching for the lipstick before Joe's amazed eyes, drew a huge red X across his own face. Then he leaned back in the chair. "Now," he smiled, "you have to repair the damage. Remember, it's your responsibility to get me onto that set, made up, and ready to shoot in ten minutes. If you don't, they'll cut your dick off. So, let's get going!"

*     *     *

Steve swung his leg over the shoulder of the man hunched in front of him on the huge "Glitter Baby" checkerboard set. The hot lights drummed energy into him, making his feet and steps lighter than usual. Synchronizing his lip movements with the recording, he kept up the fleeting pace. When he got to the rear of the colossal set, the men all stood up stiffly and collapsed, on signal, to await his white-body-stocking-encased legs slashing the air about them.

"Cut!"

Everything stopped. Steve swayed backward, but then regained his balance.

Over the bullhorn came Ben's voice: "Pick up your legs, Jennie. Hold them straight out, and keep the toes pointing. Keep your fingers together. They were flipping out like popsicle sticks."

He had never been better! Ben was crazy. Crossing his arms in front of him, Steve waited for the signal to restart.

The long take began again, over the bodies of the chorus boys. The hot lights drove needles into his body, contributing to his nervous excitement, making him want to get rid of the energetic frenzy inside his gut.

"Cut!"

Steve's hand shot up to his head, and he groaned. Was that son-of-a-bitch never satisfied?

"Please, Jennie. Let's try it again, with just a little more ... vitality." Ben stopped speaking, and the set became very quiet.

A surge of white heat flashed through Steve and ran down his legs.

"And, remember," Ben reminded him, "bring those legs into perfect extensions, please."

"If I do it any higher," Steve yelled back, his voice cracking in anger, "I'll kick the fillings out of my mouth! You're having me do all this for nothing. I'm damn good just as I am. Why in hell are you riding me?"

Ben's voice was soothing: "This is the last segment of this number. Let's get on with it. Just a little more work left."

"You'll bury me before it's over!" Steve crossed his hands in front of his face. Joe ran toward him to check for any makeup damage. He removed a smudge and retinted the cheeks. As Joe walked away from him, Steve caught the sound of the word "Cunt."

Steve's retort was interrupted.

"Ready?" Ben called.

He nodded from the edge of the immense checkerboard.

The clapboard was slapped shut, and Steve faced the crew, a glimmering shooting star. Across the set on flying feet he moved, making sure Jennie's smile was ecstatic—and always aimed at the camera.

He was still caught up in the rhythm's incessant pounding when he heard Ben's voice boom, "Cut!"

Once more, Steve's skin writhed underneath the tight gown.

"When you come past Jimmy," Ben began, "don't waste so much time getting into your forward pattern,"

Silence descended on the set like an ominous cloud once more.

"What do you think?" Ben asked, more as a matter of courtesy than a point of information.

"I think you should go fuck yourself."

The words charged across the set. "And when you do, be sure to call me. I'd like to see it. You've got to know a little bit about something else besides the fine art of psychic sabotage." Steve stalked toward the trailer, leaving the crew, mouths agape, wondering what the hell would happen next.

*   *   *

Across the marquee, in front of the entrance to Grauman's Chinese Theater, were the words:

YOUR DARLING IN A SNEAK PREVIEW

On either side of the heavy restraining cords were crowds that had arrived too late to purchase tickets. The limousine carrying Steve, Stella, Mike, Ben, and Wesley pulled up, and the door was opened by an usher in full dress.

Steve looked at the people sitting on the overcrowded bleachers that had been erected that afternoon and wondered if any stand had ever collapsed at a preview. The faces of the fans who'd come out tonight all wore the same expression—a rather dazed-looking curiosity. The glances of these spectators followed the celebrities, who walked into the forecourt, then veered back to speak to fans on both sides.

Carefully, Stella was helped out, and Steve followed her. The crowd paid scant attention until somebody recognized Wesley Adams. Then he heard a cheer, followed by waves and smiles. From the lobby, the trio was directed to reserved seats located in the last row.

Steve nudged Stella as she moved around to get comfortable. "The film isn't even dry."

She leaned over to give him a kiss of reassurance.

He braced his knees against the seat posts in front of him. A debilitating weariness overrode his nervousness. Would the audience be fooled? Gooseflesh erupted in patches on his chest, and he wished he could run from the theater.

When the credits came on, his name, of course, was not among them. Wesley shot him an encouraging look and slapped him on the shoulder while the audience applauded. Against a black background, a sprinkling of diamonds exploded all over the screen, and *Star Fire* began.

Several minutes in, "Jennie" was slowly being lowered from a tree branch on a swing, singing "One More Time." A rustle of applause swept through the audience, coupled with a sigh of loss. But not wishing to miss a sound, the crowd quickly became quiet again.

There she was: tousled hair, bangs falling across her forehead, liquid brown eyes, calling out to her audience in the dark. The throb in her throat massaged the lyrics as they came out, mellow as thick syrup.

Steve looked around at the smiles on the faces of the people nearest him, at the same time fighting an overpowering urge to sleep. He was barely aware of Stella holding his hand.

A sharp burst of applause yanked him back into the theater as "Hey Out There" was belted from the huge white rectangle in front of him. "Jennie's" leather-strong voice transformed that song into a personal statement. When she reached her last note, the audience shivered in a communal thrill and rose to its feet. As the house lights came up, the crowd cheered.

"God damn it! It *is* the ultimate Jennie Darling picture," Wesley shouted amid the clapping and yelling. "She was *never* greater, *never* better!" Wesley turned to Steve, eyes full of unabashed wonder.

The entire theater was filled with an emotional glow. As the excited throng left their seats, Steve's need to sleep left him. He was aware of a shifting of emotions and light-headedness.

"It's not me up there. It's her." He turned back to Wesley. "I was *never* that good."

Stella started to say something—then her look turned to confusion. She clutched him, and her nails went down his jacket sleeves, leaving a trail of four deep ridges. A rush of fluid ran down her legs.

"The baby," she panted. "It's coming! Get me to Cedar's fast!"

He carried more than helped her into the waiting limousine. The audience busily filling out preview cards took no notice of Stella, her face contorted. Their joyful comments filled the air as the cab door shut and the limousine sped away from the curb.

# CHAPTER TWENTY

Carlo Castegna finished his scotch and walked around his penthouse apartment atop the Windsor Castle Club in Canada. The fringe of black hair barely covering the tops of his ears would have made him look comical, if not for the hawk nose standing sentinel over his slit of a mouth.

"Why won't you do Jennie?" he rasped. "They all ask for her." Carlo flung the motion picture advertisement section across the table. "*Star Fire* is doing great business. You don't have to read *Variety* to know that."

God damn it all. Steve's first job since leaving New York, and already he was getting static.

"Everything looks good at roadshow prices, Carlo. Wait until it plays the small theaters. That will tell the story. This hard-sell stuff is just a come-on. The real money," he rolled a fist inside his hand, "is what pays back all the expenses plus." As he faced the irate nightclub owner, he wished he were back in Ohio with Stella and her parents. He should have extended their vacation a month more, making it a full year since he'd set foot on a nightclub floor.

"Why in hell won't you do her?"

"I can't dance," he muttered, remembering the weeks of bone-breaking rehearsals. Why was he being pushed? Carlo had already agreed to the terms of the act. Christ, you couldn't trust anyone, even after they signed on the dotted line. "And I don't sing as well as she did."

"Better, from what I hear. Hey, what *are* you without Jennie?"

Steve drew a deep breath. "You have Lily Jannings—"

"Yeah—"

"And Myra Dormann—"

"Crazy Jew-broad from Brooklyn."

"Sherri Pickens—"

"Blonde jackass," Carlo said, almost allowing himself to smile.

"And, finally, me! As me! We're doing nice business." The muscles in his back tightened. He hoped this would be the end of it.

Carlo's eyes narrowed. "We've got *turnaway* business if you do Jennie!" Suddenly he quieted down and waved his hand, his smile revealing slightly yellow teeth. Slowly, he took a cigar from his humidor, snipped off the edge with a cutter from his pocket and rolled it around his fingers, his eyes on the ceiling. "What do you owe her?"

"Respect."

"Respect?" Carlo guffawed. "Go see *Star Fire* and, while she's up there waving her keester in front of the audience, ask for permission to do her. Christ," he roared, "You're not a fucking Boy Scout. She's dead almost two years and bigger now than when she was alive!"

Steve sulked in his chair, wondering when this conversation would be over.

"Her picture is breaking records in every city where they're burning a bulb behind a moving strip. You'd be doing her a favor. And here you are, fresh out of retirement! In this business, kid, you're forgotten before you're remembered. But you're not selling yourself like you should."

"He's doing all right," Stella said from a sofa at the far end of the living room. They'd been so intent in conversation that they'd forgotten she was there. She looked at her watch.

Steve nodded. "In a few minutes," he told Carlo, "our baby has to be fed."

"Are *you* going to breastfeed him?" Carlos' lips curled around his cigar, squeezing it.

"Mr. Castegna," Stella reminded, "business is good—you said so yourself."

"Everybody begs for Jennie." Carlo stretched out his arms and his bright red face turned toward the ceiling; he looked as if he were about to make an ascension. "You could be the biggest draw this club ever had!"

"Jennie is out and that's that!"

The finality of Steve's remark struck the nightclub owner like a wet towel across the face. Carlo was not used to being rebuffed. "Kid, one of the things you have to learn in show business is that when you're hot, you're hot, and—"

"Look, you've talked to me about this almost every day since I got here."

"I'll hike your salary. You're closing up a gold mine—"

"No Jennie!"

Paul sneered. "Are you sure she wasn't your mother?"

Steve clenched his teeth. "She was a good friend."

"She had to be … more than that." The man's eyebrows rose as he looked over at Stella.

"Nothing more," Steve said flatly, his patience turning to anger. "We've got to go now. Don't waste my time. Or yours."

"When is your agent coming in?"

"Tomorrow afternoon," Stella interjected, and started to get up. "We pick him up at the airport at two."

"I want to see him," Carlo told them. "Maybe he's got smarter talent on the string. Have him call me."

"I sure as hell will!" Steve helped Stella with her coat, and they left Carlo glowering at them, still chewing on his cigar.

*   *   *

Stella had tried to make the dinner a gay affair, but Steve and Sam were both waiting for the opportunity to discuss the future.

Sam speared his last bit of turkey with his fork and used his knife to mound cranberries over it. He put it into his mouth and made satisfied noises.

"I'm glad I'm not working tonight," Steve said, impatience getting the better of him, "if it's going to take you this long to come to the point. You haven't said anything all evening." Sam had something up his sleeve. He wouldn't have flown up to Canada just to see how they were getting along.

Stella, clearing away the dishes, headed for the kitchen. "Steve promised me a year in Ohio. We were going to listen to the grass grow." She tried to sound angry but couldn't manage it.

Sam shot Steve an inquiring look, which he returned with a "What could I do?" expression. A furtive grin crossed Sam's face.

"I'd like to listen to the grass grow," Steve said loudly enough for Stella's benefit, "but we need money for fertilizer."

Sam's tone was respectful: "You'll be very rich when *Star Fire* begins to pay off."

"I'll be very *old* when *Star Fire* begins to pay off!"

Sam shrugged.

After Stella poured coffee, Steve lit a cigarette and blew perfect smoke rings into the air. Then, taking a sip from his cup, he stared at the tablecloth. "OK, Sam, what have you got lined up for me?"

"I can get you the Liza Jane in Newark, the Gateway in New York. Helga's in Chicago—"

"They're joints," Steve howled in disbelief. "You should know that! You're supposed to get me into the Big Room at the Pyramid. The Lotus Room! In Las Vegas! Remember? Mike's promise? Remember?"

Sam leaned forward slightly as if he were remembering something. Then he straightened up. "I can get you into the Camel Driver Lounge."

"That's where I started out!" Steve yelled. "That's chasing my ass. Stella," he shouted, "I need a drink."

Sam lowered his voice: "You don't *have* to go around in circles. If you'll do Jennie, I can get you into any Big Room."

"Is that right?" Steve grimaced, then changed his tone. "Sam, there must be some other way to get me into those places."

"I can get Jennie into those rooms, but not you." Sam reached out for Steve's hand and held it firmly. "Steve, you defied detection. No one knows the way the film was completed. Nobody! That shows what kind of an acting job you did."

Steve's shoulders sagged. He took a drag on his cigarette and looked back at Sam. "Get me there with the material I'm working with."

Sam's face pinched tight with concern, and his voice turned soft: "Everybody's been after me for you —but it's Jennie they want. They won't be satisfied with less."

"Never."

"Can I promise them Jennie twice a week?" Sam pleaded.

"Once?" His tone was hopeful. "That's all you would have to offer."

"Absolutely not!"

"I can't swing it then, and there's no sense trying to get another agent. Clubs only want your act with Jennie as the headliner. Reconsider. Don't you have any sense at all?"

"I won't do it."

"Think about it. Call me when you decide where to work. The top, or the bottom—it's all up to you."

"Sam, I respect Steve for his stand," Stella cut in. She ate a bit of pie before continuing, "Let Jennie rest in peace."

"No wonder you left the business," he smiled.

The baby began crying in the next room, and Stella excused herself.

"The Big Room is yours," Sam said. "Don't make up your mind about it right now." He raised his hand to forestall Steve's burst of anger. "But don't sit on your ass too long, either, because—between you and me and no one else—I was sent here expressly by Nate Komanek to get you for the Lotus Room at the Pyramid as soon as you finish your gig here.

"Steve," Sam lowered his voice, "I have eyes and ears in this place, and I know what's going on. The audience at every show catcalls Jennie's name. I know it, Carlo knows it, and unless you're deaf, dumb and blind—you know it, too! Give them Jennie. They want Jennie. Don't do her, and you'll be outta the business in less than three years!"

# CHAPTER TWENTY ONE

S teve pulled the white convertible up alongside the luxurious house lent him by the Pyramid Hotel. Vast expanses of grass were set in front of gleaming white desert boulders on the far end of the sculptured golf course. He thought of Sam: they had just finished an eighteen-hole round and Steve had come in five points above par. As he removed his bag of clubs from the trunk, he noticed his darkening skin. It would take real effort to cover that desert tan with makeup. From now on, he'd better stay out of the sun during the middle of the day. Leaning on the fender, he looked across the street and stared at the gigantic marquee in front of the hotel:

THE ILLUSIONS OF SINGER STEVEN DENNIS

Sherri Pickens   Lily Jannings   Myra Dormann   Jennie Darling

He'd insisted on Jennie being at the tail end of the billing to minimize her importance to the act. He'd been rehearsing for a week, but he still was not ready to do her.

On the shelf in the garage sat the trunk containing her signature swing. Steve snapped the locks open and lifted the lid. In the dim light, he ran his hands over the metal rigging and smoothed down the plush velour of the seat, recalling her descent in "The Sleeping Princess."

He closed the lid sharply, flipped the locks shut and quickly stepped into the breezeway.

Kevin, all gurgles, sat in his playpen, fascinated by the string of plastic toys strung across the top. A flood of warm pride coursed through Steve, and he quickened his step. Kevin smiled broadly as his father came close. Steve placed a fingertip to Kevin's nose and was rewarded by a series of "Da's." The kid sure was a happy little butterball. Steve began tickling him under the chin and darting his fingers into Kevin's brown curls. Kevin broke into laughter, and his face—remarkably like Stella's—flushed red with excitement.

"Hi." Stella came up to Steve and kissed him lightly on the cheek.

He held her close for a moment, then stepped back to gaze at her. She looked great in her bikini, just as pretty as she'd been at Jones Beach, before they'd married. There was no flabbiness, yet enough substance under the skin to give her body a smooth, molded look. Her hair was already sun bleached in a scattered pattern.

"Be back in a minute." She returned to the kitchen, then reappeared with a tea cart set up for two.

"How about the patio?" He held the door open.

Carefully she wheeled the cart past him.

He followed her, then sat down heavily in one of the empty chairs, interlacing his fingers around the back of his head.

Stella smiled, brushing the hair away from her face. She watched Kevin through the glass door, then turned her attention to Steve. She pursed her lips. "Are you still smarting because they asked you to shorten *your* part of the act?"

"I told you," he said sharply, "I'd end up taking too much time changing clothes and identities. Plus, a shorter act means the customers won't be away from the tables for too long. Management loves that." He thought of the substantial income he would be getting for the next two months. "Business is business."

"Sure," she replied.

He wasn't certain how she meant that. "I was just looking at Jennie's swing in the garage as I came in."

She gave him a wry look.

He pretended not to see it. "I still have hopes of persuading them to take her name off the front sign."

Stella crossed her legs with an air of deliberateness.

"I mean it," he said emphatically.

The words rushed out of her: "The sooner her death is accepted as a reality, the better for all of us."

"I already started to work on Sam at the golf course today. I can drop her from the act slowly so it's not noticeable. You'll see. People will lose interest after a while." He paused. "I'm not planning to do her at all for a couple of days, at any rate." He gazed over her shoulder at the oversized inflated toys floating in imperfect circles around the pool.

"You still get a good bit of mail asking where Jennie's hiding out." She reached for her cup of tea, and shivered.

"Will you be at the late show again tonight?" he asked.

"Uh-huh. Tell Sam to save me a ringside table." She looked toward Kevin again. "I want to be sure he's tucked away before I leave. Last night was the first since we've been here that he slept the whole night through. Who's scheduled for tonight?"

"Myra."

"Both shows?"

"Yep." He reached for a glass of iced tea. "I've got to remind myself to take a diuretic before I leave for the hotel. Stella—"

"Yes?" She turned her head to look at him, her eyes a mottle of gray and green.

"Are you happy? I mean, now that the dollars are finally coming in?" She had said little about finances lately, now that they were on their way up.

"I don't think about it any more." Her eyes took on a faraway look. "As long as *you're* happy, that's all that counts. We're more comfortable than we've ever been. But somehow … that doesn't seem to be as important as it once was."

"It is still as important as it once was."

\*     \*     \*

Behind the curtain in the Lotus Room, the clatter of silver and glass blended into a pleasant background sound. Steve stepped up to the conductor's stand, checked Myra's arrangements, then left for his dressing room.

Slipping into Myra's brocade gown, he had difficulty with the zipper and reminded himself to take an appetite killer. He reached for a cosmetics case. After studying Myra's pictures for several minutes, he confidently started applying makeup. He outlined Myra's generous lips, filled them in with an additional coat of color, then applied a light covering of vaseline: his lips turned luminous.

He took the wig off its stand, put it on, and brushed it carefully from the center part until the hair curled at the ends and poked forward at the cheek.

A knock on the door, and a voice: "Fifteen minutes to showtime." Steve mouthed the lyrics to "Picadilly Circus" as he finished his preparations. A second knock on the door meant he had to get to the wings, fast.

The musicians whistled at him and he waved back appreciatively. On the other side of the curtain he could hear the crowd quiet down when the orchestra played Myra's theme song. The huge stage began moving forward as the curtains parted and the Master of Ceremonies' driving voice introduced the star of the evening. Faster and faster the drummer pounded until Steve stepped toward the microphone and into the hot spotlight.

A smattering of polite applause greeted him. He stepped back uncertainly and started to sing but could not seem to establish any kind of rapport with the audience.

If he could keep on working them, allowing them no time to think, he might still get them. His movements became stilted and awkward. Myra was slipping away from him. Behind his professional smile, panic was rising, for he could keenly feel the crowd's displeasure. He gestured to the orchestra, and they went into the next song—fast.

The thought of forty minutes more of performance time started a series of pains inside his stomach. Beads of perspiration ran down his face, and he wondered if the makeup was smeared. When he finally got to the end of the second number, he took a deep bow. A smattering of applause greeted him. They were being absolute bastards out there.

"You're OK, Myra," a female voice yelled, "but we came to see Jennie."

A chant began on the right side of the room: "'One More Time'—'One More Time'." Another group on the left side started pounding on the tables with their glasses and utensils. Steve held onto the mike tightly for support as, over and over again, they called out Jennie's name and shuffled their feet.

"It's Myra Dorman's night, friends," he said in an attempt to humor them.

"We paid a pile to see Jennie," a deep, masculine voice called out. "Where the hell is she?"

"Fuck Myra," a ringside drunk spluttered. "I wanna see a real movie star on that stage."

"I paid to see Jennie and I want to see her," a husky Texas-accented voice thundered in the darkness.

With the cries of "*Star Fire,*" "Melinda," and "Jennie" ringing in his ears, Steve was grateful when the heavy purple drapes came between him and the frustrated mob. He kept clenching the microphone in disbelief until Sam pulled him off the stage. He heard the angry crowd's insults all the way to his dressing room as Sam pushed him inside.

"A scotch," he barked, and hit the sofa with a thud. A cold glass was placed in his outstretched hand; with his eyes shut, he drank silently. At the sound of a sharp hammering on the door, Steve leaped up. Sam opened the door slightly, but Nate Komanek, the hotel owner, barged in and shoved Sam against the wall. He stood there, furiously strangling a cigar with his lips. His breathing was punctuated by snorts that made his speech come out in angry, jerky phrases.

Steve raised his hand in a protest while he downed the remainder of his drink.

Nate brought his palms together in a loud explosive clap, signaling ominous news.

"Now take it easy," Sam started. "He *is* fulfilling his contract! There was no promise as to when he would do Jennie."

"Then what the fuck is that eight-by-ten-foot poster of her doing in front of the Big Room?"

Perplexed, Steve turned his head swiftly to face Nate. "How did it get there? It's supposed to be in the basement." He brought his hand to the sides of his face. "Christ, those idiots brought up the wrong one!"

"Yeah," Nate raved, his attention riveted on Sam, "that poster shows her with her legs hanging out of a short tux. Sam, he's been here four nights and he hasn't done her yet!" he yelled, his cord-like veins sticking out of his neck. "What's he trying to pull? Sam, you son-of-a-bitch! You promised me!" He glared at the agent. "You want them to go away mad and find their way into another joint?" he screamed. "They're supposed to stumble over the crap tables when they leave the Big Room." He curled his meaty hands into fists. "You'd better do Darling," he growled, "or we'll carry you out of Las Vegas a helluva lot faster than when you came in. Motherfuckers. I should have kept better tabs on this operation." He thrust his hands into his trouser pockets; the material made a tearing sound.

"Steve didn't *promise* to do Jennie tonight," Sam protested.

Nate gripped Sam's lapels and slammed him against the wall. "Is that oversize glossy in front of the entrance to the Big Room your idea of a joke?" Nate turned to Steve. "How long does it take you to get dressed up like her?"

"At least an hour and a half," he answered flatly.

"Then you've got enough time to get ready for the late show. We'll give out rain checks—for the first time in our history. Whoever wants back in *gets* back in." He strode to the door, his head shaking. "You have no mind to make up, fella. We're not paying you in Crackerjacks." He jerked his thumb toward the hall and sneered. "They're baying like hyenas in heat out there."

"They put the wrong picture up." Sam's eyes rolled around in their sockets. "It's a mistake, Nate. We'll laugh about it one day."

"I already am!" Nate shouted, then turned to look back. "See you soon, Jennie. That is, if you want to keep breathing." Then he left the room.

"Steve," Sam said quietly, "You know what you've got to do."

Steve nodded weakly, then swung his feet up over one sofa

arm; he let his head fall back over the other, and wished to hell it would drop off. He tried to stop the tremors surging inside his body by holding his breath for as long as he could. He looked around the huge, brightly lit room with its built-in cabinetry and wardrobe closets along one wall, and its floor-to-ceiling brown and black mirrors on the other. He was drowning in an ocean of opulence.

"Steve, I'm leaving. Do you need anything?"

He shook his head.

"I'll be outside the door. Knock if you want anything." At the door, Sam hesitated. "Steve, give a little. They don't come any bigger than The Pyramid."

"Don't waste your time trying to convince me." Steve pushed himself up from the sofa and unzipped Myra's gown, then dipped his fingers into a jar of cream and wiped them across his face: his features emerged as Myra's disappeared. One by one, he tacked three photos of Jennie's alongside the mirror, then painstakingly went to work.

*      *      *

Sam had already knocked three times on the door and was becoming concerned. The door suddenly opened, and an arm encased in a glittering, flame-colored sleeve shot forward. Another arm came around the jamb, propelling Jennie, wearing her most dazzling smile, into full view.

"Sammy!" She posed dramatically. "Baby!" Her voice rang out in delight at seeing him.

Sam smiled nervously; he hadn't expected this kind of entrance.

"Jennie is ready," the familiar voice announced, accompanied by an impatient glance. "Are my numbers stacked?"

Sam nodded dumbly.

"Then let's show them what the hell this business is all about!" Head held high, Jennie pulled the door shut and strode toward the wings.

*   *   *

The whistling and cheering that had started when she'd come onstage would not stop. The crowd was boisterous, jammed together over every inch of floor space, with more people standing against the walls. Then the band segued into "One More Time." She motioned for the crowd to stop, but their applause only grew louder.

Myra could never command a reception like this.

Before Steve knew it, Jennie's stint was ending with the plaintive singing of this, her signature song. He felt in control again. Then he realized how much he'd missed all the admiration and warmth, the patrons demanding "One More Time," again and again. When they released Jennie, almost in relief, he threw grateful kisses at them as the curtains closed.

The musicians stood up in congratulation. Jennie was back, and everyone knew it! She shoved her tousled hair back carelessly, theatrically. Then, surrounded by admirers, she made her way on spike heels to the dressing room.

A beaming Sam stood there rubbing one hand over the other—while Nate Komanek, eyes jack-o-lantern bright, held out his hand. "Kid, that's the greatest job I've ever seen." Nate looked him over as if he were deciding something, then said, "From now on, you do her exclusively!" Nate bit sharply on his cigar, which broke in two. The lighted end fell to the rug, and he unmercifully smashed the embers out with his foot. "Do you hear me? Or, you're out! And I'll see you don't work anywhere else."

Entering his dressing room, Steve slammed the door shut and placed his hand on the makeup table to support himself.

A knock on the door made him stiffen—but then he heard Stella's voice. The door opened, and she entered. "I didn't know you were going to do her tonight," Stella said, voice cracking in bewilderment.

The reply was sultry: "Honey—no business like show business!"

"Drop her voice, Steve—"

"Stella, it's real," he cut in, "as real as anyone you know."

"But *you're* not. You're a first-rate imitation—"

"You couldn't have seen the show," he said in bewildered disbelief. "They gave me five minutes of applause out there. Don't give me that first-rate imitation crap. Are you so blind you don't recognize a tour de force when you see one?"

Stella walked up to him. "Now, let me tell you something," she snapped, eyes afire. "Even Jennie Darling couldn't live up to the Jennie Darling legend. What gives you the gall to think *you* can dance to that tune?"

"Because I pay the piper," he yelled—in Jennie's voice.

Stella's laugh turned into a scoff. "You damn fool! That piper will slice you to ribbons, when and as he pleases." Stella crossed her arms and stepped back, staring.

Suddenly he lifted the wig from his head, and Jennie was no longer in the room. He pulled off his artificial nails. His hands slowly moved to the back of the gown and unzipped it. Slipping out of costume, Steve stood in front of her in his shorts, then walked to the dressing stand where he cleaned the makeup off his face in silence. He turned around and smiled.

"Steve," Stella said, "no more tricks like that again. They're very bad jokes."

Voice low, he confessed, "I *had* to do her tonight."

Her expression changed from anger to surprise when he told her what had happened at the dinner show. He omitted the scene with Nate in his dressing room because he didn't want to frighten her. "There was no way I could do anything else."

He stepped behind the dressing screen and put on a maroon turtleneck sweater over slacks of the same color. What agitated him now was the fact that he could barely remember what had happened from just after he'd gotten into Jennie's makeup until Stella had confronted him.

Stella kept looking at him, waiting for him to say something.

"Honey," he grinned, "all I want to do now is relax, not think, not do anything except squeeze a little relief out of what's left of the night."

"Steve, she's big trouble. Can't you see you're better off without her in the act?" Stella's eyes filled with tears. "Can't you feel it?"

"I *feel* like taking a few passes at the crap tables. My luck seems to have returned." He tried to sound as if he didn't give a damn. "What do *you* feel like doing?"

She spat out the words: "Throwing up. Take me home, Steve. I want to go home."

"If you want to go home, drive yourself back." Christ, if she would only get off his back. He'd had enough thrown at him tonight to last a long while, and he didn't need any more. "I'm going to hang around here and loosen up a bit."

At the door, he kissed her quickly on the lips, then watched her disappear down the corridor. His body relaxed somewhat as he realized the evening was finally over. Suddenly the brightly lit yellow and white room looked cheap and sleazy. Pulling a bottle of scotch from the bar, he half-filled a short glass. Alone, he sat down and sipped the drink until it began blunting the hard edges of the last hours.

\*     \*     \*

When Steve woke up, his mouth tasted like it was filled with lint. He gazed about their living room and realized that he never had made it to the bedroom last night.

In front of him, on a huge black pedestal, sat a small Chinese stone head that supposedly saw and knew everything. If his own head were made of stone, would he know everything, too?

Attempting to get off the sofa, he listened for the usual sounds around the house. There were none.

"Stella?" he called.

There was no answer.

He called her several times more, then leaped up from the couch. Where was she? He moved from the living room to the dining room and kitchen, finally ending up in the bedroom. The bed hadn't even been slept in. Kevin's playpen stood empty in the hallway, its colored ornaments swaying back and forth on the string tied across the top. Steve ran to the patio and looked out at the pool: Stella was not there, either.

Back in the kitchen, on the table, sat the oblong diuretic he'd forgotten to take last night. Steve turned away, toward the refrigerator: a note in Stella's familiar handwriting was anchored there by two magnetic replicas of the hotel. With effort, he focused his eyes on the paper:

*Steve—*

*I love you—very much, but I sure don't love what's happening to you. I heard Nate Komanek tell you he wants you to do Jennie exclusively for the rest of the engagement.*
*You didn't even try to argue him out of it.*

*I could barely stand 25% of the act devoted to Jennie. If you are going to do her full time, I don't have a chance.*

*When the insanity ends and your Horror Act is over, I'll be waiting for you in Ohio.*

*Nothing is worth the orange diet pill, the yellow happiness pill, the red pep-up one, and the blue diuretic.*

> *Love,*
> *Stella/Kevin*

Damn it! Obviously she'd left as soon as she'd come home. He had been alone all that time. He tried to drive out the hurt in back of his eyes by slamming his hand against the refrigerator. When the telephone rang, he grabbed the receiver off the wall. It was Sam, the characteristic rasp still in his voice, even after a full night's sleep: "We've got to be at Nate's office in an hour. Should I pick you up?"

"Somebody's got to," he said weakly. There was no response. "No; never mind. I'll drive myself."

"Nate wants to bill you as 'The New Jennie Darling'."

Steve's laugh was at once triumphant and ironic. "I'll be at the hotel as soon as I shower and get cleaned up. Meet me in the Safari Room for a quick lunch before we go in to see Nate."

"OK. How's Stella and Kevin?"

"They're great," he said and replaced the receiver.

In the darkness, to one side of his white convertible, sat the trunk containing Jennie's swing and rigging. He looked at it closely. The brass locks at either end were unsecured. Yet he clearly remembered having snapped the locks shut the day before, when he returned to the house after playing golf. He slowly lifted the lid: the necklace of giant links sparkled in the compartment alongside the swing. He ran his hands over the cold metal and smoothed down the plush blue velour.

"Jennie," he said softly, "you never ran out on me. Right?" The sound of his own voice startled him a bit. It didn't sound like his own …

Steve closed the trunk and locked it. He didn't feel alone any more.

# CHAPTER TWENTY TWO

T he sunlight bounced off the clouds into the Lufthansa airliner, almost blinding Steve, as he arrived in Berlin— as Jennie. He lowered his head, stubbed out his cigarette in a grapefruit half, and pushed away the uneaten food on the tray in front of him.

With the plane due to land shortly, it was time to get into character. Being Jennie came effortlessly now that she was his full-time act. He relaxed and made his mind blank as her character began to take over. "Jennie," he sighed, "Jennie … "

Eyes half closed, he reached out for the liquor alongside the tray and thought about the opening at the Club Jonquil in ten days. That week of rest beforehand would be a release. Fumbling in Jennie's bag, he came upon the telegram from Sam confirming a series of U.S. concert dates, beginning with the Winter Garden Theater in New York. He slowly folded the paper into a neat square and put it back in the purse.

The pace never really got easier—only a little more frustrating with each engagement. Every date meant starting out new, and every city except London had taken time to get used to. Had the PR staff arrived in Berlin on time, he wondered, to take care of all the preparation details? He would give a week's salary to be rushed to the hotel with no fanfare.

*I feel as much like having a press conference at the airport as I do about climbing Mount Everest,* he told himself. Yet the club had insisted he arrive in Berlin in character. He lit another cigarette; it was the wrong thing to do, but that smoke was so damned tasteful. He rubbed his back into the seat, searching for some comfort.

The stewardess, in German-accented English: "Miss Darling?" She held a nightclub program in her hand.

Feeling trapped, he reached for the outstretched pen and, in the right-hand corner of a picture of Jennie posing against a column, scrawled:

Best Wishes

JD

He smiled tightly as he handed the program back to the stewardess, then watched her deliver it to a man at the other end of the First Class section.

He looked at his hands. It would have been a bitch to glue the nails on that morning; it was easier to just sleep dressed, rather than dress up before leaving. The farewell party in Paris was still going strong when he left. Had he taken today's appetite killer? For good measure, he took another. If he didn't eat the rest of the day, that wouldn't be so bad.

It was too much trouble to think about anything more, he decided, and checked his seat belt. Templehof Airport was only minutes away. Had the crew sent the car out to meet him? They were supposed to! *"Please, God, I'll believe in you if you don't let them forget. I'm not up to getting there by myself!"*

Soon, the huge wheels touched down and, eventually, came to a halt. Steve waited until everyone else on the jet had disembarked. When the moment could be put off no longer, he settled the mink

coat across his shoulders and walked stiffly to the open door—
only to back away. This army of photographers was larger than
any he had seen before. He gripped the sides of the doorway, then
shot to the top of the moveable staircase.

From behind his bone-tired weariness, he somehow brought
out Jennie's magnificent smile. Cameras clicked continually,
making little punctuating noises as he walked down the stairs,
allowing time for their pictures. The bright blue sky forced him
to squint.

"Mister Dennis?" a voice close by called out.

Steve could not identify whose it was but he turned in the
general direction from which it had come.

"Miss Darling," Jennie's voice cracked back. "Miss Jennie
Darling." At the bottom of the steps, facing the battery of microphones,
Steve caught the black eyes of television cameras, and he waved. It
seemed that everyone in Berlin had come to the airport.

"But you *are* Mister Dennis," the voice persisted.

"I am Jennie Darling."

"Are you returning directly to the United States after your
Jonquil commitment?" A tall, angular woman in a frayed mauve
tweed suit with a mannish hat drawn over one eye stepped forward.
Her eyes never left her notepad. "What about additional concerts
in Europe? What about more movies?"

He let his head go back and then brought it up again slowly,
as Jennie did when she was thinking up answers to questions.
"I'm returning to my homeland. Concerts? Of course; I work
best when I have an audience. My throat's dry. Does anyone have
anything?" Someone slipped a glass into his hand as pens glided
across reporter's notepads. "I hope it's not alcoholic," he grinned,
and tested the drink. Damn—it wasn't! He set the glass down on
top of a nearby airport luggage vehicle.

"Movies? Of course! Where would I be without them? Without Melinda?" He gazed around at the intent throng and brought his hands out for emphasis. "After all, it all started with *The Sleeping Princess.*"

A chauffeur broke through the crowd and said he was from the Berlin Haus. Great! No screw-ups! The crew was on schedule, doing their job. Jennie waved the man away: "I can't leave just yet."

A rotund man in a caramel-colored leather jacket asked how she liked Germany.

Jennie glanced at her wrist. "I've only been here fifteen minutes. Give me five more to make up my mind." She looked at the amused expressions on the faces of the nearest reporters. She winked at them, and they smiled back.

"Do you mind?" She pulled from her bag a pair of oversized sunglasses and settled them onto her nose. Immediately, there was another burst of flashes. Steve couldn't top that moment, and so decided it was time to go. With his back to the photographers, he wound his way to two large glass doors with the word "Visas" gold-lettered on them in several different languages. He let the mink drop halfway down his back, and the bulbs went off again. Christ, he thought, the act was flawless.

In the VIP Lounge, publicity photographs were taken with the airport's vice president, a short, balding man with a kind expression. This official told Jennie he would "personally" take charge of getting her through Customs.

Steve motioned toward his myriad trunks and wig cases.

The official appeared to be perturbed at the task of getting them through the doors, but then good-naturedly broke into soft laughter.

At a photographer's request, Steve perched atop one of the

trunks, gams crossed, and made sure he faced downward from the left—counting the seconds until he could bolt out of there.

"I'm thirsty," he complained again, and someone shoved a paper cup into his hands. He lifted it to his lips and sipped: it was great-tasting wine, and Heaven seemed closer. "There's a friendly soul out there somewhere," he said gratefully, and waved the cup.

"Did you know *Star Fire* has been playing here for the last two weeks?" a voiced called out.

"*Star Fire*? Playing here? Wonderful! I can't wait to hear myself speaking German." The tickle in his throat bothered him, but he didn't feel he could ask for another drink.

Going without sleep the past two nights was taking its toll. The muscles in his calves were beginning to tighten into knots. The inside of his costume seemed to have been lined with small pebbles, each one digging into him with its own particular pain. He shut his eyes. It felt good to escape the incessant prodding, if only for an instant.

"I have to go now." He ran his right hand down his left shin until it almost touched his ankle, then lifted his face; everyone got the message! He nearly went blind with the number of flashes going off at once, and at such close range. Then he ran into the waiting limousine. Looking back, he waved and moaned loudly in relief.

At the Berlin Haus he was escorted to the elevator by the hotel manager, who assured him the maid would take care of the luggage when it arrived. If anything was not up to Jennie's expectations, the hotel would "consider it a compliment" to correct the matter.

Steve was too tired to reply, so he nodded in agreement. He felt imprisoned in the small elevator. He could hardly wait for the doors to open so he could breathe.

Waiting outside the apartment door, an athletic-looking blond bellhop held his suitcase. He placed it on the luggage holder inside the bedroom, with its green and beige moiré tapestried wallpaper. After Steve signed for the tip, the bellhop clicked his heels, uttered "*Danke schoen*," and wished Jennie a good afternoon.

The suite was right out of a 19th Century interior decorator's textbook, with its high-domed ceiling, crystal chandelier, and arched doorways leading to the living room and bath.

Steve picked up the phone by the bed. "No calls," he told the hotel operator. He walked to the suitcase, opened it and pulled out a pair of pajamas.

He stared for a long time at Jennie's reflection in the mirror. Then, pulling off the eyelashes, he shoved the hair of his wig behind his ears and reached for a box of cleansing tissues. Wiping with brisk strokes, he removed the makeup, then lifted the wig off his head.

He slowly removed the rest of the costume until he stood alone in the large bedroom in his jockey shorts.

"Godamn *beat*," he mumbled, and returned to the mirror, looking at the tiny red veins lacing his eyes. When he was Jennie, he was positive they were not there. Christ, he was hungry! When had he last eaten? The walls of his stomach must be touching each other.

"Suite twelve-one-four," he told Room Service. "Something light … Chicken salad? Great! With a bottle of vodka! *Mach schnell!*" Would their customary efficiency also extend to such matters as room service? Moving across the floor, he kicked the skirt he'd just worn into the air; it landed across a nearby chair.

There was no evidence of the spirited Jennie who'd come into the suite a half hour ago. He felt the tiredness around his chest fade away, and at the same time, his heart began beating irregularly. He stretched out full across the bed, hollow and exhausted.

How long? Nearly a year since he'd last seen Stella and Kevin in Vegas? It seemed like a decade. He remembered the last time he'd played with Kevin. He yearned to reach out, grab his son and toss him into the air. He could hear Kevin's chuckle as he realized his father would never really allow him to fall. He missed Stella, too—when he had the time. But he didn't have that kind of time any more. His merry-go-round was going too fast.

Stella's infrequent letters from the farm usually included snapshots of Kevin and were full of his latest discoveries. She never included any pictures of herself. Absence didn't make his heart grow fonder—only more desperate.

Here it was, almost Christmas, and Steve was both more successful and lonelier than he had ever been in his life. The only time he felt alive lately was when he was Jennie.

He thought about his upcoming engagement. The sound man at the Jonquil *had* to be better than that jackass in Amsterdam. How could such incompetents manage to hold onto good jobs? This band should be more disciplined than the one in Copenhagen, too! He could well believe the Danes were fun loving, for no one at the Varieteen Theatre ever took the music seriously. But he had slaved over his act, and he was determined to put it across.

Would his dressing room be like the flea trap in Paris? He would see about that tomorrow, or even tonight when he met the band leader. He tried to stop the twitch in his eyelids. Suddenly his body began to tremble, and he dug his fingers into the sides of the mattress. Once the shaking subsided he worked his way under the spread and pulled it over his head …

A knock at the door awoke him. His food order was softly wheeled in on a glistening chrome cart. Inside an ice bucket stood a chilled bottle, water drops sparkling like silver crystals on the outside. After the bellhop had left, Steve helped himself to some of the salad. He poured the vodka and brought the glass to his lips. The cool liquid ran into him, and he began to feel better.

Sitting on the bed, he caught his reflection in the mirror. Gradually, the reflection separated, and he saw two of himself vacuously grinning back. Then, suddenly, Jennie's smiling image dominated the frame.

He lifted his glass to her—and fell back onto the bed. Chilled vodka ran over his underwear and onto the sheets, wetting them in large circles that were, in time, completely absorbed.

# CHAPTER TWENTY THREE

Sitting close to the blazing fireplace at the Krystal Bar of the Berlin Haus in the late afternoon, Steve flicked his nails at his whiskey glass and listened to its tone. He rubbed the bridge of his nose with his thumb and forefinger and thought about the immediate past. He'd managed to sleep through his first two days in Berlin, then drink to a comfortable satiation and go out for a late dinner on the third. Rehearsals had started on the fourth day, and they'd been at it for nearly a week.

Jennie's pace was accelerating; already, he had been asked to model furs by Helmut for the West German Children's Orphanage. (In France, it had been for *Ma Cherie* Magazine.) The thought of tramping down a runway, even for charity, made him snicker. If he did that, he would see about picking up a mink coat, at cost, and Expressing it to Stella. Dayton got pretty cold in the winter.

In West Berlin, the spirit of Christmas already permeated the city, helped along by the light snowfall of the past two nights. Steve wondered if it had snowed in Dayton.

The morning's run-through went almost well. The band's style was less spirited than that of the French, but their timing was superb.

Steve wanted to investigate the sound booth early the next day and check the equipment; he didn't like the flat sound of the current system and wondered if the electrical wires were held loosely by their connectors. He also had to again remind Herr Hauptmann, the manager, to make sure the overhead speakers located on each side of the stage would be moved far forward so that Jenny and her microphone would be well in back of them, thus preventing feedback.

He motioned to the waiter to refill his glass.

Conditions at the Jonquil left a lot to be hoped for. The club's operation was not great, and those damn waiters never stopped moving. Steve had told Herr Hauptmann that serving food and drinks during his act would result in him putting on a lousy show. Herr Hauptmann listened until Steve started getting angry and threatened to pull out. Then, the man's angular face began showing some signs of emotion, the blond eyebrow perpetually lifted over his left eye came down to rest, and they began earnestly talking business.

Herr Hauptmann's thin, expressive fingers had shot out in stabbing movements as he explained that no one had ever complained about the club's equipment before. He insinuated that Steve was being unnecessarily priggish.

Steve had been ready to haul off and separate him from a couple of his front teeth, but instead he'd explained that the technical standards of his act had to be faultless.

After an hour's discussion, Herr Hauptmann agreed that during Jennie's show, there would be no unnecessary distractions—no serving of food or drink or cigarettes—but only if Steve would consent to doing one additional show, at four in the morning—with no increase in salary.

A half hour later, after more discussion and no progress, they'd let the matter rest.

At the Fire Bar in the lobby of the hotel sat a blonde Steve had noticed the past several afternoons. Her hair was sleek and short, side-parted with a wave rolling across her forehead. Thickly shaped eyebrows rested above two dark brown eyes. Her chin was strong, almost square. A nose that would have been considered too long for most women looked just right on her face, accentuating Teutonic ancestry. She smiled at Steve indifferently, then gazed past him into the flames.

He asked the waiter to serve the woman a drink with his compliments.

She was startled by the unordered drink placed in front of her. When the waiter pointed out Steve, she looked at him again and smiled warmly.

He lifted his glass.

Almost but not quite toasting him, she lifted her glass to her lips and sipped. Then she took a long blue glove from the seat next to her and began putting it on.

Before he realized what he was doing, he was standing beside her, asking if he could sit down.

"Let us sit over there." She motioned to a nearby table. "The fire is much prettier from that view." Her voice had just enough of an accent to sound intriguing.

They stepped over to the table. There were perhaps ten customers in the gigantic rococo bar so early in the afternoon. Overhead, the heavy, carved beams complemented the prismed mirrors and crystal chandeliers. "You speak English," he said.

She grinned. "Doesn't everyone in Berlin?"

He toyed with his glass. "You live here?"

"In the suburbs."

He looked at the plain gold band on her left ring finger. "You're married" came out as a fact, though it was more of a question.

Her chocolate-colored eyes reflected the flickering light. "I have two children, a boy and a girl, ages nine and seven. And a husband."

"What does your husband do?" There was something about her that reminded him of a lighted torch imbedded in a block of ice. He could feel the heat of the flame through the cold.

"He works and works." She twisted her body in Steve's direction and frowned. "For recreation, he's found something new: more work!" She traced the rim of her drink with a gloved fingertip. "And that's such a pity."

"Do you come here often?"

"Oh, yes," she replied, matter-of-fact. "I come here after shopping. You see, a drink makes boredom bearable. It softens the hard edges of …"

"Of reality," he broke in, and they both smiled.

She took a pack of cigarettes from her purse and removed one; he lit it for her. She drew back her head, inhaled the smoke, and released it slowly. She looked at the watch on her left wrist and, without lifting her eyes, asked, "What do you do, Mister—?"

"Dennis," he volunteered, "Steve Dennis." He waited for a moment. "Does the name mean anything to you?"

There was no change in her expression. "Should it?"

"Don't you read the papers?"

She smiled. "I try not to. What passes for news is most often just daily irritation. I'm much too busy—"

"Shopping?"

"Exactly." She circled her neck with her gloved arms, which looked like twining blue garlands. Closing her eyes, she said, "You must be American. You are definitely not British, and you must have come here recently or I would have noticed you before. And," she continued, "you seem lonely." Then she gave a shallow laugh, and her smile disappeared. "I know, because it takes one to recognize another. Will your business keep you in Berlin long?"

She seemed almost sad when he told her he would be leaving in about seven weeks.

The waiter reappeared with two filled glasses on a tray. She waved hers away, but he took his as he asked her name.

"Silvi Teller." She brought her forefinger to the side of her nose. "And you are Steven Dennis. You are married?"

He told her that Stella had stayed in Ohio because traveling with Kevin was too difficult.

"She must trust you. Why, I wonder. You are much too attractive to be wandering about by yourself." She shoved her honey-colored hair in back of her ears and stared into the fire, studying the darting flames. "This reminds me so of our fireplace at home. It's a lovely old house. If we were there, I would invite you in for a coffee. But Harmstadt is so far away."

"Let *me* extend the invitation then." He felt a quickening of his pulse and a warm stirring. "I have a suite on the twelfth floor. It has a fireplace in the living room. Imitation, of course—but a fireplace nonetheless."

She brought her fingertips to her lips. The fire gave her features a glowing softness. She glanced at him, and her look turned pliant, "I guess the twelfth floor isn't all that far away, is it?"

\*   \*   \*

As they stepped through the suite door, Steve put his arm around her shoulders, and she leaned into him. They walked to a large window looking down on the city below. Through sheer drapes, the sun cast a silvery gloss over the suite, turning the light green walls a soft gray.

"You are very beautiful," he said, caressing her ear.

"No, I'm just attractive—enough to be noticed but no more than that."

His hands pulled her earrings gently from her ears and he began unfastening the top buttons of her dress. She unbuttoned the others, and her dress fell to the floor. As he unhooked her brassiere, her soft breasts fell down against him in a graceful arc and she tilted her head back. She loosened the catch on his belt and unzipped his fly, almost in one movement. She pulled him closer, and he smelled her perfume. She suddenly seemed terribly fragile.

He slid out of his shorts and undershirt. Their kiss was slow and natural. His hands ran over her body. With the tip of his index finger he outlined the large, round circles around her nipples. Then, he took one in his mouth and rolled his tongue around it while she kissed the top of his head. He pressed his cheek against her and moved down to her navel. She pulled off her girdle and stockings; he placed his arms in between her legs and gently forced them apart. He pressed his face into her crotch and slid his tongue into her.

Her cry of pleasure told him he had struck home. She shook fitfully, grasping his shoulders and, with a guttural moan, fell across his back.

Getting up, he carried her over his shoulder to the bedroom. Holding onto him, she kissed the small of his back and rubbed the curves of his buttocks. He sat her on an armchair and opened her mouth with gentle caresses as she opened her legs wide. The height was perfect, and he effortlessly slid into her. Resting her arms on the chair's edge, she brought her legs around his back, and he began a lazy thrusting. With each forward shove she opened her legs wider, then grasped him tighter.

He could feel her hurtling into a frenzy of abandonment. She leaned back, allowing him to pummel into her with wild, jerking thrusts as she convulsed in orgasm … and then was still.

The silence now surrounding them was too heavy to bear. She brought her arms around to circle his shoulders and cried quietly. With her legs locked around him, he carried her to the bed, where they remained coupled until sleep softly nudged them apart.

They fed upon each other twice more during the afternoon. She kissed his hair, licked his nipples, marveled at the smoothness of his chest, surprised to find that he had no hair under his arms.

When she checked her wrist watch, he protested, "Stay just a little longer." She had fortuitously stumbled into his life, and he didn't want her to leave. Something more than just a sexual adventure had just occurred.

She drew her legs up under her, "Leibchen," she murmured, "I told the maid I would be late getting home, but I hadn't counted on anything like this." She hummed a tune as her fingers danced up his stomach to rest just under his chin.

He playfully snorted and kissed her, then rose and went to the bar off the dining room. He came back with a snifter of brandy for each of them. "I drink too much," he said flatly as he set her glass down on the hand-carved nightstand beside the bed.

"Everyone in Berlin drinks too much," she said with a hint of mischief in her voice, "so, you are among friends."

"How long have you been coming to the Krystal Bar?"

"At least a year." She turned away from him and sprawled out comfortably across her side of the bed. Even in repose, her back arched beautifully.

"Is this the first time you spent the afternoon in one of the hotel's rooms?"

"Yes, except in my imagination." Her voice lightened.

"Frankly, I am as amazed as you are." She hesitated. "I guess I am here because you looked sadder than I felt." She paused again. "Maybe the word I am looking for is lost."

"Sadder? Probably." He pointed his finger at her. "But lost? No! You really don't know who I am?"

She drew back and studied him, her features drawn together. "No, but I like very much of what I already know."

She got off the bed with her drink in hand and sauntered across the huge blue-and-green-colored carpet. When she opened the closet door, a light shown upon several gowns, wig boxes on shelves, and matching shoes sitting directly under the hanging formals. She looked at him, puzzled.

"Open the wig boxes," he urged.

"All of the wigs are the same color, red," she said more to herself than to him, "but they are styled somewhat differently." Her forehead wrinkled. "Didn't you say your wife was in Ohio?"

He pulled himself up against the headboard and crossed his legs, tailor fashion, in front of him. Elbows on his knees, he said quietly, "They're mine!"

"Yours?"

"I'm an actor," he added, enjoying her confusion.

"But what about the gown? The hairpieces?"

"You've heard of Jennie Darling?"

She drew in a deep breath, then sighed. "Now I understand." She peered back into the closet, then turned to him, almost smiling. "At the Club Jonquil. I can hardly believe it!"

"Look at the maroon scrapbook on the coffee table." He motioned to a huge Moroccan leather-bound volume.

Inside she found pictures of Jennie and of Steve as Jennie.

"Can you tell the difference?"

She grinned. "Only with your clothes off."

He reached for her.

She flipped shut the cover of the scrapbook, then came back to the bed. They held each other close, warming themselves and one another with body heat.

There was more. He had to get everything out of his system. He spoke rapidly: "I've got to see you again. We don't have enough time today, but we have the whole day—every day; I don't work until late at night, and—"

"You don't have to plead," she cut in; her resonant voice seemed to float throughout the room. She kissed him lightly on his face, then tapped the tip of his penis in a gesture of farewell. "You don't even have to ask."

He pressed his face into the hollow of her neck for a moment, then released her.

She stroked the top of his head as she might a child's. "Do you ever get your identities mixed, up?"

"Never."

"Jennie was such a tragic figure," she said, soft-eyed.

"She never really died. You'll understand what I mean when you see the show."

She curled into him, her back against his chest, and brought his hands around to her stomach.

He grasped the tiny cushion of belly fat just under her navel. It felt warm, comforting.

"Fantastic," she said. "I would really like to see how you transform yourself—before you go on. It's too incredible a feat for me to imagine."

"No," he said sharply in spite of himself. "I don't want anyone to see that!"

A shiver ran through her body. She said nothing, but then she slowly began to relax. She turned around to look at him.

"I'm very superstitious about the whole thing." He brought her back into the hollow of his neck. "The only living person who has ever seen me undergo the transformation is my wife, Stella. In fact, she used to help me. The other person was Jennie, who first showed me how to do it. It would be impossible for me to let anyone—"

"Anyone?" she questioned, then turned away. "Never mind; I didn't mean to upset you. The whole idea just isn't worth it."

"But it is! I mean, you are!" He bit his lower lip. "Maybe, before I finish the engagement, you can come to my dressing room and watch me do it, once." He knew that sounded less than convincing, and so added, "Let's see how it goes."

He rolled over onto his side and she lay alongside him. He ran his fingers down her back and gripped her around her waist.

He wasn't quite sure just when he'd dropped off to sleep, but when he awoke, she was gone. The only evidence that she had been there was the smell of her perfume, which floated above him.

# CHAPTER TWENTY FOUR

It would be a long time, Silvi mused, before she'd drive down Kurfurstendam Strasse again. She passed The Zwei Schwester's Konditori where she'd introduced Steve to coffee *mit schlag*. The cafe's blue-checkered curtains were drawn across the windows, and a faint light shone through them. A vignette flashed in front of her: She and Steve sharing a Viennese pastry piled high with whipped cream. Silvi began to smile.

The news that she'd decided to leave Berlin with Steve couldn't wait until after his late show. She wouldn't remain in Germany for three more months as they'd originally planned; that would be entirely too much time to spend away from each other. Besides, he'd said Stella would give him a quick divorce.

The feeling of being loved and needed, for herself alone, was one she had not experienced in years. If ever.

She should have called Steve at the club, but this news was too exciting to give over the phone. Besides, she couldn't get to him anyway: he was too keyed up at work and never took calls unless it was an emergency.

Maybe she should just wait for him at the hotel and surprise him. No again—Steve would be as overjoyed at the news as she. Then again, he was superstitious. In all the time they had gone together, he'd never let her into his dressing room—never let her see him undergo the transformation into Jennie. The only two people who had ever seen him do that belonged to his previous life. She'd read in *Stern* that theatrical people had their peculiarities—she would learn to live with his.

She pulled up to a red light, grateful for the pause. The pain in her forehead over the past days was finally leaving; it always left once she'd made a major decision. She placed the two Berlin Haus luggage receipts in her bag, then pressed her foot firmly on the accelerator.

Soon, she reached the Jonquil. Parking her grey Audi in back of the club, she guessed the early show would be just about ending. She knew her way to the stage-door entrance as well as she knew the way home. She also knew that Steve's dressing room was about twenty yards straight ahead, then a sharp turn to the right. She opened the stage door quietly, walked toward his dressing room, and saw him as Jennie, still onstage.

She stopped. The act was as astounding from backstage as it was when she and Helmut had seen it from the audience the second week Steve was at the club. Steve was really marvelous. Even Helmut admitted that he'd enjoyed the show.

Helmut! Well, Helmut would survive; he could survive anything. He had his work and never did need anything else. Once things settled down, the children would spend vacations with them and, ultimately, come to the States to live. Steve had even spoken of adopting them! At first, Helmut would be too proud to let them see her, but eventually he would capitulate.

*   *   *

"It's been absolutely wonderful being here with you the past few weeks at the Jonquil," Steve said in Jennie's voice with its little-girl lilt. "It's my first time here, but it won't be my last; I'll return, and soon." He smiled and waved to the audience.

With the exit music of "One More Time" in the air, he bowed low, and the curtains came together to cut him off from the crowd.

A man came up to him from the wings. In his wide-lapelled pin-striped suit, he looked like a 1930s Chicago gangster. "They want another encore," he informed Steve.

"Is that right, Herr Hauptmann?"

"Yes, it is—and it is also your last night. One more late-night show, then that is it." He added, "We are most relieved that it is!"

"Not as much as I!"

Herr Hauptmann was being unfair. Steve deserved some consideration. The Jonquil's current show was its most successful one in years, according to the entertainment section of the *Berliner Zeitung.*

"Quiet! They'll hear you!" Herr Hauptmann grabbed Steve around the shoulders, shaking him slightly, then faced the curtain and listened to the sounds on the opposite side. The orchestra went into Jennie's overture again.

Steve drew one side of Jennie's face up in a smirk. "OK, I'll do it. If I don't, you'll probably tattoo my forearm and clamp me into a gas chamber."

Silvi became momentarily embarrassed and angry. It was wrong of Steve to make a remark like that. It reminded her of the time in high school she had gone to dinner at the home of one of her friends. Hildegarde's father was in his forties but looked seventy. On his forearm were the dreaded tattoo numbers of Dachau. Hildegarde noticed Silvi staring at her father's arm and later volunteered to tell her about his experiences at the camp, but she stopped Hildegarde before she got started.

Herr Hauptmann quickly left Steve's side, and a thunderous roar began as the curtains separated.

"'One More Time'," the audience pleaded in accented German.

Steve signaled the orchestra leader to speed up the child-like melody, then raced through it. At its conclusion, he threw the audience a kiss and ran to the wings as their shouts became louder. He clenched his jaws in disgust and strode up to Herr Hauptmann amid the backstage clutter of scenery.

"My friend, what you don't know about the successful running of a night club could fill volumes. You promised you would not serve drinks during my show, and you went back on your word. The club's atmosphere the past few weeks has been brutal. What the hell is the matter with you? Don't you understand? I can't compete with the clink of glass—"

"Those clinks," the man cut in, "pay your very large salary."

"Let them clink afterward."

"They will leave! They did, the first few weeks!" Herr Hauptmann rocked back on his heels and stared Steve down. "My patience with you is at an end. You say every night there is something wrong with the way the club is run. But one thing I do know is that the people here will leave if they are not served during the performance."

"Then they don't deserve a first-class attraction! My contract reads 'Artist,' in great big letters. Or don't you know what that is? There has been nothing but backstage blundering connected with the show since it began."

"We pay you well—"

"Well, then," Steve mocked him, "you ought to be able to afford an up-to-date sound system with an adequate technician. Anyone can operate a mike. All you have to do is turn a switch on and off."

"He is *our* man." The tall, goateed orchestra leader, who had been following the conversation from a distance, walked over to them. "And we have *all* gone through this before with Miss Jennie Darling."

"But it didn't sink in." Steve glared at the swarthy, black-bearded man. "I sound like a screeching eagle out there." Steve strode away, then turned abruptly. "I pulled every goddamned trick out of my hat to make us all look good."

"We won't bother you any more," the orchestra leader retorted.

"And I thought God was dead," Steve muttered.

What an ugly, ridiculous scene. What was he trying to accomplish at the end of a successful engagement?

Silvi clutched the sable wrap that Steve had given her a week after they'd started seeing each other and made her way to his dressing room. Steve was having a hard night, but Silvi had never been happier, for the desperation that had plagued him when he'd first arrived in Berlin was nearly gone. "It *is* gone," she heard herself say, and shut his dressing-room door behind her. Sitting on a chaise with small holes in its once-luxurious blue covering, she picked at some stuffing that came through the fabric. The room looked somewhat grim, but a fresh coat of paint could fix that.

Kicking the door wide open, Jennie lurched inside and caught herself on the back of a chair. Her gown swayed on the current of her angry motion. Then she noticed the occupied chaise.

"Steve!" Silvi's enthusiasm was too much to bear, and she started to get up.

A look of consternation crossed Jennie's face. "Silvi, you had no right to come here! Ever! It's my dressing room!"

She bit the inside of her lip. The fringe on the black beaded gown Steve wore rippled back and forth. In the mirror behind him, she could see the back of the dress, cut to reveal the top curve of his buttocks. Or Jennie's? The figure was so shapely, she was having trouble separating the identities.

"I can't argue with you this way, Steve. Take off the makeup."

Jennie pointed a finger at her. "I never did extend the invitation for you to come to my dressing room. That's where I drew the line. Why in the name of God did you barge in here? I've got trouble enough with incompetents in this joint—I can't handle one more!"

Helmut yelled at her that way when he was excited—when a business deal tanked. He made her feel useless, cheap. She wasn't afraid, but she was shocked to see Steve behave that way. He and Helmut were opposites.

Or were they?

"You loused up my work from day one, and I could kill you for it. You made me gain over eight pounds! Do you know what that means when you have to slip into a second coat of skin?" Jennie quickly shoved her hands down the sides of her body.

"Stop talking like her or we'll never get anywhere," Silvi blurted out. Calming him down was the first step.

"I was all right until I hit this dumb-ass town."

Silvi opened her mouth but Steve didn't give her time to defend herself. "And what did you do? Don't look so innocent! You made me forget my work. My timing is off. But what the hell do you know about anything artistic, anyway? Culture? You Germans gave that up when you drove the brains out of your country in the '30s."

"You're irrational," she said to the shimmering creature in front of her.

"I am not irrational. It's not me—it's you. Don't think you are getting another chance to louse things up around here."

"Steve!" she half shouted.

Jennie snapped her fingers. "I've worked too goddamn hard for this success." She grabbed at the air in front of her with both hands, the red nails flashing. "Jennie did, too!"

"Jennie's dead!" It was time to get this matter onto solid ground, into a sense of reality.

"No." She leaned over and brought her face directly into Silvi's. "Jennie never died. Ask anyone out there whom they come to see. Who brings the money into the front offices? Who paid for all your good times during the past weeks? Jennie, that's who!" The skin around her neck tightened, the muscles jutting out in bold relief. "Jennie, Jennie, Jennie!"

Silvi lowered her head. The nightmare would end soon; she would wake up and find herself listening to Helmut's snores through the thin wall that separated their bedrooms.

She looked back up at Steve. The fringe on his costume, always in motion, made him look as if he were moving, even when he stood still. His breathing was so rapid that the gown seemed to pulsate.

"You are completely out of your mind, Steve! What have you taken this time?"

"Every goddamned thing I could shove down my throat. I had to because you haven't let me rest since I've been here—and I was exhausted before I came. Who the hell do you think I am? Samson?" He turned his back on her. "I don't leave the club until daylight! I don't relax until I take a couple of shots. I'm so busy shaking the sheets with you, I have no time to get enough sleep." He circled back, confronting her. "Jennie can wing it easy, but I need all the help I can get."

"Jennie is taking away your life!" she shouted. "You are beginning to sound more and more like her. You are even acting like her. There's no need for any of that." She planted her feet firmly on the floor. "You are in your dressing room, not on stage. The act is over!"

He opened his eyes wide. "I *had* no act until she came into the picture," he explained. "I need her more than I've ever needed anybody."

"You have a wife and child."

"That Mouse?" He clapped his hands together and began to laugh. "She's all gingham, sugar water and cotton candy. The only thing she is sure about is being a sharecropper. She hates show business."

"I can understand why."

"Get out of his life, Silvi."

"For God's sake, stop speaking as if you were Jennie. Let me know you are still in back of the makeup." She was beginning to feel very uncomfortable. It was almost as if she were carrying on a conversation with Jennie. But Jennie was dead.

"Get out of his life," the figure in front of her shouted. "Go back to your husband and family. Stay where the cards are stacked in your favor."

She wasn't getting anywhere by antagonizing him; she'd have to try another approach. She knew well how to do that: after all, it was her and Helmut all over again, at a different time, in a different room..

She started out in a low voice: "You are not really equipped to run Jennie's race."

Steve's hand struck the side of her face quickly. Her head twisted to one side. She was stunned, but only for a moment. His eyes were hard and full of hate. "You damn fool, get the hell out of here!"

Silvi stood her ground. "Give Jennie up!"

"No!"

"Let the act go!"

"*Never!*"

"For the last time, darling," she said through a film of tears, too demoralized to go on fighting. "If you really love me, come out from behind that makeup."

"No!"

She shuddered and closed her eyes for a moment, then rose unsteadily to her feet. "I lost," she said, her insides convulsing. Suddenly she felt very cold and wanted to run from the room. But instead, she folded her hands and bent her head back, ashamed to let Steve see her pain. She remembered him telling her, in their walks through the zoo and park, that he was almost drained from the grind of continually working, paying bills, being someone else. He surely needed help—but not the kind that she could give. She felt helpless to help him.

She didn't know to whom she would deliver her sorrowful thanks—Steve or Jennie. She stifled a wry laugh. "In the long run, I guess I owe you a vote of thanks." Her voice was saturated with a wet heaviness.

"Who doesn't?" Steve countered in Jennie's honeyed voice. "Everybody feeds off me!"

Silvi forced her features into something that resembled a smile and looked at the sable stole. Flinging the fur piece across the seat of her now empty chair, she stood tall. "Jennie needs this more than I do."

"Of course she does, Silvi," came the casual reply. "This scene is getting bad for both of us. Would you leave, please? There are people waiting to see me. After all, this *is* my last night here."

*   *   *

The gray, frizzy-haired old woman made her way to the counter again and again, lugging Silvi's suitcases one at a time.

Silvi placed both palms flat on the counter top, steadying them. "Leave the luggage here. I can't—I can't leave just now." She went directly to the Krystal Bar and, not waiting to be seated, sat down at an empty table next to the dying fire. She gave her order and stiffened her legs to keep them from trembling.

Fingering her long-stemmed glass, she gazed at the fireplace and remembered the day they had driven to Tegel for a sail in the nearby lake. A sudden downpour had drenched them thoroughly. They pulled into a wharf, soaking wet, and dashed into a nearby park building, where a fireplace was being tended by a park attendant. Since it was the middle of the week and no other guests were present, the attendant murmured that he could accommodate them, then left the shelter, locking the door after him.

Steve and Silvi took off their clothes and draped them along the backs of wooden chairs placed near the fire. They ended up making love on fireside floor cushions, furtively, like children afraid of being caught in a forbidden game.

An hour later, the attendant came to the door with beer and pretzels. They told him to wait and, laughing, dressed as quickly as they could, helping each other into their outfits.

It was one of many unexpected adventures they'd had. It was so like Steve to take every disturbance in stride, turning it into something they could immediately laugh at and enjoy. That capricious air about him was so exciting. Yet now … Well, thank God she hadn't been so stupid as to leave a note for Helmut. She'd planned on calling him from London as soon as the plane landed.

When her drink was finished, she ordered another, then lit her third cigarette. A soft tap on the shoulder startled her, and she turned her head.

At her side, with the stole in his hand, was Steve. "Forgive me," he said. Sliding into a chair, he called a waiter to order a drink and helped himself to some nuts from a center bowl.

Everything seemed unreal.

He placed the stole on her lap, but she moved her legs to one side, and the fur fell to the floor in a serpentine heap. After a moment, she said, "Give it to Jennie."

"Forget about her, damn it."

In the half darkness, she could see his ashen skin, his bloodshot eyes.

"Look," he began, "the past weeks have given both of us a new view of what life can be like. Don't take those times away from us. Don't let anything spoil them, Silvi. Don't let *her* spoil them, either! She's only an illusion." He placed his hand over hers.

His grasp was tight, almost painful, but she made no effort to draw away. She leaned forward and her hair fell across her cheeks. "I can never be what you need, Steve."

"Let me be the judge of that! I'll work up a brand new act," he said quickly. "Baby, come with me. I can make it as a single. Who the hell needs Jennie Darling, anyway?"

She finally drew her hand away. "You do."

"I don't! Silvi, your family can get along without you, but I can't!"

"Steve, I saw you every day, as soon as I could get away from the house. When I got to the hotel you were so tired that I would be beside myself. Then you would come out of it and be full of enthusiasm and vitality. I thought I helped you, and I was flattered." She tried to smile. "But it really was your friends in the medicine bottles that did the trick. And now," she could hardly go on, "this crazy incident tonight. Steve—"

"It won't happen again. I promise."

"No." She felt a tear slide down her face. Perhaps she hadn't played fair with Steve. She brought her fingers over her mouth. No, that wasn't true. She had been as fair to him as she had been to herself. What she had seen tonight brought back memories of Aunt Greta, committed years ago to a mental institution in Munich. Aunt Greta always pretended to be someone else. One day, she gave up her identity altogether—and never regained it. "I suddenly realize a few weeks is not long enough to really know anyone."

His voice rang out: "A few weeks is a lifetime!" He glanced at the other patrons, who were now looking at them, and he spoke more quietly. "I know I've been entirely too wound up in my career."

"Steve, you are as committed to your work as my husband is to his." She bit her lower lip; the pain was almost pleasant. "Whatever choice I make, I lose."

He slid his chair closer to the table and leaned over the small, circular top, bringing his thumb to his chest. "I'll tell you what I'm prepared to give up if you will come with me. I'm supposed to do a show called 'Jennie In Winter' at the Winter Garden Theater in New York City. There's a fortune to be made on that show." He gave the information time to sink in. "I'll give it up."

She looked at him in silence.

"You said you loved me!"

"I did. I do. But now I am afraid for you."

He pushed himself away from the table and drew his eyebrows together; deep furrows creased his forehead. "I know I have been hard to be around sometimes." It was getting difficult for him to remain calm. "I know I have to pull myself together. That's—"

"Where I come in?" She could see the words sting him.

He banged his fist on the table. "You would be with me. That's all!"

"No: I would also have to learn to live with Jennie. That's an impossibility."

"I won't ever do her again!"

"That's another impossibility."

He brought his chair around the table next to hers and pressed his face against her cheek.

If she didn't get away from him soon, she just might relent. She had to leave now.

"Just you and me," he whispered, "from now on. I'll get the plane tickets."

She jerked away from him. "You didn't do your midnight show! You won't be allowed to perform at the Jonquil again!" She half-smiled through her agitation, knowing how ridiculous that statement sounded.

He narrowed his eyes. "Who wants to?"

"Jennie would have acted the same way."

"Silvi, we can catch a plane out of here in a couple of hours. I'm all packed. I sent the bulk of my stuff to New York ten days ago."

"Steve, after I finish this drink, I am going to get into my car and leave. Don't try to stop me. Don't mar the past." She made an attempt to grin, but it didn't work. "The children do need me, and Helmut still thinks he does. One day, he will know better. Until then, I can live on what you and I have had."

"I left the club for you—"

"No." Helmut, too, blamed her for things that did not turn out right for him. "If you want to *think* you left it for me, go ahead, *Liebchen.*"

"Then I am your love."

"Yes—but in love, too, one has to fight for self-preservation, and I am fighting desperately for mine. You would eventually destroy me, Steve. Darling, I'm going back to my home. Give up the act and return to your wife—for your own salvation."

"That's pretty practical German behavior," he taunted.

"Absolutely right," she nodded. "Go back." Silvi stood up and kissed him on the forehead. Her kiss was as warm as she could manage.

He pushed the fur piece into her.

She clutched the soft wrap and looked at him.

He reached out for her, only to grab a handful of air.

"Don't leave Templehof as Jennie," she warned, continuing to move away. "Don't arrive in New York as her, either, no matter how they urge you."

"Only if you come with me tonight."

"Darling, turn away, or watch me walk away, but don't bargain with me. Go home—before it is too late!" Holding his gift, she turned around and stepped quickly through the bar's ornately carved dark-oak doors. She heard the doors swing back and forth behind her in successive shallow arcs.

Once she'd crossed the lobby and reached the hotel's entrance, she glanced back over her shoulder. The large doors had come to a complete stop.

# CHAPTER TWENTY FIVE

The BOAC airliner smoothly touched the ground at LaGuardia Airport. Once the huge engines had stopped whining, the forward "Fasten Seat Belts" light went off. Steve heard the clicking of released catches throughout the plane but kept his own belt locked. Passengers surged forward, eager to leave the confining cabin, but he sank back into the seat until everyone else had left. The hard part of the trip was still to come. He had to tell Max the Winter Garden deal was off.

He pulled the collar of his coat around his neck. A group stood off to one side, holding a hand-lettered banner that read "We Love You, Jennie." Another one declared, "Jennie is Forever." Silvi was right: this whole business had gotten out of control. He'd played on the public's imagination by encouraging it to the hilt. Slowly, Steve walked off the plane toward Customs.

Sam, wearing his ever-present grin, happily waved from the balcony.

Lifting his hand slightly, Steve returned the gesture. Usually impatient about staying in line, he welcomed this delay. The flight across the ocean had seemed long at first, but it had gone too damn fast. He wished he had taken a ship. That would have given him time enough to think about his future. Giving up a career going at full tilt was going to leave him floundering around for some time.

Sam's cable was still in his pocket. Buying out of his Winter Garden contract would cost a fortune, but it would be worth it. If Silvi were here with him, the fight with Sam would be bearable. He missed her so much, already.

The people who had come to the airport to see Jennie groaned with disappointment. How much had the newspapers played up the time of her arrival? The crowd eyed the passengers clearing customs, hoping somehow to spot her. Carefully, the inspector rifled through the contents of Steve's plaid airweight suitcases, slapped stickers on both lids, and motioned him forward.

At the cab stand, Sam hugged him, pointed to the crowd and winked. "They're waiting for you."

"Her, not me."

"I was kind of disappointed when Jennie didn't come off the plane. You saw that mob—"

Steve tilted his head to one side and barely nodded. "It's been happening all over."

"And she's a 'no show.' Hell, she always was one to pull that trick."

The white-haired redcap smiled widely as Sam overtipped him, then put the luggage in the trunk of the cab. The redcap wished them well as they silently pulled away. A cold, gray mist covered the road directly ahead. Idly, Steve watched cars passing them or falling behind. When would Sam start the barrage?

"You could have at least answered my cables," Sam finally began.

Steve almost smiled at the man's irritation.

"The grunts I got over the transatlantic phones weren't worth either my effort or the cost. And now you want me to cancel the whole thing? Are you out of your head? You don't have that kind of money; they'll sue you, for sure."

"Can't I do it later—in a year or so?" Sam, of all people, should understand. Couldn't Sam see that he needed some time off—to breathe—to get Jennie off his back?

"You're tossing away a four-hundred-and-fifty-thousand-dollar opportunity. That's not beans, even with inflation!"

"But *I* pay for the orchestra, scenery and costumes!" That seemed like a sour enough note to start on.

"There will be plenty left over."

Steve didn't reply.

"Where in the hell is the hustling kid who wanted his big chance and did everything he could to get it?"

Sam nudged him in the ribs, his face florid.

"He's around somewhere." Steve looked out the window at the dirty mist that surrounded them. The dampness stayed in the cab's interior in spite of the noisy heater's efforts to keep it dry. He felt wet and chilled.

"I thought he was *here*. I didn't think he was fool enough to turn away a chance to make millions—"

"Millions?" He brought his head to one side and looked at Sam through almost closed eyes. "For doing Jennie?"

"I know fucking well what I'm talking about." Sam jackhammered him in the shoulder.

Damn it, that hurt! He wished to hell Sam would get over the habit of overselling everything.

Glancing at the floor, Sam said almost in defeat: "But I can't force you—just as I couldn't ever force her. What gets into you people? Is it something the manufacturers secretly add to the greasepaint?"

Irritated, Steve looked away. "There is nothing more to talk about. I'm going straight to Stella and Kevin. That's the story, Sam!"

"But you *told* me to have your stuff sent to the Americana when it arrived, days ago. Steve," Sam patted him on the knee, "have I ever steered you wrong? You're tired? Rest! Call Stella." His voice became persuasive. "Suggest she come here with the baby."

"She won't travel."

"But that's a necessary part of the business you wanted very much to be in." Sam fidgeted around in his seat, took a fresh cigar from his inside coat pocket, bit off the tip and lit it. "Face it. You are one of the few people today who can pry them away from television, poker and mah jong. Don't fight me. Stay at the hotel, and give it a think. All you need is a few days' rest." Sam turned to him and dropped his voice. "I was really disappointed when Jennie didn't come off that plane."

"Go on, Sam. It's easier listening to you than arguing with you."

Sam lowered his voice in defeat: "Jennie was always one to take the easy way out."

"She worked her ass off," Steve reminded him. "All agents do is sit back and collect."

Sam pointed his hand out of the cab toward the pedestrians. "Those people out there work hard. Every one of them falls into bed bone-ass tired. If you ask them, they will tell you they work like horses. I work like a horse, too." His voice bounced off the walls of the cab: "You think it's easy being all things to all people? *Especially* show people? They're sharks once they're operating on a head of steam! On the way up, they'll do anything for a chance. Once they realize they have pulling power at the box office, their demands increase. The more power they get, the more demands they lay on us until we end up diapering them."

"For a percentage, Sam. For a percentage!"

"Everything in life costs, Steve!"

"I've noticed that, but you don't bust *your* balls every night turning in a razor-sharp performance."

"Steve, let's stop for lunch. I've got to be back at the office most of the night, checking over stuff before I leave for the coast. I'll see you tomorrow, and we can talk." Momentarily appearing to forget him, Sam looked through his attaché case, then pulled out an envelope and placed it in his inside suit pocket.

"No thanks—no lunch. Are you still at Rockefeller Plaza?"

"Same old forty-fifth floor, but we've enlarged." Sam snapped his attaché case shut. "See me tomorrow in the early afternoon for a short drink. Maybe you can come with me to the airport." He became serious again. "But you've *got* to get into action at the Winter Garden. Everybody is lined up and ready to start in days."

"How many numbers would I have to prance around in?" Christ, couldn't Sam tell by the sound of his voice that he was only killing time until they got to the hotel?

"Seven. Maybe eight, but you could fake it once you got the essentials down. You can't use any of the numbers from *Star Fire* except 'One More Time.' The studio wouldn't go along with any of the others. The footwork would have to be adapted for the smaller stage anyway. Tom Gennero said he would work with you day and night to get the new stuff whipped into shape. *Star Fire* is proof you can do it." Sam's voice was full of praise.

"They shot that in fifteen-second segments. I can't ask the audience to close their eyes to every mistake." He grinned at his own joke. "You're asking the impossible."

Sam glared back at him.

Every so often, the cab driver brought his head back sharply to the right, and Steve wondered if at those points the man was losing track of their conversation. He hoped the talk sounded more interesting than it actually was.

"Is it or is it not the way you make your living?" Sam took the cigar out of his mouth, blowing the smoke to the roof of the cab.

Christ, that cigar smelled really bad. Steve thought about asking if it were made of manila hemp.

"We all have our crosses to bear, Steve. Don't forget that!" For the first time, his voice carried an edge. "You didn't think it was asking the impossible when you signed the preliminary contracts. There are important things we have to tackle now. We've got to move like it was three months ago."

"Look, Sam, I'm going straight to Ohio, where one and one still makes two." He hit his thigh with his open hand. "I may be a better somebody else, but I've got to learn to be myself all over again. For whatever I'm worth."

"You can't leave. You will be paying people off for the next six years." Sam brought his hands up between them to forestall any further arguments. "I'm not going to listen to any more craziness. I'm not going to do anything until I hear from you tomorrow. I know you're tired," he admitted, "but you are not insane!" He breathed heavily. "Welcome home, Stevie!"

The cab slithered through the heavy traffic and stopped at the entrance of the Americana Hotel. Steve gave his suitcases and his name to the bellhop, then shut the cab door without saying anything more. He walked up the broad cement stairs into the sparkling glass lobby.

His room on the fifth floor was almost sparse, furnished with a double bed and the usual dresser, mirror, and desk on the opposite wall. Off to one side, sheer floor-to-ceiling drapes cut out the glare of the late-afternoon haze. The bedspread was an off shade of orange that matched the drapes and walls. Hell, he didn't care. Turning on the television and listening required too much effort, so he opened the door to the adjoining room, where Jennie's wardrobe was being unpacked and hung. Where could he store it all?

Sitting on the floor was the swing in its huge black case. Steve opened it, then picked up the swing and chain, feeling their weight. Suddenly he saw Jennie clearly, singing vibrantly. She waved and reached out to him. He wanted to tell her to hold onto the swing with at least one hand, but it was too late! She fell and screamed in panic, tumbling over and over again in the air.

He quickly let go of the chain, which clanked back into the case. The room became very still.

"Fuck you, Sam! Fuck you, too, Jennie!" He walked to the bed without closing the lid on the case, then fell on top of the covers—but not before swallowing a red, a blue, and a yellow capsule.

*     *     *

Sam's afternoon had flown. Seated behind his huge circular teak desk, he munched on his cigar. He smoked it too far down, then stubbed it out in the heavy glass ashtray in front of him. He had managed to squeeze in two new client interviews before beginning his paperwork, and as he now glanced out at the darkened sky, he remembered he had not eaten lunch.

From the reception room came the noises of a cleaning woman. Sam yawned. All he could think of was a hot bath and a cold drink, followed by a room-service salad and Porterhouse steak—rare!

Sam's door flew open and hit the wall with a bang. The strong light in the reception room behind the shapely female figure cast it into bold silhouette. Her arms extended; her gloved hands touched both sides of the doorway. Her legs looked as astounding as ever.

Sam brought a hand up to his mouth as she came forward. For a crazy second, he forgot Jennie was dead.

"Sammy! Baby!"

That crazy jackass. What the hell was Steve doing here, tonight, in costume and makeup? A few hours ago, he was dead set against doing *anything* associated with Jennie.

Steve flashed Jennie's long red beetle nails at him. "Guess who's back in town? Sweetheart, did you miss me?" Steve carelessly placed one hand on his hip, just as Jennie used to do. He even included the slight upward turn to the corner of the mouth that she affected when she was triumphant. "Now, where does little old Jennie sign for all those great big deals you've got lined up?"

Without waiting for an answer, Jennie crossed the huge expanse of room, swinging her hips. She sank into a chair, crossed her legs and slid her skirt far back over her knees. "Lost for words, Baby? You never used to be." She reached for a cigarette and picked up an expensive lighter from an end table; she blew the smoke directly at Sam.

Sam pushed the blue stream away from his eyes and placed his hand over his heart. It was racing. He tried to speak, but nothing came out. Steve was carrying the act a bit too far.

"Sammy," she sang out in her throaty voice, "Jennie's next in line for a grab at the gold ring. Stick around! We're going to make everybody rich!"

Sam studied the figure in front of him, conscious of the way it delicately took off its gloves. Everything about it was consummately female. He could almost believe Jennie had come back. No one could do her that perfectly, up close—not even Steve. Yet underneath the arched eyebrows and faultlessly applied eyelashes, a man *was* there.

He drew his mouth to one side, biding his time. Steve would

slip out of the act soon, and that would be the signal for them to get to down to business. "Steve—"

The figure looked around the room vacantly. "I don't see any Steve around here. You're losing your touch, Sammy." She half-closed her eyes. "You might at least offer me something to whet my whistle."

"A joke is a joke, Steve," he began.

"Are you calling Jennie Darling a joke? I am not a joke. If my acting is good enough for the world, it's good enough for you. I am thirsty, Sam," Jennie drawled, "real thirsty."

From the small, well-stocked teak bar next to his desk, Sam poured a glass of scotch.

"Three big fingers," Jennie said, eyes opening wide. She brought her hands together and interlocked her fingers. "Jennie likes three rocks in her drink. One for each finger," she told him as if explaining something to a child, then leaned into the chair and rubbed her palms across its leather arms. "Life has been good to you, Sam. But I'm going to see that it gets even better." She leaned forward. "I've learned a lot, Sammy, and I'm not going to be the problem I once was. I'm very pleased that Gennero is going to work with me again. He's a genius."

"Gennero has never worked with Steve," Sam said quietly.

"*I've* worked with him and that's enough," Jennie replied, then began calculating how long fittings would take. "New costumes are no problem. New York is full of odd people wanting to do odd things at odd hours." She brought herself upright, her lacquered fingertips curling into her palms. "Where are those goddamn papers?"

Sam laid out the documents, and Jennie scribbled "Steven Dennis" across the bottom signature lines. "It's a real shame I have to use that name instead of mine."

Sam brushed his hands over his ears and shook his head.

Jennie handed the papers back with a flourish. Seating herself on the desk, she leaned forward, and her well-shaped lips parted in a wide smile. "My act's greater than ever! Isn't it, Sammy?"

"Yeah …" He backed away, the paper in his hands fluttering. What the hell was this apparition in front of him talking about? For a million bucks, right now, he couldn't tell who was real and who wasn't.

Jennie eyed him coldly. "Just be sure Gennero is here from the Coast tomorrow." She pulled her forehead into a frown. "You heard me. You expect me to make the soufflé rise, don't you? And, not to worry: Dennis will never get away from me the way he did in Berlin." She got off the desk to walk away. "No sirree, Dennis is strictly Jennie's boy now!"

Sam searched again for some trace of Steve behind the façade, but there was none. The pain in his chest began to subside as he savored the success of his just-completed deal. But then, against his will, concern for Steve surfaced. He needed more proof than a signature that Steve was still inside there, somewhere.

"Maybe you *shouldn't* do the Winter Garden after all, Jennie. You've been working entirely too hard!"

"God damn you!" Jennie slammed a book down on Sam's desk, making the papers rise up in a flurry. "I'm indestructible. Before you leave, set everything up for me. I'm taking a two-day holiday; after that I expect a rehearsal hall and the theater open to me. By the way, I've got to call Iris. She doesn't know I'm back, and she will be absolutely delighted to see me."

Sam shuddered.

"You sure you wouldn't like to make the rounds with Jennie tonight?" The provocative lilt in her voice was warm and inviting.

Sam explained that he had too much to do and kept his attention fixed on his desktop. He had to get Stella here to straighten Steve out, fast—very fast!

"Well then, Jennie is going to have to stir up some excitement all by herself." She threw him a kiss and backed out the door, tightly clutching her copies of the newly signed contracts.

Sam picked up the phone and began dialing long-distance information for Dayton, Ohio.

# CHAPTER TWENTY SIX

On a bare gray stage, amid patches of crumpled paper waste and a thin layer of dust, Tom Gennero tilted his face upward, observing the action on the catwalk above. Two mechanics were reinforcing the securing clamps to the part of the grid where the swing would be anchored. The swing dangled in the air like a limp snake as the men shoved the top hooks back and forth until the distance between them was equal to the width of the seat.

Tom sighed. Leaning against the battered stage piano, he rested his face in his hand. Progress so far was great, but paid for at the price of slaving like a son-of-a-bitch almost every waking hour. Steve was no slouch when it came to working hard, and he caught the new routines almost as fast as Jennie had. It was uncanny working with him this way. Since he'd arrived, Steve had rarely been out of costume and makeup, thereby bringing the illusion of a living Jennie to its ultimate peak.

Even the slack suit Steve was wearing now reminded Tom of the one Jennie had worn when they were blocking out the steps for "Lady, Don't Love" so many years ago. Jennie always wore brightly colored outfits when they rehearsed. She said they lifted her spirits when she was too tired to lift her legs. This one was an eye popper that could be worn to any smart supper club. During the past weeks, when Tom went to bed, there were times when he'd asked himself if Jennie were not really alive.

"Are you sure it will come down slow enough?" Jennie—
Steve—called up to the men on the catwalk, hitting the floor
with her heel the way Jennie did when she was preoccupied with
a production detail.

"We set it up for normal running, but you can use the side
levers for any other adjustment you want, Mr. Dennis."

"If you remember the name is Miss Darling," Jennie's voice
stridently reminded, "we'll all get along better around here."

The larger of the two men in overalls, a heavy red-faced giant,
brought his shoulders up in a shrug, squeezed his features together
and shot them a sloppy salute.

Turning his attention back to Tom, Jennie said, "I've got
fittings this evening after we finish. Greg Damon is coming over
with the costumes basted together. He's got some women straight
from Guadalajara doing the lace beading. What an artist! And he
is so damned accommodating."

"You have got to slow down," Tom cautioned the pacing figure
in front of him. "Don't you ever stop?"

"Can't. There's too much at stake. Besides, I work better when
I'm keyed up. Let's run through 'So Glad You Came Tonight'."
She went to the rise at the far end of the stage and pointed her
left arm toward the ceiling. She swept her other arm high in the
air and brought it down to rest gracefully on that same shoulder.
Jennie's opening stance had never been done better. "Hit it!"

In resignation, Tom started the tape again. As Steve undulated
toward him, singing almost at full volume, Tom stopped the tape.
In disbelief, Steve stepped out of his pose.

"For Christ's sake, don't give it all you've got now," he warned.
"You have almost a week before you open. Save yourself, Jennie!"
Startled at his own words, he broke into a half-smile.

"What the hell are you laughing at?" Jennie's voice, edged

with a hint of anger, suddenly softened: "I'm sorry, Tommy. I got carried away." He dropped his hands to his sides and settled his shoulders back. "I've just been racing my motor for so long, I don't know when to stop—or how. Christ," Steve looked around the theater, "it's so damn hot in here! Can you get someone to turn up the air just a little?"

Tom walked up to Steve with a towel.

Jennie took it and patted it lightly around her face and hairline. A hint of a grin started to make its appearance. "Thanks," she muttered, just as her hand unsettled the wig. Automatically and quickly, she adjusted it.

The man needed rest. He was as tight as a bow string. "How about getting out of the get-up you're wearing?" That would slow him down. "How about some pants and a shirt?"

Jennie looked down at herself. "No, even though this outfit might be a little too showy for rehearsals, and—"

"That isn't what I meant," Tom interrupted.

"What are you talking about, then?" She snapped her fingers, once, in a gesture that ended the conversation. "Got a cigarette?"

"No, I haven't, and you know you shouldn't be smoking."

"I know. I shouldn't be doing a lot of things, but I'm edgy about opening night, even though I know I shouldn't be. And, I'm dealing with this infernal headache. I've got to get something for it. Wait a second; I'll be right back."

"Why don't you just go to bed and get some sleep?" Tom called out. He couldn't remember ever having worked with anyone who had such nonstop drive. It was also uncanny and brutal for Steve to use Jennie's voice constantly. He had almost never stepped out of character. Was he a consummate artist or a consummate fool?

Jennie stopped just before she disappeared behind the dust-covered curtain and yelled back: "Tom, it's got to be a helluva show for the New York crowd. And there's only one way it will be! We have to keep at it."

"If you don't kill yourself before we open, you sure as hell are going to kill me," Tom called out. Picking up a dummy program waiting for final approval, he looked at the words "Directed and Choreographed by" on the cover. His name was almost the same size and type as Jennie's." Tom audibly grunted. For all the effort he was putting out, there was no type anywhere in the world big enough for his name.

# CHAPTER TWENTY SEVEN

As he walked down an empty aisle of the Winter Garden Theater, Tom paused and looked at the show's newly arrived props. Off to one side of the bare stage, the glittering outfits looked incongruous hanging on a long plumbing pipe. He laid two brown paper bags on a nearby seat, adjusted a shoelace that was giving him trouble, then picked up Jennie's lunch and his own.

Since the day Steve had told the mechanics to call him "Miss Darling," Tom had gone along with the joke. It wasn't until a week later, when they were getting the first number into final shape, that it was no longer funny. On a darkened stage, in front of a purple velvet curtain, wearing a gown of the same material, Jennie's legs and upper body had seemed to float in space, barely moving, until her voice swelled into the first measures of "Begin The Bolero For Me." Then, she sold that song for all it was worth—and it was worth plenty!

When he went to bed that night, Tom was almost positive she had come back. He had worked long enough with Jennie not to be fooled by an imposter.

From behind the wings, Jennie screamed at Greg Damon in the first row before she charged onto the proscenium.

"If I make my entrance from stage left, the slit has got to be on that side. There are three reasons why I am in the business, and

I'm dancing on two, so let's give the legs a big play." As she came toward center stage, she cast an eerie shadow on the brick wall behind her. "That way I can get a lot of action out of the costume." She placed her hands on top of the skirt and ripped the material midway between the left side and front.

Greg moaned and flung up his arms in exasperation.

"Don't worry," she appeased. "Rack it up to production costs."

Greg stood up, a small, thin, gray-haired man, immaculately dressed in a black suit. As he walked up the makeshift ramp to the stage, he looked all of a piece with a black tie hanging out of his black shirt. Every time Greg came to the theater, he looked like his entire outfit had been cut out of the same bolt of cloth.

Jennie brought her hand above her eyes to block out the overhead glare. "I really don't like it at all any more. Greg! I need a caftan with a slit!"

"Caftans are long, graceful and flowing," the irate designer yelled back, matching her temperament. "You can't have them hugging your ass like the rest of your outfits. Two days ago, you *hated* caftans!"

"That was two days ago." Her eyes narrowed. "Make it long, graceful, and flowing, and slit the goddamn thing so my legs will show. I'll work it so everyone gets a peek now and then. That's the idea of the game, Honey!"

Tom jumped off the ramp. From a brown paper bag, he handed her a large plastic cup and a hamburger wrapped in waxed paper.

Opening the lid of the cup, she closed one eye and scrutinized its contents with the other. "Is the egg in it?"

He toasted her with his own drink.

As she downed hers, shuddering in distaste, she held her head and hands well forward so nothing would spill on her. Abruptly she drew her head back and looked at him straight on, the thick off-white fluid outlining her mouth. "What the hell—let it spill. We're not going to use this damn thing the way it is, anyway." She wiped her mouth daintily against a skin-tight sleeve.

Tom looked away. Christ, that was one expensive napkin! Didn't she have any regard for what that number cost—let alone what that gesture was doing to Greg?

"Sweetie." She refocused her attention on the costume once again. "Jennie wants a caftan. Run along and make it. We only have three days left, so for God's sake, don't go to any kinky four-night parties. Unzip me, will you, Tommy?" Holding onto her burger, she turned her back to him and reached for a scarlet kimono lying across the top of a chair. She tied it around her waist with a gold-corded belt.

"You are one first-class bitch, Jennie," Greg shouted over his shoulder, turning away quickly. "Nothing you do on stage compares with what you do off!"

She watched him disappear into the lobby. After drinking the health cocktail, she finished the burger. Crumpling up the waxed paper, she spotted a dab of meat on top of a splotch of mustard. She brought the paper to her lips and ate the meat, then threw the paper into the wastebasket. "God, Tommy, this headache hasn't left me for a week. Wait a minute; I need to get something from the dressing room."

What she *didn't* need, he thought, was something she could spill out of a bottle and count. He glanced at the stage, noting the stairs, trees, and papier-mâché animals from the various production numbers. Out of context, they looked like odds and ends from a jazzy junkyard, but in a few days they would create another world.

"It's time you unwound," Tom said firmly. He *had* to force her to relax.

"Just one hour more," she pleaded. "Blast-off time is here!"

"You'll drop," he warned her. "Right in front of the curtain."

"Never mind," she snapped back. "I'll work alone. I'm no stranger to that." Leaning against the stage piano, she raised an eyebrow. "Do you think Iris would come if I sent her tickets and plane fare?"

He nodded. "By the way, I'm not going to be here tomorrow until late afternoon."

"That's all right. You'll find me either here or in my dressing room." She glanced at her watch. "Ready? I'll start from the top again. I've got almost everything nailed down."

"Is there going to be anybody here tomorrow that I should see?" Tom asked.

"No—I'll take care of everything. By the time you get here, I'll have run through the program at least twice. Joe Fields is one fantastic conductor. I wish I'd had him with me in Europe." She brushed her hand through her hair. "That guy can make a hoot owl sound good!"

"OK, Jennie. Now show me all the talent you can stuff into the next ninety minutes."

She clicked the phonograph on, saluted him, and started the quick climb to the swing.

Tom wondered if her headache still bothered her.

\*    \*    \*

When Stella asked the theater doorman if Mister Dennis was in his dressing room, the portly man drew his bushy white eyebrows together and tucked both thumbs behind the top band of his discolored coveralls. He held them there for a minute. "She's in her room." His voice was gruff. "You got business here? I ain't seen you here before."

Very slowly, she said, "I'm his wife."

"Jennie Darling has a wife?" The doorman hunched forward, the hint of a smile crossing his face.

"No," she retorted, "but Steve Dennis does." Had the insanity of Steve's act gotten to everyone?

"Down the hall and make a quick left when you pass the men's john." His reply was surly, and he didn't even point the way.

Stella started walking. She held her handbag with both hands, her knuckles turning white. Where was Sam? He was supposed to be here, waiting for her. Last week, when he'd called for the third time, he'd told her to get to New York as fast as possible. Steve wanted her back. More than that, he *needed* her back. That was all she'd had to hear.

Was it only two days ago that Kevin had been released from the hospital recuperating from a concussion he'd received when he'd tripped and fallen into a shallow abandoned quarry? She couldn't possibly leave until this morning. While he slept, she'd kissed his forehead and left instructions with her mother regarding his medications. At the airport, she'd told her father she would call them just as soon as she knew her plans.

All the speeches she'd prepared on the plane boiled down to one: I WANT YOU BACK, NOW. She was more lonely for Steve than she'd ever expected to be.

When Stella reached the men's washroom, she turned left, pausing a moment to look around. The light of one naked, low-watt bulb hanging from the ceiling made the corridor seem forbidding. How unattractive the rear of a theater could be. It was so dark, she couldn't tell whether the walls were gray or green.

The big door at the end of the hallway bore the usual star, with the name "Jennie Darling" carefully lettered onto it. Even death wasn't strong enough to take that woman out of circulation. Stella knocked on the door.

No answer.

Stella knocked again.

"For Christ's sake, stop that banging and come in." That wasn't Steve's voice. It was Jennie's!

She opened the door and stepped into the large room in one motion. The area was divided into sections by eye-level opaque glass panels and was hot and overlit. Jennie was standing up, facing the mirror.

Stella stared at the scarlet-sequin-clad body in front of her, from the copper-colored hair down to the ruby pumps. But she knew that the illusion in front of her was Steve.

Jennie stood up rigidly, without turning around. "What the hell are *you* doing here?"

Stella looked at her watch. It was ten in the morning. "Steve, what are you doing in costume so early?"

"Costume?" Jennie turned around and brought her hands to her waist. "Stella, this is what I wear when I get up."

When Sam had said Steve needed her, he had not added the word *desperately*. The windowless room was blinding in its silver, white, and black décor. Stella felt stifled and had to get to the studio couch against the wall before her energy completely left her.

"If you are looking for Steve, he's not here!" Jennie moved toward a small rococo white-marble table, took a cigarette from its hidden drawer, and lit it. She inhaled the smoke deeply and let it out in a lazy stream. "What the hell did you have to come around for? I don't need extra aggravation right before an opening."

"Steve," she said, walking closer, "I want to talk to you." She set her handbag down and folded her hands. "About your future. About ours!"

Jennie laid the cigarette in an ashtray, picked up a nail file, and made a series of quick passes at one of her artificial nails, then laughed. "You didn't want him when you had him. He got smart, eventually, and left."

What Sam hadn't said was far more important than what he'd said. Steve was sick; very sick. Perhaps she could still save him. Suddenly she loathed herself for leaving him after the Lotus Room fiasco in Las Vegas. None of this would have happened if she had been more patient, more understanding. "I should have come when Sam first called, but Kevin was in the hospital." That seemed the best point to start from.

"Tough!"

The word bore through her like a bullet.

"Look, Stella, nothing of that kind matters to me now. Least of all, news from Ohio."

"Steve, remember I'm with you. I always was, when nobody else was—and I still am. I love you." She moved forward very slowly, so as not to alarm him.

"Well, he despises you." Jennie's voice soared with malice: "He and I discussed it all—just before he left." She drew her fingers up to her chin in a gesture of femininity. "He went back to Europe to marry a German *hausfrau*. Weeks ago! But I stayed. And for your information, I'm not leaving—*ever*."

Stella started to speak, but nothing came out. Maybe she should run out of the dressing room and see if Sam had arrived. Finally, she whispered, "Steve, you need help!"

"I don't need help," Jennie said while backing away, "but you do. Tons of it! Now get the hell out of here before I forget that I am a lady!"

"No, you're not!" Stella lunged toward the figure in front of her and pulled off the mass of red curls, then grabbed a towel and shoved it hard against Steve's face: the makeup came off in a wide streak. "You're Steve, not Jennie!" she shouted, again and again.

"You rotten bitch," he growled in Jennie's voice. The dagger-length nails sliced through the air, dangerously close to Stella's face. "I'll kill you!" Jennie's voice screamed. One palm smashed against Stella's cheek, driving her into the wall: bursts of white and blue light flashed in front of her.

How she got her arms around him, she didn't know, but she had him momentarily pinned. As quickly as she realized it, he broke her hold and grabbed her, squeezing hard. Stella dug her nails deep into the soft flesh around his midsection. As his head jerked to one side, she screamed into his ear. He released her instantly, then covered his face with his hands and began to shake. She could hardly hear him through his labored breathing. "Where's Jennie? Where is she? Where's Jennie?"

"Look." Stella threw the wig to one side and pointed to it. "Jennie's dead! You're Steve, my husband, Kevin's father—and we want you back." She began to cry in spite of her resolve to be strong. "We want you back. We want you back. Very much!" She put her arms around his trembling shoulders. "Steve—it's me, Stella."

He brought his hands into his lap. A single tear streamed down his cheek. "Why are you so unhappy, Stella?" He looked up at her. "Las Vegas—The Lotus Room—is where I always wanted to play. But I don't have time to tell you why I'm doing Jennie instead of Myra. I have to go. People out there are waiting."

She felt totally helpless. She didn't even know how to get a good doctor in Manhattan. But Sam would. Damn him for not getting here in time! She stroked Steve's forehead and turned off the lights around the makeup mirror. "I'm going to take you to a place where you can relax for a while. You need rest, darling."

"Jennie doesn't like hospitals," he said quietly. "She was in too many."

She drew her head back. "Jennie is dead," she cried out. "You aren't. Steve!" She pulled gently at his ears, then nipped his cheek. "Honey, come back to us. You're not that far away!"

"It's all too far gone," Steve said. Suddenly he seemed to become aware of himself, and he grabbed her. "She'll be back to get me. You're not safe here, either. Leave me. Right away!"

"Jennie is *not here.*" She turned him around to face the mirror. "There is no one here but us!"

He stared into the glass, then pulled back, his mouth in a half-grin. Calmly, he reached into the makeup case and began to repair the damage to his face. His voice was soft—but it was Jennie's. "Why did you mess me up, Stella? I have to be on stage in seconds."

All she could think of now was getting help from Gus and Janet. Thank God Steve was too absorbed in what he was doing to notice her backing away, toward the door. With each step, her feet seemed to stick to the floor.

The last thing she saw before she turned and ran down the corridor was Steve reaching for Jennie's red wig.

*       *       *

Gus drove his beefy shoulder into the locked door of the dressing room. It popped open with a harsh *snap*, and Stella and Janet followed him inside.

The room was now in complete disarray. The mirror was smeared with green and brown greasepaint, and talcum powder had been thrown over it. Gowns had been pulled off the dressing rack and thrown to the floor.

"What the hell?" Gus murmured.

Stella ran behind the dressing screen and came out the other side. "But he's *got* to be here," she insisted, "he was here a few minutes ago. He must be in the theater!" She swayed into Gus' arms for a moment, then straightened up.

"Stella," he said quickly, "get on the stage and check the wings on both sides, and the orchestra pit. Search behind the props. Janet, check the first-floor seating, starting from the last row. Then we'll move up to the balcony."

Janet nodded, her hair sweeping across her face as she quickly turned and began a half run toward the door.

"Whoever sees him first—yell. Let's all move! Now!"

*   *   *

Stella tapped her foot to keep her mind off the constricting pains in her chest. Her thorough search of the stage area had yielded nothing. From near the prompter's box, she watched Gus and Janet search the main floor of the darkened theater as they made their way, row by row, toward the orchestra pit.

"There he is!" Gus abruptly pointed upward from the second row.

Stella looked up. Directly overhead, on the swing, sat Jennie, legs crossed, in a ruby-sequined tuxedo jacket with a slit skirt. The swing began moving back and forth as she shifted her weight.

"Cleaning crew?" Jennie's voice mocked them below. "Can't you do anything by yourself, Stella?" Steve squinted at Gus, who was anxiously peering up. "Hey, pervert, don't look up my dress!" Jennie's raucous laugh reverberated through the theater.

"Steve, please come down," Stella called out, praying he would listen.

"Great comic, isn't she?" Jennie's voice screeched. "I sure could use a kidder like you in the show, Stella!"

"Please, Steve, come down so we can talk." Pain cut tortuous paths through her, and she was having trouble breathing.

"Jesus Christ, Stella." Jennie drew back in the swing, then leaned forward. "If it weren't for Jennie Darling, Stevie Baby would be in Nowhere Town. He owes me, Sweetheart. And I'm here to collect. Go away, Stella. If it were up to you, he'd still be back at the post office, licking stamps. Find another postal clerk. That's your speed!"

Jennie stared off into the balcony. "Steve," she shouted, "think of all the fun we've had together. You have no room for Stella. She'll only weigh you down." She brought her thumb to her chest. "I was there myself, and it cost me years and a pile to get out from under."

The illusion of Jennie glared down at Stella. "You are a colorless, senseless, no-talent mouse." The tragic figure again faced the upper section of the theater. "Steve, when you get the divorce, pay her off in cheese!"

"Come down, honey," Stella pleaded. She could taste the salt of perspiration on her lips. Curling her nails into her palms, she dug into the soft skin. Mother of God, was he beyond hope?

"Steve, come down!" Gus' voice boomed through the blackness.

Jennie's voice was sweet, flirtatious: "You're a nice guy. Tell that crazy bitch to go away—and meet me after the show for a real good time."

"You'll burn yourself out," Janet called up to the figure on the swing. "Besides, you're too big a star to act like this."

Jennie's voice filled the theater: "I'm indestructible!"

The swing began moving back and forth. "Don't mess with me." Jennie's voice rose in fervor as the swing picked up speed. "Nobody crosses Jennie! Steve?" The apparition of Jennie looked around the theater. "Don't listen to them! You and I are going to take this town apart and glue it back together—*our* way!" The swing swayed from side to side. "And *you*," the excited figure leaned forward and pointed down, "Stella, you—"

The word evolved into a scream of anguish as Jennie lost her balance and fell forward—a marionette with its strings cut, falling from a great height. Her hands grasped the air, blood-red nails flashing in the proscenium lights. Then her legs began a running movement; a ruby slipper flew off one foot and sailed into the darkness.

Steve's life swirled all about him. There he was, singing and telling jokes on all the stages on which he'd ever performed. He was so handsome, so full of talent and vitality! Everyone in the audience was applauding and cheering like crazy. Frank was there, and Peggy, and Sammy and Joey. Then all the words of all of his songs ran together into bits and snatches that didn't make any—

He hit the stage next to Stella and bounced up, only to come back down on his back and lie completely still.

Stella had never heard a thud so full of heaviness—and the angle his neck made with his shoulders was something she had never seen before.

Stella fell to her knees and called his name. His eyes slowly opened, and she realized what great effort that took. He began blinking until she moved to cut off the harsh rays of the spotlight behind her with her body. He smiled in thanks—or was that her imagination?—and then, his eyes closed again.

Her tears, falling down upon his still face, washed the makeup off in miniature roads; she began wiping the rest of it off with her fingers. Once his own features had emerged, she gently removed the wig and placed it on the stage, very close to his head.

THE END

# ABOUT THE AUTHOR

Jerry Jaffe, award-winning writer, world traveler, and pianist, is conversant in five languages. An inveterate traveler, he now lives in suburban Chicago with his wife and Afghan hound. They have one child and two grandchildren. He has also written material for the US Army, and a one-act play for Laura Hoffman, the music director of a popular cruise ship line.

He holds three Master's degrees (Fine Art, Clinical Psychology, and Computer Technology). *One More Time, Jennie Darling* is his first novel.

His motto is "Opportunities are everywhere—just keep your eyes and ears open."

Contact Jerry at jaffe77@sbcglobal.net